Deceptive Mayhem

Deceptive Mayhem

Dakota Destruction Book 4

Millie Copper

Written by Millie Copper

Edited by Ameryn Tucker

Proofread by MDC Proofreading

Cover design by Dauntless Cover Design

Also by Millie Copper

The Havoc in Wyoming Series

When a series of coordinated attacks devastate the United States, the people of Bakerville, Wyoming, must come together to survive. Unfortunately, not everyone has the town's best interest at heart. Some are striving for personal gain during the apocalypse.

The Montana Mayhem Series

A group from Bakerville, Wyoming strikes out on their own while searching for the desires of their heart. Unfortunately, the road will not be easy, and sometimes the heart is hardened and deceitful.

The Dakota Destruction Series

After a series of coordinated attacks devastate the United States, Katie and Leo sacrifice everything to help their country. But some things aren't as they seem. Is it time to go home and start fresh, or can something good come out of this terrible situation?

Wyoming Fall Series (In The October Fall World)

In the blink of an eye, an EMP changed everything for Lauren and her family. Now they are in a fight for survival, trying to keep their loved ones alive as society collapses around them.

Nonfiction Books

Millie has penned seven nonfiction, traditional food focused books, sharing how, with a little creativity, anyone can transition to a real foods diet without overwhelming their food budget. Many of her books also include preparedness and food storage tips.

Find these titles at:
MillieCopper.com

Join My Reader's Club!

Receive a complimentary copy of *Looming Mayhem: A Dakota Destruction Prequel.* As part of my reader's club, you'll be the first to know about new releases and specials. I also share info on books I'm reading, preparedness tips, and more. Please sign up at:

MillieCopper.com/Join

Chapter 1

Katie

The soothing sounds of my husband's soft snores fill the room. I sink into the fireside chair, absorbed in the pages of a novel depicting a Norwegian family's saga in 1800s North Dakota. Despite my resolve to stay up later tonight and indulge in some extra sleep tomorrow morning to gear up for my night shift, it isn't long before I find myself drifting off.

With a sudden jolt, I whisper to myself, "Well, Katie, there goes your brilliant plan to stay up late." I pull myself upright and rub my puppy along his neck. "I can't keep my eyes open, Gerry. Let's take you outside and head on to bed."

He wags his tail and hops to his feet. During the daylight hours, we walk Gerry around the neighborhood. But at night, we pop out into the backyard and encourage him to hurry. Especially on nights like tonight, when the temperature has dropped well below zero.

Gerry also seems to hate the extreme cold and will do his business quickly. Knowing we'll only be a few minutes, I don't bother with my ski pants. But I do put on my heavy coat and stocking cap before slipping into my snow boots.

I grip the handbell mounted on the backdoor, one of our security measures, so the ringing doesn't disturb Leo. Several weeks ago, we closed off our bedroom and transformed our dining room into a cozy sleeping nook to take advantage of the warmth from the woodstove. Living through the apocalypse definitely demands some creativity, and having a bedroom in the dining area is just part of the adventure.

I step out the backdoor, and a frigid gust pierces through my clothes, gnawing at my skin with an icy bite. With a shiver, I pull my coat closer around me and urge Gerry to hurry. "It's too cold to lollygag, sweet boy."

Gerry emits a low growl, his fur bristling. I scan the yard, regretting not grabbing a flashlight. "C'mon. It's fine. Just our cold backyard." I venture off the porch and onto the snow-covered ground. My legs slip out from under me, and I hit the unforgiving surface with a thud. I let out a breath and roll to my stomach as pain sears through my right leg. "Ugh," I groan, as Gerry gives a throaty bark.

Close by, a man orders, "Grab him."

My arms swing on instinct and connect with something solid as I struggle to grasp the unfolding chaos.

"Hey! He hit me in the nose," a voice whimpers. "I'm bleeding."

Gerry stands beside me, growling and snapping, while one of the men cautions, "Watch that dog."

A high-pitched male voice remarks, "Guys, something's wrong here."

I lash out with my left leg and make contact with someone.

They emit a sharp yelp.

As I struggle to get back on my feet, Gerry lets out a pained yip. Out of nowhere, a blow lands on my head. I cry out and collapse to the ground.

A distant voice interjects, "That's not him. It's a chick."

"A girl?"

Amid the throbbing haze in my head, I strain to grasp the distant voices, my fingers digging into the frozen snow. My gaze fixes on Gerry, sprawled nearby, unmoving. Is he even breathing? As I begin to rise to my knees, my left leg sends a sharp, almost unbearable pain through me.

A foot connects with my ribs. "Stay down."

The fresh pain mingles with the existing agony as I take shallow breaths, fighting to stay conscious.

The man with the higher-pitched voice says, "Let's get out of here."

"We can't leave her. She'll freeze to death."

"Let her. Let's go."

"Sorry, lady," the man mumbles, his boots crunching through the snow as he makes his escape.

A pair of heavy boots still linger beside me. I start to lift my head. "Don't. Keep your head down, and I won't kill you. If you survive the cold, tell Oscar we're coming for him. This is a warning. We know what he did, and we're going to make him pay. Understand?"

When I don't respond, he seizes me by the hair and raises me up. I gasp for air.

"I said, do you understand?"

"Y–yes." Searing pain shoots through my tender ribs, and the relentless throb in my head intensifies, amplifying the agony.

None too gently, he drops me back to the ground. "Good luck. Better figure out a way to get yourself back inside before you freeze to death." He emits a harsh laugh. "Too bad we killed your dog. He could've been a good one. A fighter. Oh well."

"Julius! Let's go!" a voice calls from somewhere farther away. The man kicks me again, this time connecting with my hip, before he makes his escape.

I remain perfectly still, trying to breathe and gather myself as I ride the waves of pain. I feel myself slipping away as I gaze toward Gerry. Tears sting my nose, and I painstakingly drag myself nearer to him. "Gerry," I whisper, my voice trembling with despair. Then, the world around me dissolves into inky darkness.

Chapter 2

Merissa

"They're back . . ." Jacquie Haley coos. "And they're all yours, Merissa."

I wrinkle my nose and shake my head, then halt midmotion. "The Ebright sisters?"

"Mm-hmm. They've perfected their technique since we last saw them. Elaine almost looks sick this time. She even convinced a neighbor to bring her here. They transported her in a garden cart, said she was too sick to walk."

"Maybe she really is sick?"

"Doubtful. There has always been something off about those two. They're a couple of oddballs. Anyway, I'm not dealing with them. You can try out your new doctoring skills. I put them in exam three."

"Thanks," I reply, my tone dripping with sarcasm.

"Oh, you're welcome. Better you than me." Jacquie cackles and walks away.

Elaine and Marilyn Ebright are a special case: spinster sisters who, somehow, have not only survived but thrived since the power went out. These two women are frequent visitors at our hospital, often with exaggerated complaints.

Besides the Ebright sisters, there are a few others we've dubbed as frequent fliers. One man in his sixties was here just a few days ago. His daughter brings him in, often with an exasperated expression. She almost always whispers, "He's faking again, just likes the attention."

While she's usually right, we learned our lesson when he had an actual injury one time. Since then, he's returned with outlandish complaints, but we still give him a thorough exam.

When I enter the exam room, an off odor assaults my senses. I glance at the sisters. Elaine is sprawled out on the uncomfortable examination bed, her eyes closed. Even from here, I can see the slow rise and fall of her chest.

Marilyn is by her side, holding her sister's hand, worry etched on her face. "Merissa," she pleads. "You have to help her."

"Tell me what's going on."

"It started this morning. She slept in late, which isn't like her. When I went to wake her so we could start our sewing, she seemed like she might have a fever. I thought maybe she was getting that flu, but she hasn't coughed or anything like that. She's been getting worse throughout the day. I finally got our neighbors to help bring her in."

Marilyn gestures a crossed-heart sign, as if making a solemn promise. "I swear. This is serious. We wouldn't go out on such a cold night if it wasn't. It's freezing out there. Not fit for man or beast."

I give her a slight smile and move toward the sink to wash. "She was fine yesterday?"

"Mostly. She's been a little tired. Complaining of feeling off for a few days."

Once I've washed and sanitized my hands, I move to the bed. "Elaine?"

The woman's eyes flutter. Her voice comes out weak and strained. "How's your baby?"

"Fine. I'm fine. Let's talk about you. Marilyn says you've been tired for a few days?"

"Not like today. I feel terrible. Can barely keep my eyes open."

"I'm going to get your blood pressure and the other fun things, then we'll get Dr. Wolff in here to check you out."

"We can't stay long." Elaine sighs. "Mother will be angry if we don't get home on time."

"Mother?" Marilyn snorts. "What are you talking about, you crazy old broad? She's been dead for years."

Elaine shakes her head. "We mustn't make Mother angry."

Marilyn huffs a few more times and mutters about her sister, then meets my gaze. "What's wrong with her? She got the dementia?"

I shake my head and resume my exam. Checking her vitals provides me with important information. Her blood pressure is dangerously low, her heartbeat is rapid, and she's running a low-grade fever.

Recalling the odor I detected when I first walked into the room, I ask, "Has she had any injuries or cuts recently?"

"Nothing substantial. We often poke ourselves when we sew, but we know to keep the pinpricks clean."

"Elaine?" I gently touch my patient's shoulder. "Do you have any injuries?"

"Oh, no. I'd never let that happen. Mother always taught us to wash carefully. Big girls like us have to keep clean."

I rest my hand on my hip and consider what she said. "Elaine, can you explain what you mean?"

"It's not important," Marilyn interjects. "Not now with the way things are. You know we lost weight after the EMP." She grabs the loose skin under her chin and jiggles it, resembling a turkey's wattle as she manipulates it. "We're half the size we used to be."

"It may be important," I say. "I think Elaine has an infection. Possibly an infection in her blood that may have started with a minor cut or other injury. I'm going to bring Jacquie in to help me get Elaine into a gown."

Marilyn scoffs. "I'll help you get Elaine into a gown. That Jacquie Haley is a gossip. Always has been. The less we see of her, the better. Isn't that right, Elaine?"

"Jacquie Haley sleeps around," Elaine mutters. "Remember that time— "

"Oh boy, do I!" Marilyn clucks. "Lot of good it did her. She's single and alone, just like us."

With Marilyn's help, we get Elaine off the bed. Although she's obviously tired, she's lucid enough to help us remove her clothing and put on a gown. As we undress her, I look for obvious signs of injury.

Because the Ebright sisters were both obese prior to the EMP and forced rations, they have a considerable amount of loose skin. Elaine's chin isn't the only area with a sagging appearance; her arms, legs, and midsection all exhibit the same effect.

With the gown on, I help Elaine back into the bed. "Do you mind if we check a few more things before I bring the doctor in?"

"What things?" Marilyn narrows her eyes.

"Sometimes there can be a sore that isn't visible."

Elaine rests a hand on her thigh as her eyes go wide. "Promise you won't tell Mother? She'll be so disappointed in me."

"She's dead, remember?" Marilyn's voice is harsh.

With a confused look, Elaine whispers, "What do you mean *she's dead?*"

Marilyn looks at me. "What's wrong with her? Did she eat some of that poisoned wheat?" A look of horror crosses her face. "Am I going to go crazy too?"

I shake my head. "I don't think she has ergot poisoning. We haven't had an issue with that here." I look over my patient as I form my thoughts and a potential diagnosis. "I'll, uh . . . let me get Dr. Wolff. She'll finish the examination."

Dr. Wolff is in the break room, sipping a cup of tea. When I open the door, she says, "Jacquie told me the frequent-flier sisters are here. What's their story this time?"

"I think it's legit. Low blood pressure, slow heart rate, low-grade fever, confusion . . ." I lift my hands.

"Septicemia? It's the older one? Elaine, right? Has she been sick?"

"Tired the past few days. Her lungs are clear. I haven't gotten a urine specimen yet. I'm leaning toward a skin infection. With her massive weight loss— "

"She has lots of loose skin," the doctor finishes my sentence. "Panniculitis. That's definitely possible. Go ahead and start an IV. I'll be right there."

Panniculitis, or an inflammation of the subcutaneous fat, isn't exactly what I was thinking, not that I know much about it. But it's something we've touched on in our lessons with Captain Williams.

My thought was more that her apron of loose skin rubbed underneath and caused an abrasion, which went unchecked and led to a bacterial infection. *Poor Elaine.* She could have a very long road to recovery.

I take a deep breath and push down the thought that, if she is septic, which her clinical symptoms suggest, she may not recover. She'll need a broad-spectrum antibiotic, which we don't have. Stella Swenson has several herbal remedies we use as antibiotics, many with good results. But for sepsis . . . I'm not sure.

Like antibiotics and everything else in our current world, plastic intravenous fluid bags, which were once disposable, are no longer being manufactured. We reuse the bags that were previously thrown away. There's a special crew that handles cleaning and sanitizing all our medical items. IV fluid bags, gloves, syringes, needles, and plastic tubing are all reused.

Even though we're confident in the procedures used for cleaning and sterilization, the human factor is a concern. While we don't believe anyone from this specialized crew would purposely return items that weren't properly decontaminated, it could happen.

Another issue is they didn't construct the disposable items to be cleaned and reused, and many have broken down. Captain Williams has said it won't be long until we'll be looking at other options for things. Instead of IV bags, we'll use pressure-sealed jars, which were commonly used in the early 1900s for intravenous fluids. Hopefully, we won't need to go so far back in history that we're using pigs' bladders as bags and quills as needles.

Back in the exam room, Elaine is softly snoring.

Marilyn has moved a chair to sit next to her as she holds her sister's hand. She dips her chin in my direction. "She has a sore on her stomach. Underneath her flap of skin."

"She showed you?"

Marilyn makes a face. "Looks nasty. Stinks too."

That, she doesn't need to tell me. When I walked back into the room, I was once again assaulted by the pungent odor. It makes sense she'd have an infection in the apron of excess skin and fat hanging from the abdomen below the waistline.

The large, overhanging abdominal panniculus was often removed in patients who lost a considerable amount of weight, not only for cosmetic reasons but because of the health implications. Patients with a considerable panniculus frequently experienced severe limitations in their mobility and ability to carry out daily tasks. Skin infections and rashes commonly afflict these individuals due to persistent irritation and excessive sweating.

The excess weight the Ebright sisters once carried was potentially helpful in getting them through the worst of the food shortages. I'm sure there hasn't been much consideration given to them, and others like them, regarding health issues post weight loss. And while removing that excess skin may have been done in the past, it's not something we'd even consider doing now. Surgery is a last resort, something done when it's the only option for survival.

Of course, if Elaine's skin infection has progressed to septicemia—a systemic infection of the blood—her survival may be in question.

My patient stirs when I tell her I need to start an IV. She mutters something I can't quite make out, but she does give me a nod. Once we've completed the task, Marilyn asks if I want to see the sore. Trying to preserve as much of Elaine's privacy as possible, I position a sheet so we can view the abrasion without displaying anything that doesn't need to be.

Marilyn wasn't off in her assessment. The entire pubic region under the excess skin is angry with infection. The left side is likely where the issue started since it looks the worst, but the right is also inflamed. I'm surprised Elaine didn't realize what was happening and come in sooner. She had to be in considerable pain with the way things look.

"See? I told you it was nasty." Marilyn makes a face.

Within a few minutes, Dr. Wolff joins us. Her examination doesn't bring up anything new. She gives a diagnosis of sepsis caused by a bacterial skin infection. "I know Stella's herbal manual addresses both of these issues. Let's get Elaine moved to a more comfortable room."

The news hangs heavy in the air as her sister absorbs the gravity of Elaine's condition. "She's going to be okay, right?" Marilyn asks.

Dr. Wolff touches her on the shoulder. "We're going to do everything we can to take care of her."

Chapter 3

Katie

Snowflakes fall gently, brushing my cheeks. I'm shivering and confused. Why am I here? I see shapes—trees and shadows—but they're all mixed up and moving around strangely. A soft, plaintive whine breaks through the confusion, and then a warm tongue drags across my chin.

Gerry.

My hand trembles its way toward him, setting off a searing burst of agony through my head and torso. "Oh, Gerry."

He responds with another lick and inches closer, his warmth a stark contrast to the biting cold.

As my scattered memories start to come back, I look around. I remember why I'm lying here on this icy ground. It was those men. They hurt me, kicked me, and even hurt my dog. Then they just left us here to freeze. Tears sting my nose as my quivering hand finds its place on Gerry's fur. "Good dog." Slowly shifting my body triggers a surge of pain, and I can't help but release a low, involuntary moan.

It's too cold out here. Much too cold for me to remain sprawled on the ground. I'm still shivering; that's a hopeful sign. Considering the frigid conditions, my blackout couldn't have been too prolonged. Hypothermia is still in its early stages.

"C'mon, Gerry. We need to get up and get back inside." I attempt to push myself onto my knees, but it triggers a cry of severe pain.

Gerry whimpers and licks me again, remaining in a side-lying position instead of standing.

I rest my hand on him while taking shallow breaths, trying to manage the pain. "What's wrong, boy? Where'd they hurt you?"

Once the pain subsides, I draw in the deepest breath I can manage and release a piercing cry that echoes through the chilled air. "Leo!" My ribs feel like they're about to break, and my head throbs.

"Okay," I whisper, as I sink back to the ground. "That was a terrible idea. Very bad." After a few moments of shallow breathing, I attempt to move again. This time, I roll over instead of rising to my knees. The pain hasn't improved much, but there's no other option. I must escape this cold ground, which is sapping my body heat. "Please, Lord. Please help."

Gerry inches close, dragging his injured leg as he stays by my side. "Good dog. Good boy. Let's do it again. We're almost back on the porch. Even getting on the deck will help."

In this new position, I'm resting on my leg and hip, which doesn't hurt. Perhaps it's enough to enable me to rise. I brace my arms beneath me. Just as I'm about to exert pressure, a bell chimes from the back door. My heart races. "Leo," I gasp. "Help us."

"Katie?"

"Leo, we're here." My voice barely carries. I try again, but it remains feeble and sickly. Gerry emits a soft bark, his tail thumping against the frozen ground.

"Katie!" My husband quickly reaches my side. "Did you fall?"

"Help us." The world blurs as my breathing quickens. "Men. Gerry's hurt. They're after Oscar. I'm hurt."

"Okay, okay. Give me . . . I'm going to need some help. With my arm, I can't get you up. I'll be right back."

"Mm." I close my eyes.

Moments later, Leo returns and drops a blanket over me. "I'm going to the Harringtons' house. Gerry's with you." He shifts his tone. "Look after Mama, Gerry. I'll be right back to help you both."

My dog nuzzles my neck under the blanket, and a gentle warmth spreads through me. I suddenly feel overheated and fling the blanket away, prompting a small whimper from Gerry, who edges closer for comfort.

I gaze up at the stars, observing one of them becoming brighter. It starts blinking. "Oh. Look, Gerry. It's a . . . a robot." I giggle. "The robot is coming to save us." As soon as I utter those words, all the stars seem to turn their gaze toward us, flashing and blinking.

It's Morse code. If I concentrate hard enough, I can decipher their message. Gerry snuggles closer. One of the blinking robot stars grows brighter and begins speaking.

"What happened to her?"

"Welcome to earth," I respond, followed by more giggles.

"Katie? Oscar and Kirstie are with me. We'll get you taken care of."

The blinking robots shine intensely, almost too brightly. "It's a warning. They're coming for you."

"What's she saying?"

"I don't know, but she kicked off her blanket. That's not good. We need to get her inside, then to the hospital."

I close my eyes and allow the robots to lift me. Their bright lights bob away. Something feels amiss, but I can't quite grasp it. "Gerry?"

"He's here, honey. I'll get him while Oscar and Kirstie help you."

"The robots."

"What'd she say?"

"I don't know. Just get her inside."

One robot positions its face close to mine, and its mechanical voice utters, "You're going to be okay."

I float along, as though on a cloud, the lights shimmering and swaying. I close my eyes and allow myself to drift. Things don't seem quite right, but it's okay. The robots have me. I can rest. I exhale deeply.

My legs tingle, and my face feels strange. I scrunch my nose and wiggle my toes. "Ah." Pain shoots from my foot to my hip. "Oh . . ."

"Katie? Are you okay?"

My eyes want to open, but it's just too difficult. I feel my eyelids fluttering. Moving. Trying.

"It's okay, honey. Just rest."

Chapter 4

Merissa

Elaine Ebright has settled into a room to receive her first dose of herbal antibiotics. We clean her wound and generously apply a calendula salve, then she drifts into a light sleep. Marilyn has requested to stay with her sister and now reclines in an old armchair. Alongside Elaine, we treat four new patients and host three in-house. It's been a bustling night.

I've just concluded my consultation with Jacquie, who serves as the official nurse on duty tonight while I shadow her. The front doorbell chimes.

"Hey! Uh, Weaver, right?" a man's voice echoes down the hall. "We need the truck."

Medic Jesse Talbot emerges from a room. "Oscar? What's the problem?"

"Katie Burnett. She's injured. I offered to carry her here, but Leo warned of her hypothermia and potential cardiac arrest from sudden movements. I need the truck."

Dr. Wolff, now also in the hallway to investigate the commotion, instructs Jesse to proceed. Turning to Oscar Harrington, whom I recognize from the Citizen Patrol, and as Leo and Katie's neighbor, Wolff asks, "What's the situation?"

He shakes his head. "I'm not sure. I suppose she took the dog outside and was attacked. It's confusing, and she's not making much sense. But she was exposed to the cold for too long, along with being beaten up."

"Lord, have mercy," Jacquie whispers.

"Is she inside the house now?" Dr. Wolff asks.

"Yeah, of course. I helped Leo get her inside and covered her with a blanket. But she keeps kicking the blanket off."

"Is she conscious?" the doctor probes.

"On and off. She's disoriented, and Leo mentioned she isn't shivering."

I exhale and shake my head. From the sound of things, Katie's in the second stage of hypothermia. "Do you want me to go with Jesse?"

Dr. Wolff purses her lips and seems to consider the question. "No, let's prepare for her arrival."

Within minutes, Jesse returns, bundled up to face the harsh cold of the night as Oscar had described. The severe weather necessitates extra layers, and Jesse has taken appropriate precautions.

Before they even step out the door, Dr. Wolff instructs me to set up a cot in the break room and bolster the fire in the woodstove. "Gather a pile of blankets and warm a few towels."

My stomach churns at the thought of Katie's injuries. Hypothermia is a serious matter. If her body temperature is too low, rewarming her could pose complications. When I arrived at work, the thermometer in the guard shack read ten degrees below zero, and that was hours ago. I'm sure it has dropped further.

If Katie was exposed to these frigid conditions for an extended period, she could face grave issues. Selecting the break room was a wise move on Dr. Wolff's part. I stoke the fire and place freestanding privacy screens to trap the warmth. Once we have the room set, plus the towels warmed and stored in an old food cooler to hold in the heat, I survey the area. I can't think of anything else we could need.

I leave the break room and hurry to Elaine Ebright's room. She occupies one of the three beds in the hospital's most spacious room. A twelve-year-old girl who slipped on the ice and broke her leg is in another bed. We're keeping her overnight for observation before sending her home to ensure no further complications arise.

The third bed belongs to a woman injured in the explosion at our local ration center back in November. Similar to Elaine, she suffers from an infection. Fortunately, the infection remains localized to the wound on her leg, which refuses to heal. We've conducted all available tests to uncover the reason behind the delay in healing, but nothing has surfaced. She's been receiving herbal antibiotics in the hospital for three days now.

Marilyn sits up in her chair when I enter. The patients, along with the mother of the little girl, are asleep. I first check Elaine's vital signs. Her blood pressure, although still low, is no longer dangerously so. Even her heart rate appears more stable, though it remains elevated.

Whether it's the herbal medicine beginning to take effect or the additional intravenous fluids, only time will reveal.

"She seems better," Marilyn whispers. "Sleeping more comfortably."

"She does. You should sleep too."

"I'll try. I heard the ruckus earlier. Someone got caught out in the cold?"

I offer her a faint smile. "I'll be back to check on you both later. Try and sleep."

She snorts. "I was just asking. No need to make a federal case out of it."

And there she is, the sassy Marilyn Ebright I know. While both she and her sister may come across as busybodies and occasionally make snide comments, I genuinely believe that beneath it all, there's goodness in both of them. Some days, it's buried deep indeed.

Elaine was supposedly experiencing seizures the last time I saw them, which, like all the previous instances when they had visited the hospital, turned out to be fabricated symptoms.

The sisters are almost legendary for their hypochondria, to the extent Captain Williams has used them as case studies in several of his lectures. The constant reminder he imparts is to always believe the patient until there's a reason not to. Tonight's severe illness is a prime example of why such a principle is necessary.

I quietly check the other two patients, visually examining the girl with the broken leg so as not to disturb her, before moving on to the woman with the infection. She's progressing well and is likely to be discharged tomorrow. When I assisted Jacquie in changing her bandage earlier this evening, the signs of infection had diminished, and she's been fever-free since yesterday. Now if we could just figure out why she isn't healing as she should.

I return to the hallway, and Jacquie inquires if the room is ready for Katie. I confirm it is.

"Go ahead and finish your rounds," Jacquie says. "If you hear the doorbell, wrap up whatever you're in the middle of and then help us with Katie. We take care of our own."

As I start to respond, the flash of headlights filters through the large front windows of the hospital.

"Never mind." Jacquie is already moving. "We'll stabilize Katie first, then you can check on the others. Go get the doctor."

Jesse and Oscar each have an end of the stretcher. Leo is at Katie's side, holding her hand, when Dr. Wolff and I reach the front waiting room. A woman joins them, cradling the Burnett's medium-sized puppy.

"We're taking her to the break room," Dr. Wolff says. "Was the dog with her?"

"He was," the woman confirms. "He's hurt and cold as well."

"Bring him along," Dr. Wolff decides. "Leo, what can you tell me?"

As we enter the break room, Leo explains how he went to bed before Katie and woke up later to find her missing. He heard a noise and checked outside but wasn't certain how long she was exposed, potentially up to an hour.

Katie's face shows signs of exposure on her nose and chin. Inside the break room, the woman places the half-grown dog on the couch. Jesse covers him with one of the lighter blankets.

Once Katie is on the cot, Dr. Wolff directs Jacquie and me to remove her clothing. "Keep any area you aren't working on covered. I want her to start warming up. Be careful. Minimize any unnecessary movement. Simply bringing her here . . ." She shakes her head. "Leo, you can stay. Tell me about the pup."

The woman, now seated on the couch with the dog's head resting on her leg while her hand soothes its shoulder, remarks, "I think they hit him, just like they did Katie. He's not moving much and seems quite sore."

Dr. Wolff sighs. "We'll see what we can do for him too. Let's clear the room."

Jesse pats Leo on the shoulder. Oscar asks if Leo would like him to stay. "Nah, man. It's fine. Thanks for helping me with her."

"Jesse, why don't you give Oscar and . . ." Dr. Wolff motions toward the woman.

"Kirstie," Oscar interjects. "My wife."

"Give them a ride home. No need to risk anyone else getting frostbite."

Once they have followed Dr. Wolff out of the room, Jacquie and I begin our work. Katie stirs a few times as we remove her winter parka. She's only wearing a light T-shirt underneath, along with sweatpants covering her legs.

"I already removed her boots," Leo says. "She wasn't wearing any socks. She was dressed for bed and took our dog out. I . . . I didn't . . ." He chokes on his words as he shakes his head.

"Why don't you tend to Gerry?" I suggest. "He looks like he could use some comforting." I refrain from mentioning that the dog might provide Leo with solace as well.

Leo sits on the couch and gently pets his pup as it lies on his lap. The dog moves slowly but doesn't appear to be in severe pain. We undress Katie and cover her with a blanket. When Dr. Wolff returns, she performs a brief examination, noting the obvious bruising on Katie's ribs and hip. After finishing the examination, she sits on the other end of the couch with the dog nestled between her and Leo.

"I don't think anything is broken, but they definitely worked her over. Jesse has reported this, and I suspect someone will be coming soon to take your statement."

"What about the hypothermia?"

"It's fortunate you found her when you did."

"But she'll recover, right?"

I scrutinize Dr. Wolff's expression as she maintains a steady demeanor. "We'll warm her gradually. We've placed hot towels around her neck, as well as on her chest and groin. Merissa will stay in here and monitor her temperature every fifteen minutes. Now, let's examine your dog."

Dr. Wolff enlists my assistance as we give the dog a thorough once-over while Jacquie keeps a watchful eye on Katie. Like Katie, the dog suffered a beating and endured the cold. Also, like Katie, we don't suspect any fractures but definitely bruising. The dog exhibits signs of minor frostbite on its nose, both ears, and one of its paw pads.

"Let's keep him warm. My guess is he'll be fine, but he'll need some time to heal. How about you, Leo?"

"Me? I'm fine."

"Your arm? I see you're not wearing your sling." She motions toward his arm with the external fixation device.

Leo shrugs. "I was in bed. I didn't think about it."

"Merissa, find something to fashion a sling for him. Let's secure that arm so we don't have to worry about further adjustments."

With Leo's arm properly slung and the dog resting on his lap, Jacquie excuses herself, reiterating Dr. Wolff's instructions for monitoring Katie.

We face a tough night ahead, but Leo's steadfast determination reflects his commitment to support Katie through her recovery journey. The path to healing, for both Katie and the dog, will undoubtedly present obstacles.

Chapter 5

Katie

"I think she's coming around again." The voice is soft and friendly.

"Katie? Honey?"

"Mm-hmm?"

"Hey, how're you feeling?" Leo asks while squeezing my hand.

I open my eyes. Bright light. The robots. I squeeze my eyelids tight. They helped me. My head throbs. My back aches. "What's happening?"

"You're going to be okay. We're at the hospital. We're getting you warmed up."

I open my eyes again, remaining perfectly still. The robot's light has vanished. "Where'd they go?"

"They? Uh, Gerry? He's here. Resting on the couch. Nettie checked him over. No broken bones. He needs to rest, but he'll recover. We've set up a bed for him in the corner."

"Good. Good. The robots?"

"The robots? I don't . . . I'm not sure what you mean, honey. The man who attacked you? Was it Geoff Landers?"

I furrow my brow. "Geoff Landers? More than one. I think there were four." Something more. Something about the men. A message. "It's Oscar."

"What'd she say?"

I close my eyes and attempt to identify the new voice. Deputy Shaw?

"Katie, were you attacked by someone who knows Oscar?"

"I think they believed . . . maybe I was him? They targeted the wrong house." I let out a laugh, which quickly turns into tears. "The wrong house. They want to kill him. They want to kill Oscar. Is Gerry all right?"

"He'll be fine. You'll be fine too. Just close your eyes. Rest a bit more and continue warming up."

<center>~~~~~</center>

Several hours later, I'm on a much-too-narrow cot by a roaring fire in the hospital break room. Leo's in the chair next to me. Gerry is lying on a blanket at Leo's feet. It's close to suppertime, and I'm finally feeling better.

Most of last night and today are a blur, with things really only coming into focus within the past hour. Deputy Shaw just finished taking my statement, which is probably a confusing mess, but it's the best I could do. Before he left, he said he'd stop in to see me tomorrow, and maybe I'd remember more about the men who attacked me.

"How long was I asleep?" I ask.

"Only about half an hour this time. Supper should arrive soon. Are you hungry?"

"Is Oscar safe?"

Leo's expression eases, a subtle reassurance in his gaze. "They've taken him and his family somewhere secret until they can sort this out."

"Did you already tell me that?"

"Yes, but it's all right. I don't mind repeating. Confusion is expected after hypothermia. Plus, you probably have a concussion."

"You told me that, too, huh?"

"Captain Williams did."

"What else did he tell me?"

Leo drops his hand on my arm. "That you'll be just fine. He doesn't think you broke anything, but your ribs, hip, and leg are severely bruised."

"He kicked me. Gerry too."

With determination, my husband nods solemnly. "I know. You'll both be okay in a few days. We're going to stay here tonight. Then, like Oscar, we'll go someplace else until they find them."

"You came for me."

He shifts his hand from my arm to my cheek. "I'll always come for you."

"How'd you know?"

20

He shakes his head and swallows. "I'm not entirely sure. I woke up, you weren't in bed, and it was too quiet. You weren't in the chair either. I couldn't find Gerry anywhere, so I started searching."

"How long was I outside?"

He clears his throat. "Around half an hour, perhaps a bit longer. It's hard to pinpoint exactly. I can only estimate based on when I went to bed and your body temperature when we brought you here."

Tears fill my eyes. I don't even know why I'm crying. Leo grabs a cloth to wipe away the tears before they trickle down my cheeks and into my ears. It takes several minutes to regain control of my emotions.

I've just managed to compose myself when Williams enters the room. "Sergeant Burnett, it's good to see you awake."

"Captain," I croak in response, trying to hide my tears.

He tightens his lips. "Emotions are to be expected after what you've been through."

"Yes, sir."

He spends a few minutes inquiring about my pain level and other matters. Even when I stumble over the day of the week, he seems satisfied with my cognitive abilities.

When he asks about the president, I let out a laugh. "I'm not sure anyone truly knows the answer to that." Radio broadcasts from the president have become infamous for his ever-changing voice during speeches.

"Very true," he acknowledges with a nod. "Did Leo mention your dog is doing well too?"

"He did. Thank you for letting him stay with us."

After a few more minutes of conversation, Williams informs me that Merissa is on the overnight shift again and will soon arrive to check my vitals before allowing me some rest. A cot has already been prepared for Leo to spend the night. He tells me to get some sleep and he'll see me tomorrow. Before Merissa arrives, Kerry Hendricks brings me a bowl of stew along with a couple of slices of bread.

It's about twenty minutes later when Merissa comes in. As she monitors my vital signs, Leo and Kerry carefully escort Gerry outside for his needs. When Leo returns, Merissa reports everything is progressing well. My temperature remains slightly low but is on the mend. All three of us should get some sleep, and we'll likely feel much better soon.

Merissa winks, a hint of humor in her voice. "Of course, we'll continue to wake you up every few hours. Hospital stays aren't known for their restful nights."

Chapter 6

Merissa

When I return to my shift at 1800 hours, I'm pleased to find Katie in much better condition. During the few instances she awakened last night, she had been disoriented, rambling about robots and spaceships. Confusion can often accompany hypothermia, and given the possibility that she may have sustained a head injury, it could be a contributing factor. She remains in considerable pain, and her body temperature has not yet returned to its optimal range, so she's currently staying in the break room.

As Katie's core temperature rises, the signs of frostbite become more apparent. Her nose, one of her ears, and the cheek on the same side bear clear evidence of frostbite. Fortunately, she had her boots on, and her toes appear to be unharmed. The pinky and ring fingers on her left hand have sustained some damage, but the others remain unscathed.

Leo mentioned her hands were tucked into Gerry's fur when he discovered her, which is likely why only two fingers were affected. The damage to the ring finger is mild, but the pinky doesn't look good, and she may end up losing the tip. We're acutely aware that the extremely low temperatures could've led to a far more dire outcome.

At some point during the day, both the girl with the broken leg and the woman with the infection were discharged. A young boy suspected of having Respiratory Syncytial Virus, known as RSV, was admitted.

Elaine Ebright continues to receive treatment. Her condition appears to be improving, and she's responding well. Deeming her sister on the mend, Marilyn requested a ride home from Deputy Shaw after he finished interviewing Katie for the umpteenth time. Both Elaine and Katie will likely remain hospitalized for several more days.

Officially on duty as a medic tonight, rather than shadowing other hospital personnel, I check in with Captain Williams. "Is there anything specific you need from me?"

"I think we're good. So far, it's . . . well, you know." He raises his eyebrows.

The superstition surrounding the word "quiet" looms large in this hospital. It's widely believed that uttering the word will invite chaos and disruption. I've experienced this phenomenon myself and fully subscribe to the notion.

"Understood, sir, and I agree. I like the way things are going right now."

He chuckles. "Indeed." Resuming a more serious demeanor, he adds, "Ms. Ebright seems to be improving. You were wise to take her complaints seriously. It's a valuable learning experience."

Captain Williams has used both Elaine and Katie as educational opportunities today. While formal classes have been somewhat suspended during this challenging period—until the arrival of a new doctor to ease the workload of the captain and Dr. Wolff—we still receive assignments and shadowing opportunities, and also hold daily meetings.

Today's meeting lasted from 1500 to 1700 hours, allowing me just enough time to grab a meal and put my swollen feet up before commencing my regular shift. After enduring the long shifts during the flu epidemic and an overnight shift last night, I'm thoroughly exhausted. Selfishly, I've considered how Katie's injuries will only increase my workload.

"Should I continue to oversee both Katie and Elaine?"

"Please do. I understand it's not the typical duty for your medic shift, but Elaine responds positively to your care. It's nice that she and her sister are making baby clothes for you."

I freeze, blinking rapidly. "Um . . . they're not making baby clothes for me."

"Really? Elaine mentioned it." Captain Williams tilts his head. "Perhaps she's still experiencing some confusion due to the sepsis."

"Must be. I'm sure I'm not the only one in this condition." I gesture toward my stomach.

"You're certainly not alone. I must say, the birthrate has slowed down a bit. The first year after the attacks was something else. I suppose, when the lights first went out, people— " He abruptly stops himself and clears his throat. There's a slight tinge to his cheeks and a drawn-out pause before he says, "Never mind about that."

I maintain an even expression while suppressing my laughter. "Is there anything else?"

"Keep me informed of any changes with either Sergeant Burnett or Ms. Ebright. Thank you, Mrs. Weaver." He gives me a brisk nod and limps away, his partially amputated foot now snugly encased in a walking boot, supported by a cane for balance.

As the night progresses, the hospital settles into a quiet rhythm. Katie is now resting more comfortably, thanks to the use of a variety of herbal remedies. Leo is sprawled out on the couch, finally succumbing to his exhaustion. I glance at the wall clock; it's approaching midnight.

With Katie's temperature close to normal, she no longer requires constant monitoring. Before leaving the room, I extinguish the oil lamp, leaving only the soft glow of the fire. Gerry lifts his head from his bed by the couch and emits a soft whine. He, too, is feeling better, although he's far from his usual energetic self.

As I engage in cleaning the examination rooms, weariness creeps in as the day's events catch up with me. Just as my eyelids grow heavy, the radio on my hip springs to life.

"Guard District Hospital, come in, over."

The voice on the other end is unfamiliar, but that's not entirely surprising given the recent influx of new personnel into both the National Guard and the Citizen Patrol following the Camp Rapid explosion.

"This is Weaver. Go ahead."

"Uh . . . Weaver, are you the medic?" the voice on the radio queries.

I purse my lips and respond evenly, "Affirmative. Go ahead, over."

"This is Deputy Garcia from the Main Street District, over."

Wondering why a deputy from a different district is contacting our hospital, I slip out of the examination room to find Captain Williams. "Go ahead, Garcia, over."

"We've received reports of a group of raiders making their way toward your location. They've been targeting survivors, stealing supplies, and causing mayhem wherever they go."

Raiders? While there are plenty of squabbles and arguments among the residents of Rapid City, raiders haven't been a concern in the area since the early days of the EMP. Moreover, it's odd that Deputy

Garcia, an unfamiliar person, is delivering this information. Typically, our own sheriff's deputies keep us informed about such matters.

"Garcia, please hold for a moment. I need to locate our head physician."

"Um, well, I guess I can hold. But don't take too long. This is important."

I give a firm knock on Captain Williams's office door and pop it open as soon as I hear him call, "Come in."

"Captain, there's someone on the radio. Deputy Garcia from Main Street District says raiders are heading our way."

"Raiders?" Captain Williams's disbelief is evident. "Let me speak with him. You said his name is Garcia?"

I raise a shoulder. "That's what he said."

He moves the radio to his mouth. "Garcia? This is Captain Williams. Please repeat the information you provided to my medic, over."

After a prolonged silence, Captain Williams repeats his transmission. When there's still no response, he remarks, "This is strange. Can you recap what he said?"

I reiterate the contents of Garcia's transmission.

Captain Williams shakes his head. "Raiders haven't been a problem for us, not here. There have been a few issues in the outlying areas, and it may still be a concern in some places, but not in our immediate vicinity. Perhaps there's an issue with the handheld. Let's try the CB base."

Even with his walking boot and cane, Captain Williams practically sprints from his office to the base radio at the nurse's station. When he reaches the base radio, he presses the talk button, causing feedback through my handheld radio. Equipped with an antenna on the roof, the citizen band radio provides decent reception, although not as robust as the few ham radios in the area. Nevertheless, it allows us to communicate with several other hospitals and provides relay options for more distant ones.

After attempting to contact Garcia on the base radio and receiving no response, Williams switches to the channel for the sheriff's deputies for our district and requests a supervisor.

Within seconds, a response comes through. "This is Trooper Schroeder, go ahead."

Captain Williams furrows his brow and asks me, "Is that the baby-faced highway patrolman?"

"I believe so, sir. That's his name, and it sounds like him."

"Schroeder, do you know Deputy Garcia from Main Street?" Captain Williams inquires.

"Garcia? He's one of the two regular deputies in that district . . . you know, from before the EMP. A good guy, but a bit gruff and overly sure of himself."

I make a skeptical face. The voice on the radio didn't convey a particularly gruff tone, and there seemed to be more than a hint of uncertainty in his words.

Captain Williams shakes his head before addressing the radio. "Garcia mentioned reports of raiders and the possibility we might be a target."

Schroeder snorts out a laugh. "Raiders? I haven't heard a thing about that. Garcia didn't call me, which is standard procedure. Let me investigate this. I'll get back to you, over."

"Copy that. Williams, out." Captain Williams eases into a chair. "This is interesting. What are your thoughts, Weaver?"

I shake my head. "I don't know, sir."

"Well, that makes two of us. Perhaps this Garcia fella stumbled upon a bottle of moonshine and is making prank calls."

I cock my eyebrow in response. "Could be, sir."

Despite prohibition being the unofficial law of the land, moonshine and other homemade spirits are readily available, along with various hallucinogenic drugs. Since mid-December, a wave of illness and death has swept through the area due to a drug called Ploy being sold on the black market.

There were even concerns that our late doctor, Chastity Morrow, had succumbed to Ploy use, though it remains unclear if it was an overdose or the flu that led to her death. Captain Williams is determined to uncover the truth behind her death.

Initially, suspicions fell on Geoff Landers, a former medical student romantically involved with Chastity. They were known to party together, indulging in alcohol and drugs. When Williams learned of the drug use, Landers was expelled from the medical school and left the area, while Dr. Morrow was placed on probation. The exact details of his expulsion and her probation remained confidential until her death, sparking rampant gossip.

After Landers returned to the area and learned of Chastity's death, he blamed Captain Williams and vowed revenge. According to Katie, Landers believed Williams had killed Chastity because she advocated for district hospitals to be freed from the South Dakota National Guard's control—a convoluted narrative.

While Chastity, Landers, and others—including Landers's uncle, Sheriff Melvin Cabal—were vocal about wresting control from the National Guard, the governor of South Dakota supported the existing system. Sheriff Cabal seems misguided in targeting local institutions instead of the state level.

Landers's belief that Captain Williams is behind Chastity's death is almost laughable. Given what I know about Landers—young, arrogant, and unpredictable, along with his penchant for mind-altering substances—it's conceivable his threats against Williams are an attempt to divert suspicion from himself.

"Williams, this is Schroeder, come in." The sudden radio transmission causes me to jump.

Williams leans forward to activate the desktop mic. "This is Williams, go ahead."

"I've reached Garcia. He claims he didn't contact you and has no knowledge of raiders or any other issues."

Williams runs a hand across his neck. "So, it was a prank? Someone with a radio who knows our channel?"

"That seems likely. Follow protocol to switch your team to alternate channels. I'll inform the guards. I'm en route to conduct interviews and get proper statements."

"Understood. Williams, out." He reclines in his chair once more. "I wonder what that was all about. Why would someone impersonate a deputy? And a more pressing question: how'd they access our channels?"

I remain silent, understanding that he's thinking aloud rather than seeking my input.

He leans forward again. "Landers. I bet he's involved in this."

Chapter 7

Katie

After two days in the hospital, I was released and we moved straight to Captain Williams and his wife's home, our safe house. Like Oscar and his family, Leo, Gerry, and I will stay here until they find my attackers.

We've been here for three days already. Although I do feel better, my recovery is slower than I'd prefer. The first few days after the attack, any movement was almost unbearable. Once my body temperature improved, I shifted from the break room with the uncomfortable cot to a regular patient room with a somewhat comfortable bed.

Nevertheless, I couldn't wait to leave the hospital. I eventually convinced Captain Williams that I'd heal better outside of the hospital, where I could get uninterrupted sleep.

Jesse drove me to the Williamses' house in the hospital's truck. We usually try to save fuel by using handcarts or the wagon, but the captain didn't want me to risk getting chilled.

I was right about sleep; it's mostly what Gerry and I have done since arriving here. We're both doing much better but are still taking things slow. At least both Gerry and I can go to the bathroom on our own now, which is a significant improvement from a few days ago.

As the attack became clearer, I provided Deputy Shaw with a few extra details. Nothing more than descriptions of their boots and insulated pants, but I did mention I heard the name Julius.

While the name meant nothing to Leo or me, Shaw perked up. "Really? Julius, huh?"

"You know him?" Leo asked.

Shaw replied with a single nod. "Sure do. Good job, Katie. We should be able to track them down and get you two, along with Oscar's family, back home soon."

I answered with a slight smile, not wanting to tell Deputy Shaw that I had zero desire to return to my house. With the break-in and being held hostage last month, combined with the recent attack in my backyard, I'm liking our house less and less.

The explosion at Camp Rapid left so much damage that the likelihood of us moving onto the base has almost completely diminished. There are still a few empty houses around the hospital; maybe we can get permission to move into one of them. For now, I'm happy to stay with Captain and Mrs. Williams.

Their place is plenty large, with two main-level master suites, giving Leo and me almost as much space as we have at our little house since we closed off the bedrooms. The bedroom even has French doors leading out to the patio, which is very helpful for taking Gerry out.

Leo and the Williamses are all working at the hospital today. Gerry and I are resting on a chaise lounge in front of the fire. I was trying to read, but my head still hurts enough to make it difficult. The bedroom has a beautiful fireplace with a woodstove insert that provides enough heat to keep the room cozy.

"Should we take a nap?" I ask Gerry, while rubbing his ears. "You want to go outside first?"

He lets out a moan and puts his head on his paws.

I give a soft laugh. "C'mon. Let's go potty, then we'll sleep." He stays on the chaise while I put on my coat, boots, and snow pants. It has warmed up considerably since the deadly temperatures of a few days ago. Nonetheless, I've learned my lesson about dressing for the weather, even when I'm only planning a short time outside.

I attach my inside-the-waistband holster, making sure my sidearm is in place, then slide into gloves that are thin enough to shoot with but still warm.

Before Christmas, I was on a quest to find a pair of mittens, but I kept getting interrupted. Now I realize these gloves are fine. Mittens would be a pain to take off before drawing my weapon. With these gloves, I'm not even very awkward. After RJ Cabal broke into my house, I went back to my gun draw practice.

My mom used to say, "Practice your draw or don't carry." While I've long taken her words to heart, I realized drawing while wearing gloves was not the same as drawing with bare hands. And mittens were not going to work. My fingers still show signs of frostbite and are bandaged, making the glove a tight fit on the two digits, but not enough to hamper movement.

Gerry and I stand by the glass door and scan the backyard before leaving the safety of our bedroom. I'm not going to lie; going out the French doors almost gives me a panic attack. Even though I'm sure the attackers have no idea where we are, I'm still nervous they'll find me. It doesn't matter if I wasn't their intended victim; it's still nerve-racking. Deciding it's safe, I take a deep breath and open the door. Gerry takes a hesitant step out as I follow.

Once we're outside, Gerry's still apprehensive. He stands near the door for several seconds, his nose in the air as he samples the surrounding area. He finally seems satisfied and limps off the stamped concrete patio to the backyard. Like me, my pup moves slowly and carefully.

He's finished his business, and we're making our way back to the house when the backyard gate squeaks. My hand automatically goes to the butt of my gun, while my dog steps in front of me, the coarse hair on his back standing up.

"Hey!" Merissa gives me a wave, then crinkles her brow. "Sorry. Did I scare you? Leo said I should come around back and knock on the glass door."

I move my hand away from my sidearm. Gerry must recognize her since he also relaxes his stance.

"Uh, hi. We were just . . ." I motion to my dog.

"It's warmer today at least." Merissa gestures around the yard. "Wow. This is beautiful. It was probably really amazing when the electricity was still on. Did the Williamses live here then?"

I shake my head and explain they lived in a different area. This was his brother and sister-in-law's house. His sister-in-law was the dentist who co-owned our hospital, which used to be a dental surgical center. The offices had been closed the week of the first attacks, with most of the staff volunteering as part of a medical and dental mission in East Africa.

When planes were grounded, they were stuck there. Williams last heard from them before the cyberwar took out the phones. Not only did Williams's sister-in-law go on the mission, but so did his brother and nephews.

When the district hospitals were being set up, Captain Williams suggested the dental office due to its location near Camp Rapid and the way it was designed, with large windows and other features. He and his wife moved here then. Probably a good thing, too, since the neighborhood where they originally lived was essentially destroyed in a fire that swept through parts of Rapid City.

"You look good," Merissa says as we move into the house and take off our coats.

"I'm feeling better. Still a little off, but better. How are you feeling?"

She opens her arms up to show off her well-rounded stomach. "Huge."

"Your weight?"

"Better. Dr. Wolff is happy with it."

When Merissa and her mother-in-law, Pearl, arrived in November, they were both too skinny. Merissa especially. She said she'd always had trouble keeping weight on, even before the EMP and food shortages.

While their town was doing okay, there certainly wasn't an abundance of anything. Like my home in Wyoming, they mainly survived on what they could hunt, forage, and grow. We all know how blessed we were, just like the people of the Black Hills, to have an abundance of wild game and a community of hunters.

Merissa passed through Billings, Montana, on the way here. They were only there for a few days while awaiting the rest of their party to arrive on horseback, but she saw enough of the once-bustling small city to know just how terrible things were for them.

"She measured you?"

"Yep. Still estimating the end of March for my due date. Earlier than I expected, for sure. I really thought late April to mid-May." She shakes her head.

"Barely over two months. It'll go fast."

She lets out a sigh. "This entire world goes fast. You'd think, with everything we do taking so much time, it'd be slower. But it's not. It amazes me that we've been living in the dark for over a year and a half. Some days it feels like just yesterday when we got the bomb alert. I still remember what I was doing—having breakfast with my husband on the balcony of our condo. We were separated then; he was living with Mother Pearl at her place, but we were trying to work it out."

"Why were you separated?"

She snickers. "He wanted children. I didn't." She rests a hand on her belly. "Now he's gone, and I'm going to have his child. It doesn't really seem right."

We stare at each other for a few moments. I want to say something comforting and helpful, but nothing comes to mind. "Um . . . do you want to sit down?"

Gerry and I take the chaise while Merissa takes a padded rocking chair. She comments about the room and how wonderful it is we have so much space. Once we're settled, she asks me what I was doing the day of the EMP.

I let out a laugh. "I was recovering from being shot."

Her eyes go wide, and her mouth forms an *O*. "What?"

"Yep. My mom, sisters, and I were attacked by a neighbor. He was . . . well, a little nuts. He kidnapped a friend of mine and killed her. My older sister had witnessed the abduction, and he thought if he silenced her, he could . . . I don't know. Get away with it? Like I said, he was a little nuts.

"Anyway, we had a doctor and nurses who put me back together. My folks had a basement at their house, and we all went there when the alerts came over the phones. I was kind of a wreck and was given some extra painkillers for the ride to their house. I barely remember anything from that day. We ended up staying in the basement for several days since we didn't know if there were bombs that hit somewhere and we had radiation."

"Same, though Braedon and I didn't think there were bombs detonated nearby. And we were extremely surprised we didn't launch any of our missiles. I'll never understand that. How come we didn't have more of a response? In some ways, it feels like we let them do this to us."

"If the rumors can be believed, it sounds like plenty of other countries shot off nukes too."

"Mutual destruction." She nods. "It kept us from bombing each other during the Cold War. I guess it's different now. Sometimes I wonder if we'll ever know who did this to us. From what we heard about the attempted coup in Billings, it sounds like the entire thing may have been an inside job—people from our own government destroying us from within. I guess that'd make sense, considering we didn't have much of a response."

"Wouldn't the president need to be involved, then?"

"Who says he isn't? Did you hear him on the last address?"

"He said he'd been sick with the flu and that's why he sounded funny."

"Sounded funny and talked completely differently. Each time we hear from him, it's almost like a different person. I don't know, Katie. It just all seems a little bizarre. There's been some weird radio stuff lately."

I nod my agreement. Even though I'm on medical leave, I'm well aware of the situation with the guy on the radio pretending to be a deputy from a neighboring district. Williams is convinced it's Landers. Well, not exactly Landers, since he's confident it wasn't his voice, but someone associated with him.

After the prank, the radio channels were immediately changed, and the following day new protocols and channels were enacted. While it's believed to be a prank, Leo says it rattled Williams. Even Deputy Shaw and Trooper Schroeder are taking it seriously.

Merissa leans back in the chair with a weary sigh. "Did Williams give you any idea when you can return to work?"

"A few more days, probably. How's Elaine Ebright?"

"Better. We've moved her to one of Poppy's care centers. Both Williams and Wolff believe she's going to make a full recovery."

"That's a miracle. Sepsis killed people when strong antibiotics were available to fight it. Now she's going to recover on Stella's herbs."

"And prayer. Stella's a big believer in prayer, too, and has spent a lot of time praying with Elaine. Not that Elaine thinks much of it, and her sister certainly has plenty of quips, but they seem to be lightening up now that Elaine is doing better."

"She and her sister are quite the characters."

"No doubt. It's obvious Elaine is better. She's hamming it up now and even doing some of her sewing while she recovers."

I laugh. "That's great that she's back to her old self."

After a few minutes of quiet companionship, Merissa says, "I'm surprised they took Leo out with them today."

I scrunch up my face. "What? Who took Leo?"

A puzzled expression crosses Merissa's face. "Um . . . Shaw. You didn't know?"

"Shaw took Leo?" My eyes go wide. "To look for the guys that attacked me?"

"He needed a medic— "

"Leo's arm . . . he isn't cleared."

"Kerry Hendricks went too. The captain ended classes early for the day so the two of them could go. I wanted to go, but . . ." She motions to her belly. "No more field trips for me until after the baby. Besides, I'm on duty tonight, so I need to get a nap in."

I give a solemn nod, forcing down the anger bubbling within me. I have little doubt Leo invited himself to go along with Shaw. I can't believe Captain Williams okayed it. "Do you know where they're going?"

"I don't know. I'm sorry I said anything. I thought maybe someone would've told you."

"Nobody said anything to me."

"I'm sure it was a last-minute thing, considering Shaw showed up at the school. Mrs. Williams is filling in for Leo, acting as the captain's aide until he gets back."

I tilt my head and take a deep breath. "I just hope he's smart about things. All he needs is to hurt his arm again."

"He's waiting for Bollinger to arrive on rotation now, right? You aren't going to the main hospital?"

"Right. Speaking of, did the new doctor arrive?"

"Not that I know of. Williams said it should be today, but he wasn't there when I left."

"Did they get the house ready for him?" I avoid pointing out it's the same house Chastity lived and died in. The same house that was the site of a murder-suicide when Bruce Blake was taken hostage. Before Blake, his brother-in-law Doctor Eugene Newsome was killed there.

Not that I believe in houses being cursed or anything, but still . . . I'm not sure I'd want to live there. I don't even want to move back to my house, and it doesn't have near the history of the house the new doctor will live in.

We talk a little more about the hospital and the new doctor, avoiding speaking of my husband going out with Deputy Shaw and his team in search of my attackers.

"Did you hear they moved Kemeera and her baby?" Merissa asks. "The rest of the children too. Even Zach and his mom."

"Leo told me. He said they've got them all in a house under guard. Leo also said the preacher and his people still aren't talking, but there's some thought maybe they didn't find all his followers."

"That's the rumor. Seems Kemeera let something slip to one of the nurses in the care center. But when questioned further, she clammed up. Zach's mom, her name's Mindy, still isn't talking. At least not to anyone outside of the children and Kemeera. Even her interactions with Kemeera seem to be limited to what is necessary."

"Have you seen her?"

"I went with Dr. Wolff to examine all of them after the move to the house. Mindy's definitely odd with her silence." She snickers. "And believe me, for me to say that is something."

I nod in agreement. Merissa is a quiet one herself. Our exchange today is rather unusual; she's rarely this chatty. I'm even further surprised when she asks if I'd be up to go with her to Opal's ranch.

"When?"

"The day after tomorrow. It's Opal's husband's birthday, and I have the day off. I'd love it if you could join us."

"Kevin's birthday? They wouldn't mind if I crashed the party?"

"Not one bit."

"That'd be great," I agree with a smile. "Will you take the wagon?"

She nods. "Either Shawn or Opal will show up around eight to pick us up. We'll come here and get you. Think the captain will allow it?"

"I'm sure he'll be fine with it." I don't point out that Leo is the one I need to persuade. I'm not particularly pleased with him for accompanying Shaw, so I'm not too worried about his thoughts regarding me visiting the ranch.

"Perfect. Bring Gerry too. You both deserve a day away."

After a good while, Merissa says she should probably go. It's her day to pick up her ration chips, and then she's going to go on to the different markets. "Can you cook in here?" She motions to the fireplace insert.

"Not on top of the insert. It doesn't have a cooktop like our woodstove at home, but I can cook inside the firebox like an oven. Mrs. Williams showed me how we could set it up. But we've had to keep the fire so hot because of the cold weather, so we haven't tried it. We've been cooking our meals on the main woodstove or eating with them. We're only staying here until they capture the men, so it may not be much longer."

"It did sound like Shaw had a hot tip." She gives me a reassuring smile. "I'm sure Leo'll be fine."

Chapter 8

Katie

The rest of my day seems to drag along as I wait for Leo or one of the Williamses to come home. I have little hope someone will arrive before the regular end-of-shift time.

Late afternoon, Gerry and I move to the living room and rebuild the flames of the still-smoldering fire in the woodstove in order to heat the leftover stew from last night. We have precooked foods to eat, like roast and bread, so I've been fine through the day.

With the stew bubbling on the stove, the yummy aroma makes my stomach growl. Even though we eat so many stews and soups, I don't mind them. It's easy to get different flavors just by combining different ingredients and spices or herbs.

When the captain and Mrs. Williams left their home, they brought all their food and personal items they thought they'd need. Even now, they still have a decent supply of dried herbs and spices, plus they grew more things in their garden last year. Mrs. Williams said she has some saved seeds she'll give me so I can start my own herb garden too.

Leo and Shaw have gone to our house a couple of times since we started staying here to not only gather things we need but to water our small indoor garden, which is going to be moved here if the attackers aren't found soon.

"You want to go for a quick walk?" I ask Gerry. His ears perk up, and he responds in his usual cheerful doggy manner. "Just in the backyard. I'm not up for anything more than that right now."

After coming back inside with Gerry, I'm tending to the stew when I hear a key turn in the lock. My heart rate quickens as my hand instinctively moves to my sidearm. Even though I'm fairly certain there's no threat, my body still reacts. I take a deep breath and force a friendly expression as Alice Williams enters.

"Hello, Katie," she greets me with a smile. "My, that smells good."

"It's the soup you made last night."

She laughs. "I am a fan of my own cooking."

"Are you alone?" I attempt to keep my voice light.

"The men are right behind me. Leo said he could push Chris with no problem. Dr. Murphy arrived. They're just showing him his house. He'll start work tomorrow."

I let out a breath. "Did Leo have any trouble with Deputy Shaw today?"

She raises her eyebrows. "You heard about that?"

"Merissa was here."

"They didn't find them." Alice rests a hand on my arm. "They will. Broderick Shaw isn't one to give up, you know that."

"Sure. Yes. Do you know if Leo will go out with them again?"

"Perhaps. It's good training for the med students. Leo can give instructions as they act as medics. Don't worry, your husband is smart about his limitations. Now let me get out of these clothes. I must say, Katie, having you and Leo here is truly a pleasure."

Gerry stands, his tail wagging.

"You too, Gerry." She kneels to pet him. "We haven't had a dog since we were first married. His name was Samson. I'd had him since I was thirteen. My parents kept him while I was in college, but he moved in with me when Chris and I married. He died a couple of years later. I still miss him."

After a few moments of giving Gerry some affection, she excuses herself to change. While she's gone, I amble through the big house. Both master suites are on the main floor, along with the formal living room and dining room, the kitchen, a family room, and a half bath. There is even a den and a library on the ground level.

Upstairs is a second family room, along with four bedrooms and two full baths. Like our house, the bathrooms have been converted to apocalyptic bathrooms. The upstairs two are completely closed off, while the downstairs ones now have compost toilets and camping showers.

I've heard people talk about how Captain and Mrs. Williams shouldn't get this big house all to themselves, how they should have others living with them. I don't really understand that since we don't necessarily have a housing shortage. With so many deaths in the first months of the EMP, due to needing medication or other care no longer available, followed by the terrible winter, housing isn't really an issue. Houses close to the dental-office-turned-hospital and Camp Rapid are limited, but there are still a few available.

Some have said this place would make a good long-term care center. Poppy Gardner approached the captain about it last summer, right around the time Leo and I arrived in Rapid City. I was shadowing Jacquie that day as part of my training when Poppy came flouncing in.

She's a tall redhead who looks more like a semi-retired supermodel than someone running a nursing home. Instead of scrubs and sensible shoes like we wear at the hospital, she was in a sundress and sandals. Her perfectly wavy hair flowed down the middle of her back, and big, round, fashionable sunglasses were perched on her perfect nose. She was even wearing earrings and makeup. I'm not going to lie, I felt completely frumpy next to the elegant older woman.

Poppy and Captain Williams met in his office. Jacquie had me doing inventory in one of the rooms nearby, and I could hear Poppy shrieking at the captain. She kept telling him he was being selfish, that his brother's home could give them another excellent care facility while the captain and his wife could move into something more modest.

When the woman left, her previously put-together demeanor was anything but. She stormed out of his office, slamming the door. In the hallway, she crashed into Jesse and declared him a clumsy oaf, only in less kind terms. She even made sure the front doorbell rang extra loudly. It was really something.

Obviously, the captain didn't give in to her request, but the next week he was able to commandeer a six-unit apartment building to turn into an additional care center. Poppy Gardner oversees that one, while her niece lives on-site, along with three other houses turned care centers.

Poppy worked as a nurse manager at the main hospital before the EMP. Captain Williams says she was instrumental in helping set up the district hospitals and care centers. Like Williams, she lived in a different area and was affected by the destruction following the lights going out. It was Williams who suggested she move to the Guard District and run the care centers here. I guess they were friends then; I'm not so sure they're friends now with her wanting to take his brother's house.

From the outside, I can see how this looks like a good place for a care center. It's huge. Not only does it have two main-floor suites, but there's also a small house in the backyard that was set up as a home for his brother's mother-in-law.

She was from Florida and would visit during the summer months. Normally, she would've already been in Rapid City, but she delayed her trip while her daughter went on her mission trip. The captain had originally offered the small house to Leo and me, but Mrs. Williams insisted we stay in the main home. I'm happy with the arrangement.

After being here for a couple of days, I don't agree with Poppy Gardner's assessment of this being a suitable care center. I mean, sure, it *could* work. There's a lot of space, but it isn't really a great layout unless you like going up and down stairs. Of course, they could turn the public downstairs rooms into dorm-style patient rooms. Maybe that's what Poppy has in mind?

In the library, I look through the books and search for an easy, beach-style read that won't tax my brain but will help the time pass. I'm just about done with the convalescing and ready to get back to my life. I'm really looking forward to going with Merissa to visit Opal.

As I step out of the library, the front door rattles. I move around the corner, sure it's Leo and Captain Williams but still cautious and apprehensive as my heart pounds loudly. I need to get my fight-or-flight reactions under control before I return to work; otherwise, every time the doorbells sound, I'll be a wreck.

Gerry isn't bothered at all and begins to do a little celebratory dance. I painfully bend to his level. "Is Leo home?"

I could almost swear he gives me a little nod and a doggy smile.

After greeting my husband and Captain Williams, Leo and I head into our bedroom so he can change. In the privacy of our room, he pulls me into an embrace. "How was your day?"

"Merissa stopped by. Said you went out on patrol with Shaw?"

"With Kerry," he replies promptly. "Part of her training."

"That's what Merissa and Mrs. Williams said."

"I was careful."

I wave a hand. "I know. It's just, I worry you'll hurt that arm again, and we'll be right back where we started."

"We won't. I won't go there again. I'm better now. Mentally, I mean."

I let out a long breath. "I wish I was. I'm a nervous wreck." I give a critical laugh. "I swear, I jump at every little sound and noise."

"We're going to catch them. Shaw got a good lead. It's just a matter of time now."

"Why are they even after Oscar?"

Leo shakes his head. "That Julius guy is a relative of someone Oscar and his dad arrested last summer. The guy had some sort of seizure or something and died."

"So, it's revenge? The guy must have done something pretty serious to be arrested."

Leo's mouth goes into a straight line. "Something very bad. Definitely deserving of arrest. I'm not even sure it's a bad thing he died."

"I don't think I want to know."

Leo pulls me close again. His breath tickles my ear. "We're going to find Julius and the others. Once we do, we can move back home."

My body stiffens.

He pulls away and tilts his head at me. "Or we can find a different place. I know that house hasn't felt right to you since RJ and Young broke in."

"It's— " I shake my head, which sends a wave of pain through it. I need to take another dose of willow bark tincture. The natural pain reliever does a decent job of keeping the pain at bay. "Let's talk about this later. *After* they capture Julius and his gang."

Mrs. Williams knocks on the door and tells us they're ready to eat. I take a dose of tincture before we join the couple in the kitchen. Even though they have a large formal dining room, we take all the meals in the kitchen where the woodstove was added.

Their woodstove is an old-fashioned style with a firebox and separate oven, along with ringed burners on top. The Williamses brought this from their old house, part of an outdoor kitchen and entertainment area. They also brought a pizza and bread oven that's set up in the backyard. During the heat of the summer, they do their cooking outside using the pizza oven and a rocket stove.

We're about halfway through dinner when the captain's walkie-talkie sounds. "Captain, this is base. Come in."

I look at Leo and mouth, "Merissa."

He nods as the captain responds. "Go ahead, base."

"We have a situation and need you back on duty, over."

Captain Williams lets out a sigh. "Be right there. Out."

Leo slides his chair back. "May I accompany you, sir?"

Williams looks to his wife, who gives a dip of her chin. "I'll stay home with Katie, unless you think you need me."

"I'm not sure what's going on. But yes. Leo can go with me, Alice. Hopefully, we'll be back soon, but don't wait up."

"I never do." She smiles at her husband.

I follow Leo to our bedroom where he quickly redresses. "Can you really push Williams in the wheelchair?"

"Yep. With the sleds on, it's easy. Sure hope this isn't anything big."

"Merissa was pretty vague."

"Very vague. She's a woman of few words."

I let out a laugh. "I like her. She's quiet, but in a good way."

"Jesse hates when both Merissa and Nettie are on. There's hardly any talking at all."

"I can imagine. Both are rather reserved. Want me to tie your boots for you?" Even though Leo's become adept at tying with just one hand, a technique taught to him by one of the nurses who used to care for stroke survivors, he's still slow at it. While I'm fast at tying, bending into a squat is slow and uncomfortable. I do it anyway.

With Leo ready to go, I kiss him goodbye and tell him I'll see him soon.

"Don't wait up." He gives me a wink and another kiss.

I playfully pop him on the arm and repeat what Mrs. Williams said, "I never do." We both know that's not true. I may try to sleep, but I won't do well at it until he's back home.

Chapter 9

Merissa

"Captain Williams will be here shortly." I motion to Deputy Shaw. "We'll prepare everything in case you need us."

Shaw dips his chin. "Thanks. I don't know why these situations always happen after dark. Maybe this time the intel is solid, and we'll finish this."

"I hope so." Oscar Harrington claps Deputy Shaw on the shoulder. "Then we can get out of your hair."

"Are you kidding? My wife loves having your kids around. They keep the dog busy. Anyone else show up?"

"The guard mentioned there are six men there now. Where do you want to do the briefing? In here, where it's warm?"

Deputy Shaw turns back to me. "Can we use your break room?"

"I'm sure it's fine, but Dr. Wolff's in charge, so you should check with her. Or wait until the captain arrives."

Nettie Wolff steps out of the treatment room, where she's examining a young boy brought in with what's believed to be the lingering flu in the area. "What's the plan, Deputy?"

Shaw gives her a light smile. "Williams is on his way. I was just asking Petty Officer Weaver if we could use your break room."

I tighten my lips at Deputy Shaw's reference to my former rank. Although I didn't share my Coast Guard background with him, he heard it from someone else and insists on mentioning it.

Like me, his dad served as a Damage Controlman aboard a cutter, aspiring for his son to follow in his footsteps. Instead, Shaw joined the Navy and then eventually moved to Rapid City and joined the sheriff's department.

Despite my repeated requests to call me Merissa, he doesn't. He prefers Petty Officer Weaver or DC Two, which stands for Damage Controlman Two, reflecting my former Coast Guard role. Maybe using my rank reminds him of his dad? He once confided in me about his concern for his parents, who retired to a coastal town in North

Carolina. Although there weren't any reports of a direct nuclear strike in their immediate area, it means little for their safety.

With the nationwide death rate ranging from 80 to 90 percent, survival seams bleak, especially in heavily populated areas. I take a deep breath. Even my hometown of Livingston, Montana, with a population under ten thousand before the EMP, suffered catastrophic losses.

I twist my wedding band, a constant reminder of my personal loss, as is my growing waistline. As I told Katie earlier today, I might not have thought about wanting children in the pre-EMP world, but now, I yearn for this child to arrive safely and healthy.

Dr. Wolff tells the deputy they can use the break room. Oscar Harrington uses his radio to call the hospital guard station, summoning the other deputies and Citizen Patrol members inside. They'll strategize for the raid and then inform the rest of us. Within minutes, half a dozen men and women, including Jesse Talbot, enter through the front door.

Jesse motions to me and Dr. Wolff. "Thanks for letting me know, Merissa. Josiah's going out with us too." He points to his brother, who's among the others. "I'm joining them for the briefing. Is the captain coming in?"

"I called him. He should be here shortly."

"I wish Dr. Murphy were trained." Nettie Wolff says with a shake of her head. "The last time we had police action, there were several casualties. Sometimes, I wish we lived in a smaller town." She gazes wistfully. "Maybe it'd be quieter."

I choose not to voice the thoughts that recently crossed my mind about the dangers in smaller towns. I'm not sure there's anywhere truly safe now.

Jesse excuses himself and enters the break room with the rest of the group. The door's barely closed when the hospital's back doorbell rings. The front skid of Captain Williams's outdoor wheelchair becomes visible, followed by the man himself. He raises a hand in greeting before transferring out of his chair and taking up his cane. Leo is right behind him. I watch for a moment, expecting to see Mrs. Williams, but she's not part of tonight's group.

Dr. Wolff says she'll update the captain on the situation. "Would you pop your head in and tell Jacquie I'll be right back?"

"Another case of the flu?"

She scrunches her face. "I don't think so. Probably another RSV."

In addition to the flu bug that's hit our area hard, we're seeing lots of children come in with RSV. It used to be diagnosed with a mouth swab or a blood test to check white blood cell counts and look for viruses. We can still do some very basic bloodwork using our microscope but tend to leave those things for extreme cases.

Now we treat symptomatically and use our arsenal of natural medicines. The captain has said more than once it's a difficult way to do medicine, but if Imhotep—a physician in recorded history—could treat people in Ancient Egypt, we can do it now.

I may understand that Williams is right, but Imhotep had the advantage of not knowing any better. Our biggest challenge is reconciling the medical advances of the past century with the methods of historical doctors like Imhotep and Hippocrates, as well as modern practitioners like my fellow med student Stella Swenson, who specializes in natural and herbal medicine.

Even Dr. Murphy, who arrived today, apparently made a few comments about our primitive setup. I didn't meet him, but Dr. Wolff did, and I was mildly surprised when she expressed her lack of enthusiasm. Dr. Wolff isn't much of a conversationalist, and certainly not a gossip, but her comments about Dr. Murphy make me wonder why he was sent here.

While I inform Jacquie about the situation, doctors Wolff and Williams make their way to the break room. Leo nods to me as he opens the door for the captain.

"Hello, gentlemen." The captain's voice carries down the hallway. "I thought I'd listen in if you don't mind." The door closes before I hear the response, but I can't imagine Deputy Shaw being anything but welcoming, especially considering this is Captain Williams's hospital, and law enforcement collaborates closely with the National Guard.

I furrow my brow. I'm slightly surprised that no one from the Guard is present at the meeting. Typically, when planning a raid, they cooperate.

Well, not always.

The Guard recently conducted a raid on their own after following a tip about the preacher and his cult, who were suspects in a recent series of explosions. One of those explosions targeted Camp Rapid and killed dozens of soldiers and severely injured many others. The Guard is still recovering from the Christmas Day explosion. Why they chose not to include the sheriff's department and Citizen Patrol in capturing the preacher and his followers hasn't been revealed, at least not to me.

Whether the preacher is genuinely responsible for the explosions is still a mystery. As far as I know, none of them are talking. One woman from the sect seems like she might want to discuss it, but she remains silent.

When I accompanied Dr. Wolff to examine everyone after they settled into the home, which is under twenty-four-hour guard, Mindy didn't utter a word. Kemeera wasn't particularly chatty, but an unspoken feeling lingered, suggesting she might be willing to confide. Yet, a lingering doubt nags at me, wondering if she'll reveal the whole truth if she does open up. My guess is she'll pick and choose what she shares.

I've just finished checking one of the patient rooms when Captain Williams calls out to me from down the hall.

"Sir?"

"I know we discussed you not going out as a medic, with the baby and everything."

"We did, but if you need me . . ."

"Do you feel up to it? I'll send Leo too. The two of you can take the red pickup truck. Shaw will station you several blocks away. Jesse will be in the green truck. We're right on the line for this being our concern. Seems the suspected location is on the border of our district and Main Street District." He tilts his head and raises his eyebrows. "There shouldn't be any danger. Not like before."

I swallow and nod. A few weeks ago, I responded to a situation where a man was assaulting his girlfriend. He ended up on the run and encountered me and Patroller McKay. He shot and killed McKay before fleeing and is still at large. "I'm sure it'll be fine."

"It's a task the Main Street District should handle."

"I understand. It's personal, with Katie beaten up and left for dead, plus Oscar Harrington being threatened."

"Everyone will handle it smartly. I'm sure. But yes, it's personal."

"When do we leave?"

"Ten minutes. Check with Leo and Jesse on the plan. Thanks for this."

"Absolutely. Do we need to call in anyone else?"

"I'm thinking about sending for Dr. Murphy. Might as well give him a true taste of life in the Guard District. I'll send Rand Hendricks after him. Maybe have him drop by his house on the way to the doctor's so he can wake Kerry and have her come into the hospital. I pray things will go fine, but if not, she'll be an asset."

"It's a good idea, sir," I say. Rand Hendricks only returned to work last week. Like many others in the Black Hills, he was afflicted with the flu. His wife, Kerry, one of the med students who also works as a janitor at the hospital, would truly be an asset if there are wounded.

It takes almost fifteen minutes for the final checks before we're ready to go. Even though Leo, Jesse, and I will be stationed several blocks away at the staging area, we're still wearing tactical gear—common for medics when going out on patrol.

I'm sure Leo and I look almost comical, with his arm in a sling and my bulging belly. At least the body armor expands enough to fully cover me. I push down the memory of McKay also wearing his body armor when he was shot in the neck and bled out before I could do anything to help him.

I drive the old red pickup while Leo rides in the cab. Jesse takes the green truck with Shaw in the passenger seat. The rest of the men pile in the truck beds. When we reach the staging location, I pull onto the shoulder behind Jesse, and everyone piles out.

"All right," Shaw addresses the group. "It'll take us a good forty-five minutes to even get into position. We'll click the radio three times when we're ready to go. As always, we're hoping this will be easy. If not . . . that's where you three come in." He gestures at me and my fellow medics.

I look around at the street signs. Skyline Drive, where we've pulled to the side of the road, is the dividing street between the Guard District and the Main Street District. Williams wasn't kidding when he said this was right on the line of something we should handle. Right on the true dividing line between the districts.

"Um, Deputy?" Leo lifts a hand.

"Yes?"

"Do the Main Street guys know we're here?"

"They know. Deputy Garcia gave his blessing on our handling of this. He has a couple of men standing by should we need the help, which we don't think we will. The closest hospital has also been alerted, though we fully intend to return to our hospital. That's why we brought the trucks instead of the handcart. Okay, final checks, then let's move."

Deputy Garcia is the one who was impersonated on the supposed prank radio call we received. Williams has mentioned it several times since it happened, but nothing further has come of it. Within a few minutes, the deputies and Citizen Patrol disappear into the night.

"Well, I guess we wait," Jesse says. "Hop in my truck. We can visit and get out of the wind."

I squeeze in the middle while the men take each side. Before moving into position, I unholster my pistol with a plan to keep it on my lap. Just being in the cab and waiting in a supposedly safe place brings the memories of McKay's death back to the surface. Jesse also mentions everyone needs to stay alert.

As usual, when the three of us are together, there's some good-natured ribbing related to our former military service. Well, *their* military service. They love to remind me I may be considered military in the broadest sense of the term, but I didn't operate under the Department of Defense but rather Homeland Security. I remind them we're still part of the Armed Forces. I get it, though. My husband, Braedon, who was retired Army, loved to tease me too.

"At least it's warmed up some compared to what it was a few days ago," Jesse says in a quiet voice as he lightly taps on the steering wheel. "Still would be nice to run the engine and turn on the heat."

"Or have heated seats," Leo suggests. "I never cared for them when they were available, but now a hot seat sounds pretty good."

"My car had heated and cooled seats," I add. "I loved them."

Jesse chuckles. "Air-conditioned seats. Man, we had it good, didn't we? Think it'll ever get back to that?"

I pull my lips into a line and shake my head. Even though I'm trying to act relaxed and engaged, I scan the rearview mirror, willing my eyes to see in the dark. Almost simultaneously, each of the men glances around.

"I doubt it," I say. "I'm not even sure we'll get back to having the lights on, let alone getting back the cars we had."

"Yeah, except we have the knowledge now, right? We know how to make all the advances we made before. So, now it's just a matter of infrastructure."

An object strikes the side window and causes all of us to jump. Leo and Jesse both grab their sidearms. My hand is already on the butt of my pistol.

"Hey, this is Daniel Garcia from the Main Street District." The voice is deep and determined. "Trooper Schroeder's with me."

"I know the trooper," I whisper.

Jesse mutters several things before cranking the window down an inch. "Not smart to sneak up on us like that."

"Yup," the deputy agrees. "That's why I tossed a pebble instead of walking up on you. I'm approaching the driver's side of the vehicle now." The deep voice is definitely not the same voice that came over the radio that night.

"Go ahead." Jesse moves his hands to the steering wheel. I put mine on the dash, while Leo moves his right hand into the same position. "There are three of us. We're medics with the Guard District Hospital."

A bearded face appears at the window. Jesse rolls the window down further as I crane my neck to catch a glimpse of Deputy Garcia and Trooper Schroeder.

"Figured as much," the deputy says. "The red cross painted on the door's a bit of a clue. Does the truck ahead belong to you too?"

"Yes, it's ours."

"You hear from your team?"

"Not yet. Probably another— " He glances at me.

I flick my wrist to check my watch. "Ten minutes."

"Hello, ma'am." The deputy sticks his head in the window, causing Jesse to push back against the seat. "You one of the nurses? Or a doctor?"

"Medic." I dip my chin.

"Hey there, Weaver," Schroeder greets me with a youthful smile, the wintry air lending a rosy hue to his smooth, whisker-free cheeks.

"You know her?" the deputy asks.

Schroeder says I was the one he was with when there was suspicious activity in a shed. He also says I was with Williams when the Garcia impersonator was on the radio.

"Not sure why anyone would want to impersonate me." Garcia shakes his head. "The other thing . . . the shed owned by the mechanics?"

After Schroeder confirms it's the same shed, the deputy asks Leo and Jesse if they're also medics. There are a few more minutes of chitchat between the men, while I sit there feeling like a fifth wheel. They sound like they're wrapping it up when the radio squawks. "This is a negative. We're heading back to the rigs."

Garcia shakes his head. "Too bad. Thought they had a good tip this time. Hope they get 'em. We can't have people threatening our law enforcement. I heard they even beat up a woman, thinking it was the Citizen Patroller they were after. Can't imagine what kind of idiot made that mistake."

Leo's tightened jaw and the sudden sharpness in his voice betray the brewing storm of his anger. "A big idiot. An idiot who's going to pay."

Chapter 10

Merissa

As the wagon rattles along, Katie's puppy sighs and rests against her thigh. She pulls the blanket closer, wincing with the movement.

"I'm glad you're feeling well enough to go to the ranch," I say, extending a hand toward Gerry, who licks my fingers. "You too, little guy." I raise my gaze. "I noticed he was limping when you came out of the house." I decide not to mention Katie also has a limp.

"Sometimes," Katie replies, her voice laced with concern as she looks down at Gerry. "But he's a tough one, just like his mama." She strokes Gerry's head, eliciting a contented sigh from the puppy. "We'll be fine in a few more days."

The bruising on her face is faded and yellowed. Her nose, cheek, and ear all have small squares of fabric secured by precious medical tape. She's wearing gloves, but I'm sure her frostbit fingers are also bandaged.

"That's right," Opal chimes in from her spot on the wagon bench. "You and Gerry will make full recoveries."

Mother Pearl, sitting next to Opal, mutters something under her breath. Although I can't hear her words, it's likely about the dangers in Rapid City.

Opal seems to have caught her sister's remark and snorts in response. "You think it's better in other places? At least we've got the hospitals and the law. And now that they caught the preacher and his group, we won't have to look over our shoulders all the time."

"Well, the preacher wasn't responsible for poor Katie getting beat up and left out in the cold, was he?" There's an edge to Pearl's voice. "I'm telling you, there's something evil happening around here. More than just that crazy preacher. And I've told Merissa she shouldn't believe a word those women who were part of that cult say. They can't be trusted."

I pull my lips into a tight line. I haven't divulged much about Kemeera, Mindy, and the children, but I did tell Pearl they seem to be recovering from their ordeal, especially the children. One thing is for certain, she's right about not trusting them.

"I'm sure Merissa knows what to believe and what not to believe," Opal responds.

"And whom to trust," I add.

As we approach the turn to the ranch, Gerry carefully rises to his feet. His nose reaches toward the sky, taking in the scents of the ranch: cattle, horses, sheep, goats, chickens, and other dogs, along with several barn cats, all mingling in a symphony of rural life.

"I wish Leo was off today," Katie says. "He didn't even hide the fact he was jealous that I was going to spend the day here. It almost feels like a different world."

Pearl tuts. "Not much safer, though. That crazy neighbor Hayward and his killer dogs . . . really, Opal, you should do something about him."

"What would you like me to do, dear sister?"

"Report him to the police!"

"That happened after the trouble on New Year's Day," I gently remind Pearl. "Deputy Shaw spoke with his counterpart in this district. They talked to Hayward, but . . ."

"They did," Opal agrees with a nod. "To him, his wife, and their hired hands. We all know that if something like that had happened before the EMP, the dogs would've been put down. But the deputy is giving them a lot of leeway. He understands the need to protect our ranches since we supply food for our district, your district, and most of the others too. While I don't agree with Hayward's methods, and I feel terrible for the way he's trained the dogs who are innocent in this, I understand his motivation."

Katie leans toward Opal. "Merissa and I were talking about Hayward a few days ago. She said he's changed, and it may be because of medical issues?"

With a weary sigh, Opal agrees he has changed. "Misty—that's his wife. She and I are still friends, but it's getting harder and harder to keep that friendship going. Gary Hayward has definitely changed. Pearl's not wrong that living next to him is like living near a powder keg." She slows the horses as we enter the driveway. "But there truly isn't much we can do about it."

"Has he seen a doctor?" Katie asks.

"Nope. Misty talked him into it before the explosion at our hospital, but now he refuses. Doesn't even want to leave his land. Says it's too dangerous."

"He's got that right," Pearl mutters.

"Maybe we could examine him?" Katie motions to me. "See if we can— "

"I don't know about that," Opal interrupts. "Maybe I can talk to Misty, see if he'd be willing, but no way can we just show up and try to make that happen."

Opal brings the wagon to a stop. "Enough about Hayward for now. Let's try to enjoy the day." She turns in her seat, her expression friendly yet strained. "I'll put the kettle on, and we'll have a cup of tea before Kevin's birthday lunch. I've even got some pumpkin scones for us."

Pearl slides forward on the bench. "I could eat."

Opal puts a hand on her older sister's arm. "Here comes Shawn. He'll help you off. Merissa, you and Katie wait for a hand too."

Shawn's face lights up as he takes my hand and helps me from the wagon. "Good you can visit today. My mom's been looking forward to it."

"Thank you. So has Pearl," I say. "We need to help Gerry down too. He's still not healed."

After Katie's on the ground, Shawn helps the dog. "He's grown," he says as he passes the end of the leash to Katie. "Is he trained to be off leash?"

Katie slings her backpack over her shoulder. "Only in fenced yards. Not that I think he'd go anywhere, but here . . ." She motions around the ranch. "There's so much he could get excited about. He may try and take off." She lifts her chin toward the ranch dogs sitting near the barn. There's no doubt they are aware of the presence of the puppy, but they seem to pay him little mind.

Pearl grasps Shawn's elbow as the rest of us follow behind. The air is crisp, and the snow beneath our boots crunches softly with each step. Gerry tugs on his leash, eager to explore this new environment filled with intriguing scents and sounds. Katie gently corrects him while encouraging him to "walk like a nice puppy." I swear he smirks at her before he lets out a whimper of disappointment.

As we approach Opal's sprawling ranch house, a plume of smoke billows from the chimney, a comforting sight in this winter chill. Opal holds the door open and ushers us inside. The warmth of the cozy, well-lit kitchen immediately envelops us. The aroma of pumpkin scones wafts through the air, and my stomach rumbles in anticipation. A solid kick from my baby follows the rumbling. It rarely fails that she, or he, seems to know when it's time for me to eat.

"Give me just a few minutes to get the water hot," Opal says as she pulls a kettle forward. "Go ahead and make yourselves comfortable. Katie, no need to keep Gerry on his leash inside. He can roam around."

After helping Mother Pearl to her chair, Shawn says he's going out to the processing shed. They butchered a cull cow earlier, and he wants to make sure their hired hands don't need help. "Did you want me to give Merissa and Katie a ride back later?" he asks his mom.

"Yes, please. Will you check on the lunch preparations for me? I'm planning on enjoying my visit." Opal explains that her ranch helpers are handling the birthday lunch today, while she made and decorated the cake. She then turns her gaze toward me. "I certainly appreciate you letting me share time with Pearl."

Pearl waves a hand. "Merissa's rarely home, anyway. Besides, once her baby arrives, I'll be too busy helping with him to come out to the ranch."

"You'll still be able to visit," I promise. "Plus, I hope to make my own trips out here." I lean back in my chair and let out a sigh. "It really is almost like a different world here."

Within a few minutes, the kettle whistles, and Opal serves the tea and scones. As we settle into our seats and start sipping tea, a distant, mournful howl pierces the air. It's a sound we've all grown accustomed to—the distant cry of the coyotes that roam nearby. But this time, the howl seems closer, more urgent. Gerry jumps to his feet, the hair standing up on his back as he releases a throaty growl.

"You're okay, Gerry," Katie soothes in a calm voice. "It's just the coyotes." She furrows her brow and glances at Opal. "Do you often hear them this late in the morning? Back in Bakerville, they usually made noise at night or daybreak."

Opal finishes the bite of scone in her mouth, then wipes her lips before answering. "Used to be that way here too. Now they seem to sing whenever they get the urge. Everything has been different since the EMP, especially the wildlife. I've even heard there's getting to be a wolf population. We've never really had any here, nothing more than the occasional transient wolf passing through, but now we may be getting a resident population. Of course, these are just rumors I'm hearing from the drayers. They've also talked about grizzly bears and bigfoot, so . . ." She raises her hands and shakes her head.

"Pshaw!" Mother Pearl exclaims. "Tall tales for sure."

As we chat and nibble on scones, the howling continues intermittently. It's an eerie reminder of the wilderness that surrounds us, a wilderness that has, as Opal pointed out, grown even more unpredictable since the world changed.

"Anyone ready for a warm-up?" Opal asks as she slides her chair back.

As I push my cup toward the edge of the table, the faint ring of a bell interrupts our conversation.

"The dinner bell?" Pearl asks.

"Not ours." Opal hurries toward the window. "It's Hayward's, but . . ." She pushes back the curtain and lets out a gasp. "There's a plume of smoke."

Opal's declaration sends a shiver down my spine, and I exchange a worried glance with Katie as I get to my feet.

"Where are you going?" Pearl points to my stomach, her mouth drawn in a tight line.

"Can you watch my dog for me?" Katie asks Pearl as she limps toward the front door where we hung our coats.

Opal is already putting her boots on; she understands there's no discussion needed about the urgency of getting to Hayward's home and doing what we can.

"I'll be careful," I tell my mother-in-law. "Please, don't worry. Keep Katie's dog, and . . ." I shake my head. "We'll be back as soon as we can."

Pearl's eyes widen, and she clutches her chest. "Those dogs, though. We were just talking about how dangerous they are. Opal?"

"We'll be careful." Opal pushes a stocking cap down around her ears. "They're only dangerous when Hayward gives the order to attack."

The front door opens, and Shawn sticks his head inside. "There's a fire at the Haywards' place. Looks like the barn."

"Grab all the buckets," Opal says, "I'll get some towels and blankets."

"A few of the ranch workers have already headed out with buckets, shovels, and hoes." He glances in my direction. "You've got your med kit ready, right?"

Katie touches her backpack. "I've got mine handy."

With more than a hint of anxiety, I say, "Let's pray there are no injuries."

Chapter 11

Merissa

Shawn swiftly brings the wagon around, and even though Katie and I suggest walking, Opal insists we ride because of Katie's injuries. She doesn't mention my pregnancy, but I catch her glance toward my stomach.

The plume of smoke thickens, becoming more foreboding. The sound of crackling flames and distant shouting reaches our ears and fuels our determination.

When we arrive at the Haywards' ranch, the scene is chaotic. Flames devour a section of their barn, and ranch hands frantically attempt to control the blaze. Misty Hayward, her face etched with worry, rushes toward us and reaches for my arm. "You're Opal's niece who's training to be a doctor, right?"

I dip my chin and gesture toward Katie. "And my friend's a nurse. Is someone injured?"

"We can't find Gary! Someone said he may be in the barn." She turns and runs toward the barn, yelling for her husband as she goes.

I take in the scene. The bucket brigade is already in action, passing pails of water to douse the flames. Men use wet towels to beat at a section of flames, while others work to lead panicked livestock away from the area.

The heat from the raging fire presses against us as Katie and I exchange worried glances. Without conversation, we grab two empty buckets and join the bucket brigade, falling into a rhythm of passing water with the others. The acrid smell of burning wood and hay fills the air, and the orange-red flames dance menacingly in front of us.

As we work to quell the fire, Misty Hayward continues to call out for her husband, her voice filled with desperation. The ranch hands search the surrounding area, shouting his name amid the chaos. The minutes feel like hours as we struggle to make progress against the relentless inferno.

Opal's husband, Kevin, was among the first of the firefighters to rush to the neighboring ranch as soon as the smoke was noticed. He wraps a wet towel around his face and yells to the men at the door that he's going in. Two additional men follow suit and race inside the burning building to look for Hayward.

"Oh, no," Katie whispers as she glances toward Opal.

The stout woman's lips move as her eyes focus on the barn door. She hands a bucket to the next man in line. I have little doubt she's praying as she works.

"Over here! We found him!" one of the ranch hands yells, his voice strained with relief. The three men shuffle out of the building, carrying Gary Hayward between them.

Katie and I drop our buckets and rush to them. Hayward's clothes are singed and blackened, and his face is covered in soot.

"He's unconscious but breathing," Katie reports. "We need to get him away from the fire."

Kevin and the others who went into the barn are coughing and sputtering. New men arrive to help move Hayward to a safe location. Misty rushes to her husband's side, tears streaming down her face. She whispers his name over and over.

As the bucket brigade continues its efforts, a voice in the crowd calls out that the barn is beyond saving. He urges everyone to shift their focus to protecting the remaining structures and the Hayward residence.

Amid the chaos, I can't help but notice three dogs nearby. Their tails are tucked between their legs as they watch with solemn eyes. These were the same three dogs involved in the tragic incident on New Year's Day, which resulted in the loss of two lives and a teenager being severely injured.

However, as they sit there a few feet away, calm and well-behaved, there's a stark contrast between their demeanor now and the violence of that fateful day. The dogs appear docile and innocent; their eyes reflect a quiet sadness, as if they carry the weight of their actions from the tragic past with them.

"Should we put him here?" Katie points to a spot at the edge of the driveway, well away from the smoke and flames.

I bring myself back to the present and nod. "Be careful with him."

I take the lead and begin my assessment of the injured man. Katie peels off her backpack and pulls out the supplies we may need. Our eyes meet as I give a light shake of my head. It's a grim scene—his skin is blistered, and his breathing is labored.

It's a scene we've experienced too many times in recent months with the explosions caused by the preacher and his followers. I glance back at the barn, now no longer recognizable as a structure. There are still directions being shouted as the firefighters work to prevent the fire from spreading.

I close my eyes and mutter a quick plea to God. "Please, Lord, please don't let the wind come up." I steel my shoulders and turn back to Katie. "Can you grab my stethoscope out of my bag?

"Here's mine." She thrusts it in my direction. I give a nod of thanks before continuing my examination. Even though the man is breathing, it's painfully clear Gary Hayward's time in the inferno has left him with critical injuries. With each passing moment, his breathing slows. His body shows signs of severe burns extending deep beneath the surface.

Misty Hayward kneels at her husband's side and whispers words of comfort and love. The ranch hands who carried him to safety rejoin the firefighting efforts.

"Can you help him?" Misty asks.

Katie rests her hands on the woman's arm. "We can try to keep him comfortable."

Misty chokes out a sob. "Please. I know . . . the last few months have been difficult, and he's changed in many ways, but he has been a good husband to me for over forty years. Please do what you can for him."

"Wild lettuce tincture?" Katie asks, offering me a small vial of the powerful herb. Although it isn't an opiate, Stella has said wild lettuce is sometimes called "opium lettuce" or "poor man's opium" because of its traditional use to treat pain and sleeplessness. While not as potent as some medications available before the EMP, we've had good results with this concentrated tincture and hope it'll at least bring Mr. Hayward some comfort.

I put a few drops of the bitter liquid in his mouth; he doesn't react. A coughing fit from nearby captures my attention. Kevin Maher is leaning against a pole fence, trying to catch his breath. The other two who went into the barn with him are sitting nearby, also looking worse for wear.

"I'll help Kevin and the others who went into the barn," Katie says.

There's little I can do for Mr. Hayward, but I run through the options in my mind as I check his pulse. It's weak and slow. His breathing is too. We need to get him and the other men to the hospital.

I scan the area and see Shawn and Opal helping to wet an outbuilding. "Shawn!" I yell, trying to capture his attention.

After a few more tries, he stops what he's doing and looks around.

I wave my arms and motion toward the wagon.

He rushes to his mom before pointing at me. The two of them dash to the wagon as Katie runs up to me. "Kevin and the others need to go to the hospital. Mr. Hayward?"

"The tincture may be helping. He's resting easier." It's not entirely true. The truth is, there's been no change, but I say the words for Mrs. Hayward's benefit.

"That's good," Katie agrees. "It looks like Opal's getting the wagon. Which hospital?"

I scrunch my face in thought. "Let's go to their district hospital since it's so close. They've got things working again after the attack a few months back. If needed, we can continue on to our hospital."

"That's what I was thinking too."

"Mrs. Hayward?" I touch the woman's hand. "We need a few blankets for the wagon. Maybe pillows too. Katie can stay with Mr. Hayward, and I'll help you grab them."

She hesitates, not wanting to leave her husband's side. Katie assures her she'll take care of him while she's gone. She gives a reluctant nod.

I follow the older woman into her tidy house. She yanks a heavy quilt off the queen-size bed she evidently shares with her husband. "Grab the pillows too?" She gestures toward them.

Outside, Hayward's dogs recline by the porch, all three with their legs stretched out and chins resting on their paws. One of them flicks his tail as we stroll past. "They seem so calm," I mutter.

"They usually are." Misty clears her throat. "Gary trained them perfectly. He alone can command them to be aggressive. With everyone else, this is their demeanor."

I shake my head as we proceed toward her husband. Opal has already brought the wagon. Within minutes, we arrange the bedding for Mr. Hayward. His breathing is shallow, and the unburned parts of his skin have discolored to a sickly gray. His wife sits beside him and clutches his hand. Kevin and the other two inside the wagon are still coughing. Opal and Shawn handle the team on the bench, while Katie and I ride in the wagon bed.

"Can we leave my dog here for now?" Katie asks. "Will your mother-in-law mind watching him?"

"Opal intends to stop and inform her of the situation. I'm confident she'll take care of your dog." As the wagon pulls out, I glance toward the three large dogs still in their spot by the porch. Their eyes trail the wagon as we take their master away.

Chapter 12

Katie

"You look good, Katie. Feeling okay?" Dr. Wolff asks without smiling.

"Still have a headache once in a while, but much better than I was."

"Captain Williams said we're easing you back into work . . . 0900 to 1500 today and tomorrow. We'll see how you do with six-hour shifts before increasing them. Hopefully, it'll go fine, and you can get back to regular shifts."

The bite in her tone catches me off guard, and I pull my lips into a tight line. "I'm sorry I've been such a nuisance. I know we're shorthanded, and— "

She lifts a hand. "Stop it. It's not your fault you were attacked and left for dead. Seriously." She huffs. "Is this going to set you back?"

"Set me back?"

"You know, shatter your confidence again?"

"I don't . . ." I straighten my shoulders. "No. I'm good to go. Plenty of confidence."

"Good. I'd hate to see you get back to where you were. You and Leo both seem to be on the right track now. I know things have been rough for you. For all of us. But there's no place now for wishing and whining."

I lift my hands and shake my head. "I'm sorry if you thought I was whining. I didn't realize that's what I was doing."

She sighs. "You weren't. I'm just . . . never mind. Merissa told me you reacted exactly as you should during the emergency at the ranch the other day. Too bad about the death of the ranch owner."

"It was terrible. His wife . . ." I shake my head.

"You'll need to get used to that," she says firmly. "At least the others will be okay. Merissa said her aunt is doing what's needed to help her husband and the ranch hands recover."

"That's what I've heard too." My voice comes out in a weak whisper. I clear my throat. "Opal will know what to do."

She gives me an irritated look, and her eyes narrow slightly. "Go ahead and change into your hospital clothes. Since you're an extra today, I'll have you do some organizing. Things are falling apart around here."

My voice is slightly strained as I reply, "Yes, Doctor." The tension in the air leaves me feeling uneasy, unable to shake the sense of Nettie's underlying frustration.

As I change out of my street clothes and into my hospital garb, I replay the conversation in my head, inserting things I wish I would've said but didn't. I'd like to blame my recent injuries for my ruminations, but it's a longtime habit. Sometimes in college, when I'd get so bogged down by something a professor or other student said, I'd rehash the event over and over, allowing it to consume my entire day.

My freshman year was the worst. Like so many others, I put on the dreaded freshman fifteen. Only my weight gain was closer to twenty pounds. I'd start my brooding and turn to food. I finally decided a healthier choice would be exercising my troubles away. Running had long been something I enjoyed, and adding biking and other activities I could do when I started to fret helped me lose the weight I gained that first year.

Now I don't need to lose weight; no one does with the food rations. But I still need the outlet exercise provides. I haven't gone running for months, since before the snow decided to stick around. The last time I went was after a particularly bad day at work, when a woman came in during early labor. We lost both her and her baby girl. I went on a hard run and got home late from work.

Leo was madder than he'd ever been at me. We were deep in the throes of our marriage trouble then, and my not coming home on time really set him off.

Up to the recent attack at my house, my exercise was walking the dog and doing some concentrated stretching exercises. Recently, I've done little but try to recover. Going to Opal's ranch was supposed to be a day of relaxation and maybe some slow walks around. That didn't turn out as expected. Not even close.

Based on my emotions during this mild interaction with Nettie, I'd better get back to some sort of fitness routine. That, or I'll be sneaking food in my efforts to control my obsessive thinking. I laugh out loud at the prospect of sneaking food. "If only it were that easy," I mutter into the mirror.

My hair is surprisingly tame today. Mrs. Williams showed me a method of wrapping and tying my unruly mane to help keep it under control by using a homemade scrunchie. She took an old latex glove and a worn-out silk shirt and turned the discards into hair accessories. The silk covers the latex and prevents the hair from catching. Plus, the smooth fabric almost glides through my messy locks.

I'll probably get a crocheted snood or hair net at some point, but I really love the scrunchie. After it's all wrapped up properly, my hair is almost smooth, and the scrunchie itself doesn't even show.

Even though my hair looks fabulous, my face is still a bit of a mess. Captain Williams asked me to leave the bandages off my nose, cheek, and ear to help with the recovery. The open spots are covered in a thick layer of salve to aid in healing. I'm sure I'd easily scare small children. My pinky and ring finger are still wrapped. While he thinks the mark on the edge of my ring finger will heal, there's still a chance I may lose part of my pinky.

Living with the Williamses has given me a peek into their life. Both the captain and Mrs. Williams have been people I've admired since we moved to Rapid City. The first time I met Alice Williams, I was surprised at how put together she was, even though we were a year into the apocalypse. She still had her hair nicely styled, and her clothes were clean and pressed.

Captain Williams is also very professional-looking. He arrives at the hospital in uniform, usually his military fatigues, then either changes into scrubs or just wears his pants and a crisp white T-shirt topped with a lab coat.

Even though they look polished in public life, I thought at home they'd be more casual. Both have said they were changing into something more comfortable, which to me meant sweats or something similar, but their at-home loungewear is anything but sloppy.

I swear, Alice Williams could've been on some old black-and-white TV show wearing a dress, pumps, and pearls to serve the family dinner. While she isn't quite that dressed up, she still always looks put together, yet suitable for the world we live in. Maybe it's part of being a doctor's wife? Or an officer's wife?

I giggle into the mirror. "Well, I hope if the National Guard makes Leo a lieutenant, he won't expect me to wear pumps and pearls."

I leave the changing room and go to one of the supply closets, figuring that's the space that needs the most organizing. We try to keep things tidy, but it tends to be a dumping ground as we drop off items before moving on to the next task.

As expected, it's in its usual disarray. I start with moving the things that are obviously in the wrong location, then work on the various labeled sections to arrange things.

When my mind tries to drift back to my earlier conversation with Nettie, I refocus on Leo and how he's been so determined to find out who attacked me. The false tip from the other night had him in a bad mood when he got back to the Williamses' house. Since then, there's been nothing new. Thinking of the situation plunges me back into the memories of the attack. I let out a breath and try to refocus by humming.

It's been about forty-five minutes since my shift started when Jacquie pops her head in the door. "Hey, I heard you were here today. Feeling good?"

"Feeling fine. Glad to be back at work."

"You teaching at the school too?"

"Not today. Just a six-hour shift here. Probably not even seeing patients, just catching things up." I gesture around the supply room. "Do you need me to help with something?"

"We're behind on files. Maybe you can work on those too? Everything is just in a pile instead of where they go in the cabinets. We've had some repeat customers, too, so . . ." She raises her hands. "You know how it is. It's been years since I worked in an office that wasn't computerized. My mom was a nurse also, and she'd often stay late just to catch up on the filing at her doctor's office."

"I'll take care of it. I'm doing this short shift tomorrow too."

"Perfect. And I'll— " The ringing of the front doorbell interrupts her words. She lolls her head to the side. "See you later. I'm glad you're feeling better."

I return to my work and have only moved a few things when the bell sounds again. This time, a man calls out, "Hey! Is anyone here?"

I drop what I'm doing and step into the hallway. "Can I help you?"

"Your guard . . . he's hurt."

"In the guard shack?"

"Hurry. He's bleeding. Looks like he was knifed. I wrapped a bandanna around his arm, but he needs real treatment. He was too big for me to move on my own."

Jesse steps out of a patient's room. "What's the problem?"

The guy repeats what he told me, and I start moving toward the front door.

Jesse puts out his hand and tells me to hold up. He grabs the radio from his belt and makes a call to the guard house. When there's no response, he tries again. The backdoor guard, nestled in a treehouse with a view of the back entrance, asks if there's a problem. Jesse relays what we know.

"Lock it down," the back guard orders. "Lock it down now."

I run to the back door to make sure the lock is engaged.

Jesse says he'll get the front. "Sir, please move away from the entryway and into this room." He motions to an empty patient room. "Stay away from the windows, and park yourself in a chair."

After ensuring the backdoor knob and deadbolt are engaged, I flip a secondary lock, like the kind used in hotel rooms, to prevent entrance even with a key. Next, I slide the door wedge into place. Jesse should be doing the same thing at the front door to keep us inside, yet everyone else out. We'll also lock down each of the individual rooms to keep everyone where they are.

Jesse and I meet in the middle of the hallway. With rooms on either side, we're well away from any windows.

"Where do you want me?" The quiver in my voice betrays my fear.

"All the rooms are secure. Nettie and Jacquie are in with the couple that arrived a few minutes ago. We only have one overnight patient. His wife was visiting. He's in the bed closest to the door. I pulled the curtains. The guy who just arrived is in the front room."

"The med school? Do they know?"

"They heard the call. They're locked down too. Hopefully, we'll know what's happening soon."

"Who's in the guard shack?"

"Not sure." He shakes his head. "It's not Josiah today. He has the overnight shift."

"Do we know if the man who told us about the guard needs medical treatment?"

Jesse scrunches his face. "I didn't even think to ask."

"Let me find out."

As I near the door to the room he's secured in, Jesse asks me to hold up a minute. He motions me to move away from the door and back toward him. With our heads close together, he keeps his voice low. "Did you recognize him?"

"I'm not sure. I only caught a glimpse. You?"

With pursed lips and a disapproving shake of his head, Jesse draws a comparison. "What if he's the Trojan horse? You know, like with what happened at Camp Rapid?"

Chapter 13

Katie

"The Trojan horse?" I furrow my brows, my doubt evident. "Do you really think so?"

"I can't say for certain, Katie. But maybe?" Jesse lets out a long breath. "Let's be smart about this. You have your sidearm?" He pulls his pistol from his holster and slides the weapon against his leg.

I follow his lead with my own 9-millimeter.

"I'll knock." He gestures toward the door. "You stay to the side. I'll go in. You stay out here and back me up if needed. Keep yourself safe. Leo would kill me if anything happened to you."

I let out a long breath. "Okay. I'm ready." I stay on one side of the door while Jesse is on the other.

He flares his eyes at me before mouthing, "Ready?"

"Ready," I mouth back.

He gives a solid knock. "Hey, just checking on you. Can I come in?"

"Yeah, man. Sure."

My heart is pounding as everything seems to go in slow motion. What's only seconds feels like minutes. Jesse turns the knob to unlatch the door, then uses his foot to push it open while staying behind the doorjamb. He spends several seconds waiting.

The guy in the room calls out, "What's up? Did you check on the guard?"

Jesse meets my gaze as he answers the guy. "We're on it." He lifts his gun slightly away from his leg and motions with his head that he's going in.

With my trigger finger indexed against my pistol, I envision what I'll need to do if things go bad. I swallow and nod to Jesse that I'm ready.

"Dude . . . what's up? Why do you have your gun out?" The fear in the man's voice is apparent.

Jesse lets out a ragged breath. "Sorry, man. We're just a little on edge with what you told us. Katie, c'mon in."

I holster my gun and run a hand across my forehead. It suddenly gets hot in here, and my head is once again pounding. I paste on a smile and step into the room.

"Hello, I'm Katie, one of the nurses here. Did you need to see a doctor?" I glance at the man. He looks familiar, but I can't place him.

He shakes his head. "I'm Austin Chambers. I'll be working with you."

Jesse lifts his chin. "You're the new medic, right?"

"Right. Dr. Wolff asked me to stop by. She said you'd have paperwork for me."

My eyebrows shoot to the top of my forehead. The new hire paperwork isn't anything more than a couple of sheets—basic information like name, allergies, and next of kin. It's not like it's a packet of information from the pre-EMP days. With our paper shortage, there'd be no reason for that.

"We'll let the doctor know you're here as soon as the lockdown is over," Jesse says. "Wait in here until we come for you. You need anything?"

"Nah, man. I'm okay. Except . . . can I use the bathroom?"

I motion to the shared bathroom between this room and the next. "Go ahead. It's a compost toilet, so follow the posted instructions. Please stay either in the bathroom or in this room, okay?"

He nods his agreement before Jesse and I step back out into the hallway. I let out a nervous laugh. "That was a nerve-racking couple of minutes."

"I'm glad we were wrong. That could've been all kinds of bad."

"Definitely. I think I know him. His mom was a patient here a month or two back."

"Yeah, I heard about him. He's transferring from the cleanup crew. That's a tough job. They get into some nasty stuff. It's better now than it used to be, but it still isn't a job I'd want."

"I was talking with Bowski once, and he told me he was on the cleanup crew when it was really bad."

"You can't even imagine what it was like that first summer and fall. So many people died in their homes. Lots of the elderly relied on medicine to keep them alive. Murder-suicides of entire families.

Starvation. It was bad. Bowski was on the cleanup crew, but he was also instrumental in getting things organized. We wouldn't have the survivors we do today if it weren't for people like him. The Guardsmen and Airmen, too, but civilians like Bowski knew how to get things done."

"Where is he? I haven't seen him since New Year's Day when we had that onslaught of flu patients."

Jesse gets a pensive look. "You know, now that you mention it, I haven't seen him around either. He may be helping with the cleanup at the base. He worked there as a special contractor or something in the past. And I'm sure Shaw is having him help track down the guys that attacked you. My guess is he's just been busy."

"Probably so."

I'm about ready to ask what's taking so long for them to check on the guard when the radio sounds, telling us they secured the area and are bringing in an injured man.

I'm already moving when I tell Jesse I'll let Nettie know and get the trauma room ready. Jesse says he'll get everything unlocked.

Within minutes, the injured man from the guard shack, one of the Citizen Patrollers, is in the exam room. The bandanna tourniquet Austin Chambers put in place is still there and looks like a decent job.

With his shirt soaked in blood and the paleness of his skin and lips, it doesn't look good for him. I get a quick set of vitals. His blood pressure is too low, as is his heartbeat and respiration. I've yet to get a temperature when Nettie comes into the room. I relay the information I have.

"Set things up for an IV," she says.

I raise my eyebrows and motion to the trauma tray, where an IV is waiting.

She pulls her lips into a tight line and turns to the men.

"Do we know what happened?" she asks.

"Knife or something similar . . . as best we can tell," the sheriff's deputy on duty today says.

I nod my agreement based on several other visible wounds. Defensive wounds.

"We didn't find the weapon," the deputy continues. "No one heard anything. We don't know who's responsible."

"I'll tell you who's responsible," the man who was carrying the other side of the stretcher responds. "His crazy girlfriend, that's who. *Ex-girlfriend.* He dumped her, and she flipped her lid. Said she was going to make him pay."

"We'll do what we can for him. You can wait out in the entryway or let Jesse know how to reach you."

As soon as the men leave, Nettie says, "Sorry I was so vague. With those vitals and what I'm seeing . . ." She shakes her head. "We're not starting the IV. He's lost too much blood. There's nothing we can do for him." She brushes his hair from his forehead. "I think his name is Mike Reno. I've talked to him a few times when I've come in."

"Me too. He's always nice. Young too. I didn't even know he had a girlfriend. He seems too . . ." I shrug. "Young."

"Will you stay with him? I'm going to check on our other patient, but I won't be gone long. I guess I'd better let the men know. I should've just said something while they were here." She rolls her head, causing her neck to pop. "Some days I hate this job. Forget what I said earlier, Katie."

"Doctor?"

"When I said you need to get used to telling the family. It doesn't get any easier." She slumps her shoulders and sulks out of the room.

Within a few minutes, the deputy and Citizen Patroller come back into the room. Both look miserable.

"Can we talk with him?" the deputy asks. "Will he know we're here?"

"You can. He might. Dr. Wolff told you he's lost a lot of blood?"

The men both say they know, and they were afraid of that when they found him.

"Who told you about him?" the Patroller asks.

"Our new medic."

"Your new medic?"

"Yes, he'll be starting . . ." I look at Dr. Wolff.

She shrugs. "In a few days. He's wrapping up his previous job."

"Is he still here?"

"In one of our patient rooms. We put him there when we locked down." I don't share the scare Jesse and I experienced when we thought he may have had nefarious intentions.

Both men perk up, and the deputy asks, "Can I talk to him?"

"Go ahead," Dr. Wolff answers. "But you may want to stay with your friend for now. Katie will remain with you." She gives me a nod before stepping out of the room.

After I check Mike Reno's vitals again and make sure the other men have chairs, I tell them just to keep him company. I try to make myself invisible on the other side of the room as I fake busying myself at the rolling toolbox containing our supplies. I don't think it'll be too long until Mike passes. Like Nettie said, some days I hate this job too.

Ten minutes later, the men say their final goodbyes to their late friend. The deputy had sent another man to find Mike's mom, but they didn't return in time. I leave them alone in the room while I let Nettie know about Mike's passing.

Nettie's just coming out of one of the other exam rooms. She gives me a tight nod. "They're still with him?"

"Yes. Time of death is 1152. Is Austin Chambers still here?"

"Waiting in the lobby. He figured they'd want to interview him."

"Do you think the girlfriend could've done that? For breaking up with him?"

She makes a snorting noise. "It's convenient that they already have a suspect."

"I'll let them know the new medic is waiting to talk to them." I pause a moment before adding, "He said you asked him to come in and fill out some paperwork?"

She straightens her back. "And?"

I lift my hands. "Uh, nothing. Just . . . his mom was treated here before."

"Yes, her blood pressure was dipping. She was one of Addison's patients." She gives me a pointed look.

I nod that I remember. The poor woman kept getting dizzy and nearly passing out. When we checked her, her blood pressure was too low. Before the apocalypse, she was being treated for high blood pressure. After everything fell apart, she ended up losing quite a bit of weight, like everyone, and substantially increasing her exercise, also like pretty much everyone.

Those changes brought her blood pressure back in line, but she was still taking some sort of herbal supplement prescribed by self-professed midwife and medicine woman Addison. We weren't able to find out exactly what she was taking, though Stella offered a few ideas.

We kept Mrs. Chambers for a few days, and everything seemed fine with her when she was discharged. When the flu hit, Addison was treating those in her neighborhood. *Supposedly.* Whatever she was doing wasn't working, and there were many deaths. When we discovered just how severe the situation was, Captain Williams wanted the woman brought in. Deputy Shaw went after her, but her house was empty, and no one has seen her since.

"I'm sure Austin will be happy to tell what he knows." Nettie dips her chin. "I'll go in and talk with the deputies. Quite the first day back, huh?"

"Definitely."

She takes a step away before turning back toward me. "And, uh, Katie?"

"Yeah?"

"I'm sorry about earlier, when you first arrived. I didn't mean to be so, uh, short with you. I was thinking about something else. You were just . . ." Her shoulders sag. "Sorry."

"I understand. And thanks for the apology. I wondered if I'd done something wrong."

"You didn't."

"We can talk sometime if you want." I offer her an encouraging nod.

"Maybe. We'll see."

She strides toward the treatment room with Mike Reno but pauses at the door and lowers her shoulders before giving a crisp knock. Nettie's definitely an interesting person. But she's a good doctor, especially considering she was only a med student when this all happened. She's so private and rarely talks about herself at all. Even Lieutenant David Paul, who was dating her, doesn't know much about her. Leo said he called her mysterious. I guess that's a good word to describe her.

Austin Chambers is more than willing to speak with the deputy. The Patroller excuses himself, saying he's going to contact Hugo, our undertaker. While I don't tell Chambers that Mike died, the deputy does, which makes our new medic even more inclined to help.

He shakes his head. "Sorry. I should've done more. I should've brought him in with me instead of just . . ." His body sags as he sighs. "Sorry."

Without any prompting from the deputy, Austin tells what he knows. He was walking toward the hospital when a woman came running in his direction. He didn't get a good look at her because of her winter garb, plus she ducked her head. But he thought at the time she had blood on her. He didn't think much of it, thought maybe she'd been in the hospital or something.

The deputy asks Austin to wait a moment before they proceed with the interview, then motions me to walk down the hall with him.

"He's your new medic? Did you know him before today?"

"I've met him in the past."

"Tell me about him coming in today."

"He alerted us about the guard—Mike—right away. Told us he put on a tourniquet. We called for help, then went into lockdown, so I didn't talk with him . . . well, not really. Until afterward.

He narrows his eyes. "What do you mean not really?"

I let out a self-conscious laugh before sharing how Jesse and I thought the man might be a Trojan horse.

"You were smart to be cautious, especially with all the troubles the hospitals, Guard, and other areas have had. Well, at least we have a starting point to search for Mike's killer. Hopefully, I'll be able to tell his mom we have an arrest before the end of the day. Thanks for your help. Hugo should be here soon."

Chapter 14

Katie

Instead of Hugo's expected arrival to retrieve Mike's remains, Bowski appears. "Hey, how're you feeling?" his warm voice greets me.

"Better." I dip my chin cautiously. A faint pounding in my head has me moving slower than I was when my shift started. I shouldn't be surprised Bowski heard about my attack; the Black Hills grapevine operates effectively.

"Heard they've had a few leads on the guys who did it."

"They haven't caught them yet, though. Did Shaw tell you? One of the guys was named Julius. He seemed to know him. Do you?"

Bowski lifts his massive shoulders. "I know a guy named Julius. My guess is it's the same one. Especially considering he disappeared from the area."

I should feel relief at the guy's disappearance, but I don't. Unless they find him and his buddies, nothing can return to normal. Oscar and his family will remain in hiding at Deputy Shaw's place, and Leo and I will continue living with the Williamses. Not that I mind staying with them. Even Gerry seemed okay with me working today; when I left, he was stretched out in his doggie bed.

"It's been a while since I've seen you. In fact, Jesse and I were just discussing how busy you must be."

"As we all are. I stopped by and saw Elaine Ebright. Seems like she's doing better."

"I heard you two were friends. It's good you could visit her."

The noise of the break room door opening draws our attention in that direction. Austin Chambers steps out, followed by the deputy. They stop in the hallway, engrossed in conversation.

In a low voice, Bowski asks, "What's he doing here?"

"He's the deputy who responded today. I guess Shaw wasn't available."

"Not him. Chambers." The name is tinged with disgust.

"Oh, he was the one who found Mike Reno. He put on a tourniquet and came in to get help. We went on lockdown, per protocol, and he's being interviewed."

"Why was he here?"

"He's our new medic."

"*Medic?* Whose brilliant idea was that?"

I tilt my head while gazing up at Bowski. The anger on his face is evident. "Um . . . Captain Williams? Dr. Wolff recommended him."

"I bet she did." He lowers his voice and bends down to my height. "You'd be smart to stay away from him."

I take a step back. "What do you mean?"

The deputy and Austin head our way. Austin's friendly expression morphs into a smirk as they get closer.

Bowski stands up to his full height as they approach.

The deputy reaches his hand in greeting. "What have you been up to, Bowski?"

Ignoring Austin Chambers, Bowski keeps his gaze focused on the deputy. "Helping Hugo, mostly."

Chambers snorts.

Bowski's head snaps in his direction. "You got a problem?"

Even though he's close to a foot shorter than Bowski, Chambers takes a couple of steps forward, invading the big man's personal space. "Nope. Funny how you neglect to mention why you're working with Hugo and are no longer on the cleanup crew."

"Wait a minute, you two." The deputy steps near them and puts a hand in the small space between their bodies. The tension in the hallway becomes palpable as the deputy tries to diffuse the growing confrontation between Bowski and Chambers. I glance nervously at the deputy, wondering what is happening here. Towering over Chambers, Bowski maintains his intimidating stance, his eyes locked onto his adversary.

The deputy squares his shoulders and attempts to redirect their attention. "All right, enough of this. We're all on the same team here." His voice is firm but measured. "We have enough problems without people who used to be friends wanting to clobber each other."

Bowski's face flushes with anger, but he reluctantly takes a step back and breaks the standoff.

Chambers grins triumphantly, satisfied with his apparent victory in the power struggle.

What in the world just happened? What could've transpired between Bowski and Chambers that led to such animosity?

Chambers turns toward the deputy. "You get what you need from me?"

"For now. Dr. Wolff said you're starting here in a few days?"

Bowski snorts before muttering, "Hope they know what they're getting into."

Chambers chuckles. "Give it up, Bowski. You're the only one who has a problem with me, and that's a problem of your own making."

"Really, guys?" The deputy shakes his head. "Let's go, Bowski. I'll help you with Mike."

Even though I want to ask Austin Chambers what the trouble is between him and Bowski, I don't. I give the man a nod and take a step away.

"Remind me of your name," he says. "I know we met when you were helping treat my mom. I remember your uniform." He motions to my scrub top with the handsewn sergeant stripes of the United Volunteers. Once Leo and I join the National Guard, my uniform will change with my new enlistment. The Volunteers don't have legit uniforms but rather guidelines as to what works to signify our recruitment.

"Katie Burnett."

"Sergeant, right?"

I nod.

"Jesse—I mean, Mr. Talbot—said the captain is a stickler for proper designations. Halfway wish I still had my Naval rank. Well, I'll see you tomorrow." He gives me a broad smile, and at that moment, his features seem to transform.

His rugged charm becomes more pronounced, and his wild, bushy, end-of-the-world beard frames his face. I sense the contours of a strong jawline that hint at a chiseled structure beneath the wildness of his beard. His warm hazel eyes twinkle with a magnetic allure, and a hint of dimples grace his cheeks as he continues to smile, adding an intriguing depth to his rugged yet attractive appearance. It's as if the weight of the world momentarily lifts from his shoulders, revealing a captivating appeal that I hadn't noticed until now.

Could his attractiveness be one of the reasons Nettie pushed through his employment?

The front doorbell announces Austin's exit, and I consider the trouble between him and Bowski. While they certainly don't seem to like each other, I thought Austin was nice. I thought the same thing when his mom was our patient and he visited her.

A few days after being released, she and Austin showed up bearing gifts. I ended up with a couple of beautiful and dainty, tatted-lace bookmarks. One, a series of hearts, I sent to my sister Sarah as a wedding gift. The second is a cross, which I use in my Bible as a bookmark.

Reflecting on that time, I recall how he seemed to spend several extra minutes talking with Nettie. She's had her share of man troubles in the past, and maybe, just maybe, Austin Chambers could bring some happiness into her life.

Leo and I consider Bowski a friend, but I've had my doubts about him. He was instrumental in setting up the Black Hills black market. Even though ration chips are now the rule in South Dakota, the black market is credited with saving many lives before the ration system was organized.

After the ration system was set up, the black market continued to operate. I've never shopped there, but many people do. It's set up as a barter system, where people trade things they hope have value for things they need.

The black market was blamed for a wave of burglaries last fall. During those break-ins, our neighbor was killed. I'll admit, I thought Bowski might have been involved in the thefts. He wasn't, but still . . . I wondered.

Returning to my closet-cleaning duties, my shortened shift is soon nearing completion. Captain Williams knew what he was doing when he brought me back part time. I'm a wreck. My head aches, and my entire body hurts, plus I'm ready for a nap.

Leo, the captain, the med students, and the new doctor are all scheduled for afternoon classes. Both Leo and Captain Williams, along with Dr. Murphy, are on the overnight shift. This is supposed to be Murphy's final training shift before he works on his own.

While the doctor was highly recommended and was a practicing physician prior to the EMP, Captain Williams didn't know him and hadn't worked with him. The man isn't even from Rapid City. He's one of many who've arrived in the area following rumors of the rebuilding. The man was smart enough to bring his credentials and records with him when he relocated. He'd been working at the main hospital since the spring and doing well. Even Dr. Bollinger, the orthopedist who's been taking care of Leo's arm, told the captain that Murphy would be an asset to our hospital.

With the flu epidemic now waning, Bollinger has asked that we make a trip to him so he can check Leo's progress and the healing of his wrist. He'll remove the external fixator once it's determined the break is properly set.

Originally, Bollinger said he'd leave it in place for six to eight weeks, but because of the flu and then my attack, we're past that point. The plan now is for Leo to make the trip sometime next week. If I'm feeling well enough, I'll join him on the five-mile journey. The captain even offered the biodiesel-fueled truck for the trip.

When my shift ends, Mrs. Williams, who had been helping at the med school, is waiting to walk me home. "Hello, Katie," she says with a smile. "Some excitement today. How are you holding up?"

"Physically, I'm okay. Achy and tired. Did you hear about Mike Reno? The guard?"

She wrinkles her forehead and shakes her head. "He was always such a nice young man. And they think it was his girlfriend?"

I shrug. "Maybe. I haven't heard anything more."

"You'd think that with the difficulties of day-to-day survival, the terrible things that used to happen would stop. But I guess that's the way of the world. There were bad things before the EMP. It's only logical those bad things would continue afterward. We're silly to think we'd be allowed to focus on growing our food and washing our clothes. I mean, look at you."

Alice has worked herself into such a state that she's almost sputtering her words. She takes a deep breath. "Forgive me, Katie. I'm just so tired of the violence."

She attempts to lighten the mood during our walk home by inquiring about Gerry. It's essentially the same questions and stories we've covered before, but I appreciate her interest in my dog.

"Which reminds me," she says, "the boy who was injured when Mr. Hayward's dogs attacked . . . you know the one?"

I nod that I do and tell her Merissa and I were discussing him the other day, at the hospital in Opal's district, while we were lingering around to help support Mrs. Hayward as her husband passed.

She grimaces. "Such a sad situation. I'm glad Opal's husband and their help weren't severely injured. Chris says the sheriff investigated. Thinks that maybe Hayward lost his balance. Fell and hit his head, knocking himself out. Probably hit the lantern on his way down, which is what started the fire."

I'd heard this rumor, too, after returning to the ranch to pick up Gerry. Pearl Weaver made it clear it sounded like a bunch of hooey and she believed someone had knocked him on the head and deliberately set the fire in retaliation for his dogs and the things he'd trained them to do.

"Anyway," Mrs. Williams continues, "Chris took everyone on rounds today . . . you know, all the med students and Dr. Murphy. In fact, they were still finishing up when I left to meet you."

"You didn't need to walk me home."

"For now, it's smart to have someone with you."

I dip my chin and heave out a breath. "I suppose. I'm sorry I interrupted you."

She waves her hand dismissively. "Chris and the others have determined the boy injured by the dogs is well enough to move to Opal Maher's ranch. He's even been able to get out and walk around. Chris said the nursing staff figures he's walking several miles most days, based on the amount of time he's gone. It was very nice of Opal to offer him a place. He'll need to continue his walking and rehabilitation, but Opal and her husband understand that. Too bad they couldn't do much about the scarring. The mental aspect of his healing is going to be difficult."

Mrs. Williams isn't wrong about that. The boy's leg was badly bitten, and he lost a lot of blood. At least he can hide the scar on his leg, though. One of the dogs got his face. Captain Williams and Dr. Wolff did all they could, but he needs plastic surgery, which isn't an option with our meager staff and supplies.

Thinking of the boy, I'm in full agreement with Alice and wish the violence would stop. It really would be helpful if we could just worry about our basic needs and not always have to look over our shoulders in fear of the next terrible event or attack.

Chapter 15

Merissa

"Mrs. Weaver, what's your assessment of Private Tillman?"

I smile at Elliot Tillman before turning to Captain Williams. "His sensations seem to be returning bilaterally, though there's still some intermittent numbness. The exercises and stretching are helping, but perhaps it's time to increase the workouts?"

"Do you think he's ready to walk?"

"I think I am," Elliot says. "Uh, Captain, sir. I'm ready to try."

The captain offers Elliot a broad smile. "I agree with you, son. It's been over a month since the explosion at Camp Rapid. I think it's safe to say a severed spine did not cause your paralysis, but rather swelling in the spinal region. I've been in contact with the main hospital. While we don't have any physical therapists, they do. They've agreed to us transferring you there for intense therapy."

"Do they have a nursing home for me to live in?" He gestures about the house-turned-care center.

"You'll stay at the hospital. Probably for a month or so. You know Sergeant Burnett, right?" The captain puts a hand on Leo's shoulder. When Elliot nods, Williams continues, "He's going to the hospital in the next few days to get his arm checked. I think you can be transported with him. One of our trucks has a camper shell we can put on it. It'll still be chilly, but not terrible."

"That sounds good, sir." The eighteen-year-old's smile is wide. "If they can get me walking again, that'd be great."

Before we leave Elliot's room, he asks if it'd be possible for his dad to ride along with them for the trip to the hospital. Since it's unlikely he'll see his dad for the duration of the time he's at the main hospital, he says he'd like as much time with him as he can get.

Elliot's dad was injured in a separate explosion when the ration center was attacked, and he has spent his own time healing. He now works in the hospital kitchen, delivering meals and helping in other ways. He's recovered considerably from his injuries, but he doesn't have the strength or stamina needed for a job as a laborer. Even the delivery work is sometimes challenging for him. The captain says he'll talk to the kitchen supervisor when they have an exact day for the move and see what they can do.

After finishing at the care center, we make our way to the house where Kemeera, Mindy, and the children from the preacher's cult are living. There isn't a guard outside, but from previous visits, I know there are at least two guards in the house. The National Guard and law enforcement are working together to supply the watchmen—or, as the case is today, watchwomen. Because it's only women and children in the house, they try to have either two women or a man and a woman on duty.

Kemeera gave birth to her baby Caleb only two weeks ago. Mindy had baby Zach back in November. Both women and babies are doing okay, though Zach is a little on the small side. We're monitoring all of them and keeping an eye on Zach's weight.

True to form, Mindy doesn't look at us or even acknowledge our presence. Using a cheap analog bathroom scale, Stella weighs herself and then takes the baby. It's not exact enough to tell how many ounces he's gained or lost, but we can estimate how he's doing.

"Looks like a full pound more from the first time we weighed him," Stella says before handing the baby off to the captain.

Captain Williams turns to Mindy. "He's doing well. Can I convince you to step on the scale today?"

Without acknowledging the captain's request, she reaches her arms out for her baby.

The captain smiles and says, "I'd like to examine him first. Can you place one of his blankets on the table?"

Her face impassive, she does as asked. When he's done with the examination, Williams hands the baby back to his mom, who leaves the room without comment. We repeat the weighing process with Kemeera's baby. Unlike Mindy, she is happy to step on the scale for her own weight, followed by the baby's. The weights of both are fine. He checks the baby over, then weighs and quickly examines the other children.

When it's just us, Kemeera, her daughter Shawna, and infant Caleb, Captain Williams asks her how she's feeling.

"Good." She shrugs. "Mostly normal. You're happy with Shawna's and Caleb's weights?"

"Yes, very." The captain nods.

She gives a brief smile. "Thank you for making sure we have extra food."

I tilt my head. While the women and children have been getting rations, it hasn't been excessive amounts. We were able to arrange for them to get a decent amount of milk, about a quart per day for each of the women and older children.

Kemeera continues, "I know Mindy doesn't say much, but she's grateful too. Her milk supply seems to be increasing. There were times . . ." She tightens her lips as her words drift off, then drops her shoulders. "We didn't have milk and eggs before. Not often, anyway. Just whatever we could get on the black market."

While we suspected the preacher and his followers weren't taking part in the ration system, we didn't know for certain. I take a chance and ask, "Did you not get ration chips?"

She shakes her head. "Those are of a world that we didn't want to be a part of. We wanted to grow our food."

When we found Kemeera and the others, they were living in a regular house with a regular yard. Not on a farm or anything. Of course, it was the middle of January. Even those who live on a ranch, like Opal and her family, aren't growing much right now. Maybe, during the summer months, they were living someplace else and able to produce their food.

Kemeera gives a furtive glance toward the bedrooms at the back of the house, then at the guard stationed in the living room. She lowers her voice and says, "I know you think you got all of us, but you didn't. There were others already on their missions."

The captain steps closer to her. "What missions?"

"I'm not sure. Only those who were involved were told the details. I didn't . . ." She swallows hard and blinks a few times. "I never did any of them. Because of Caleb. Mindy, she never did either, but she's . . ." She leans slightly to the side and glances toward the bedrooms again. "Since she had Zach, she was supposed to. There was something planned, I think. But I don't know for sure. Not about hers. Not about the others."

"How many others?"

Kemeera moves to a chair, and her daughter rushes to her side. "Several. Not everyone was there that night."

The captain steps closer to her. The rest of us hold completely still, barely daring to breathe for fear we'll frighten the woman and she'll stop talking.

"Do you know about the things that already happened?" the captain asks.

She gives a slight nod. "Some, yes. But . . . maybe not all."

Captain Williams seems relaxed and has a calm look on his face, but his hands are clenched into tight fists held close to his sides. "But you know for sure about the other places? Your preacher . . . what's his name?"

I'm certain Captain Williams knows the man's name since he was known to many in the area from before the EMP as the owner of a computer company, but now everyone refers to him as the preacher. People like Kemeera and Mindy are called his followers or his cult. While the guards are here to keep the women from leaving, they're also here to keep them safe. The trouble is, many of the guards lost friends and family in the explosions, so it's almost like the fox watching the hen house.

I glance toward the guard that's part of the Citizen Patrol; she's staring intently in our direction, obviously listening. The other guard, a tall redhead, is walking the perimeter while we do our exams. She has yet to return.

Kemeera smiles. "I'm sure you know his name. They believed it had to be done. We can't go back to the way things were before." She drops a kiss on her daughter's head. "I'll tell you all I know. Mindy, though . . ." She shakes her head. "Mindy won't speak to you."

"Will she be angry at you for telling us?"

"We have an agreement. I'll do the talking, and she'll reap the benefits."

"Oh? What benefits?"

"We want you to move us. Take us away from here to where people won't know us, won't know about our involvement. We're innocent of actually doing anything, but we understand that by not coming forward, people may be angry."

The guard snorts. "A bit of an understatement, don't you think?"

Kemeera lifts her hand in the guard's direction. "See? Even those who are assigned to protect us don't really wish to do so."

"I don't have the power to make any sort of deals, but I'll talk to those who can," Captain Williams says.

"Make it fast, Captain," Kemeera says in a snappy tone. "There's every possibility we're not as safe as you seem to *think* we are." She motions toward the guard again.

In response, the guard's lips curve, and her arms fold across her chest in a display of confident indifference.

"And when you get the deal made, I want her— " she points to me " —and Nurse Katie with me."

Williams glances in my direction, and I respond with a dip of my chin. He turns back to Kemeera. "Sergeant Burnett is recovering from an injury."

"I heard. I also heard she's doing well. I'm sure you can get her here."

"I'll see what I can do."

Silence surrounds us as we exit the house. The captain's wheelchair awaits at the base of the steps. As he settles into it, the other guard approaches. She greets us with a nod as we tread down the walkway toward the sidewalk.

About fifty yards from the house, Stella breaks the silence. "Do you think she'll actually spill the beans and share what she knows?"

"I believe she will," Leo responds while pushing the captain's wheelchair.

"I concur," the captain says. "I think she's been itching to talk all along, just unsure of the wisdom in doing so. Now, I reckon she realizes it's the right move."

A sinking feeling washes over me. "Captain?"

"Go ahead, Weaver."

"Do you think they're safe?"

"In what way?"

"Well, she mentioned the guards aren't fond of them. Given all we suspect the preacher is responsible for, it makes sense. But what if . . . could the preacher have other followers? Individuals not truly part of the cult, who are . . ."

"Hmm. I see your point. Leo, stop for a moment. New plan." He retrieves the radio from his medical bag nestled in his lap. "I'm calling

Shaw and Lieutenant Paul right away. We're heading back to the house and waiting there until familiar, trustworthy faces arrive."

Chapter 16

Merissa

Lieutenant David Paul of the National Guard doesn't respond. Someone else comes over the radio and informs us Paul is unavailable, but he'll find him and will have him reach out to the captain.

The captain then calls for a major, one of the people who works closely with the general. Instead of relaying his concerns over the radio, he asks the major if he can meet at Mindy and Kemeera's safe house. For safety's sake, he doesn't actually say Mindy and Kemeera's safe house but instead uses some sort of code they'd devised in advance. When that's arranged, he reaches Deputy Shaw with the same request, using the same code words.

As he was making the arrangements, we began walking back. When we reach the bottom of the stairs, Leo helps the captain out of the chair. He's wearing his walking boot and using a cane as he carefully mounts the steps.

After a solid rap on the door, we wait several moments, to no response. The captain knocks again. The sinking feeling in my stomach increases when a voice on the other side of the door calls out, "What do you want?"

"This is Captain Williams."

The door cracks open and reveals the face of the redheaded guard. "Why are you back?"

"Are you going to let us in?"

She grunts. "I suppose."

Inside the house, the women and children aren't in the front rooms, but the other guard, the one who'd been eavesdropping as Kemeera spoke, is sitting in the living room. She flashes her brows. "Forget something?"

Ignoring the guard, Captain Williams motions to me. "Weaver, you and Swenson go check on the women and children."

"Check on them?" the redheaded guard scoffs. "What do you think? That we offed them in the five minutes you've been gone?"

I catch the glare Williams sends in her direction as I stride down the hall. Kemeera immediately answers when I knock on her bedroom door. "Is something wrong?"

"You tell me."

She motions into her room where her daughter and the five-year-old boy are playing on the floor. The two older girls are sitting on a bed, while Mindy and Zach are in the rocking chair. "Caleb's in his bassinet."

I offer a smile. "We've decided not to wait on your request." Mindy stares in my direction. I catch a faint hint of a smile before it quickly disappears. I'd like to think the smile is because she's in favor of the deal Kemeera is making, but the cynical part of me is concerned it's for shady reasons.

"What happened to make it suddenly urgent?" Kemeera asks.

"I'm going to go back out to the front. Can you all wait here while we make the final arrangements?"

"Don't forget about Katie. I want both you and her with me when I talk."

Oops. I did forget about Katie. "Don't worry, we understand what you need."

The two guards are both in the living room; they look decidedly miffed about the situation. I notice Leo has the guards' radios, and their pistols are on the table. Two rifles lean against a nearby wall, out of their reach.

When I look at him with raised eyebrows, he gives a shake of his head. I address Captain Williams, but make sure I include Leo in the conversation. "Kemeera reminded me she won't talk unless Katie is here."

Leo opens his mouth but appears to think better of it.

"I guess we'd better honor that," Captain Williams says. "Leo, she should be off shift now and back at the house. Do you want to go get her?"

"Yes, sir." He passes me the guards' radios. In a low voice, he says, "We thought it best they don't invite anyone else to this little soiree."

I scrunch my face in agreement. Leo says he should return within thirty minutes. With the women and children in the back, and the guards still shooting us evil eyes, the rest of us settle around the kitchen table. I sit between Kerry and Stella.

Kerry and I have worked together the most since she also takes regular shifts at the hospital as a janitor, in addition to the shadow shifts required of the students. She and I, along with Katie, are also teaching very basic self-defense courses to the other women in the area. Because of all the turmoil of our day-to-day living, we've only had a few classes.

It started as something we offered to the women working at the hospital and the care centers but has grown to include anyone interested. At the last class Kerry led, there were half a dozen women from the neighborhood. In some ways, I'm surprised this wasn't offered before. Katie and I both underwent self-defense and weapons training in the small towns we lived in; the ongoing danger from raiders and other threats made it a necessity.

I suppose, as the captain mentioned when that prank call disrupted our radio transmission, raiders haven't posed a significant threat in Rapid City. Hence, the residents here never saw the need to acquire self-defense skills. While Rapid City itself remained unscathed, I know that other small towns faced their share of issues.

One such town, the secluded enclave of Black Canyon, fell victim to a brutal attack that resulted in fires and assailants shooting those who attempted to escape. I furrow my brow in contemplation.

The assault on Black Canyon bears a striking resemblance to the attack on the festival, believed to be orchestrated by the preacher's followers. In that instance, they initiated a series of explosions and followed up with gunfire, targeting fleeing individuals. Could they have also been responsible for the devastation in Black Canyon? This is a question worth posing to Kemeera.

Medical students Matt and Jeff recline in their chairs, their vigilant eyes fixed on the guards. Initially, we started our classes with two additional students: Geoff Landers, who was dismissed after his drug use was revealed, and Pamela. Pamela fell seriously ill with the flu, necessitating hospitalization and a subsequent stay in one of the care facilities. She has now made a significant recovery but remains unfit to resume her studies.

She approached Captain Williams with a request to withdraw from the medical program and enroll in the upcoming nursing training, which starts in the middle of February. I believe this is a wise decision for her. Even before falling ill, she was grappling to keep pace with the demanding curriculum and shadow rotations. Getting caught up seemed like a daunting task.

When there's a knock at the door, the captain motions for Jeff to answer while he moves alongside the door. The rest of us students get to our feet and move to the other side of the breakfast bar to put something between us and whoever is at the door.

With his hand on the butt of his pistol, Jeff asks who it is. Confirming via the peephole that it really is Shaw on the other side, he ushers the deputy inside. As soon as the two guards see the deputy, who's considered a supervisor of the Citizen Patrol, they spring to their feet.

"You know about this?" the shorter guard whines. "You know they're holding us hostage?"

Shaw ignores the guards and offers Williams his hand. "Thanks for calling me." He nods toward the guns on the table. "Playing it safe, I see."

Williams shrugs. "I don't know them. If you can vouch for them, feel free to do what you think is best."

"I think this is fine. Their radios?"

I hand the radios to the deputy, and he accepts them with a nod before turning back to the captain. "You said it was urgent for me to meet you here. You've disarmed the guards— "

"We didn't exactly disarm them; we nicely requested they give us their weapons."

The redheaded guard snorts. "They threatened to shoot us if we didn't."

Williams ignores her and inclines his head. "Kemeera is ready to talk. She has a few conditions, but she's agreed to divulge what she knows."

Shaw's face reflects appreciation. "What conditions?"

"Relocation. For her, Mindy, and the children. Somewhere they won't be associated with the cult."

"Jeez. They don't want much, do they? You know how far we're going to have to move them? The Wastelands might do it."

I suppress a smile at the suggestion. The Wastelands encompass the East and West Coasts and were declared uninhabitable by the president after direct nuclear strikes. The United Volunteers have been responsible for relocating people from these regions.

"Where's your sidekick?" Shaw asks Williams.

With a puzzled expression, the captain responds, "My wife?"

Shaw chuckles. "I meant Leo Burnett."

"Ah, one of the other conditions is Kemeera will only talk with Mrs. Weaver and Sergeant Katie Burnett in attendance."

Shaw crinkles his brow. "Is Katie well enough for that?"

"She returned to work today. Half-shift only. My wife was supposed to meet her and walk her home, and Leo went to the house to get her."

"What about us?" the redheaded guard interjects. "Are we just supposed to sit here?"

"Do you have something better to do?" Shaw retorts. "I'd think you'd be pleased about the prospect of this wrapping up. I've heard rumors about what you all call 'babysitting duties.' Personally, I wouldn't consider this half bad. It's nice and warm inside, certainly a lot better than some of the other assignments."

With a huff, the woman settles back into her chair.

Shaw lowers his voice. "They're both new. I can't see this working out for them long term."

Williams nods in agreement. "It's a delicate situation, and you'll need to figure out what to do with them once this is resolved. I don't like that they know as much as they do. But for now, we need to focus on Kemeera and obtaining the information we need."

As we await Leo and Katie's arrival, tension fills the room. The guards cast suspicious glances at us, while the rest of us exchange anxious looks.

Matt leans near me and whispers, "Do you think she will really talk? And will her information be valuable?"

I shrug, attempting to conceal my own doubts. "You heard her. She just wants a safe place. If she's right and there are still some of the preacher's followers out there . . ."

"But she said she didn't know what they were doing. How will that help?"

"Maybe she knows more than she's letting on? Or maybe she doesn't realize she knows what she knows." I shake my head, realizing how jumbled my words came out.

Matt chuckles. "I guess."

I'm about to say something else, which will probably also come out as a tangled mess, when there's a knock on the door. The voice on the other side calls out, "This is Burnett. Both of us."

Shaw raises a hand and motions for everyone to remain still, then moves to the living room window. He barely shifts the curtain before turning back to the captain with a nod.

"Matt? Want to let them in?"

Katie walks in with Leo following. She scans the room, appearing weary but resolute. Her gaze fixes on me, and she raises her shoulders toward her ears.

I send her a small smile of encouragement.

The tension in the room thickens as the captain says, "This may be the break we've been waiting for."

Chapter 17

Katie

Less than five minutes after Leo and I arrive at the safe house, a major I recognize as part of the general's detail, along with Lieutenant David Paul, joins us.

After brief greetings, Paul turns to the captain. "Thank you for including me in this."

"It makes sense to keep this limited to those who've already been involved." Williams looks at the major. "How do you wish to proceed?"

It's decided that instead of bringing Kemeera to the kitchen, we'll go to her bedroom in an attempt to keep the conversation—and audience—as controlled as possible.

Stella is tasked with caring for the children while we visit with Kemeera. Mindy could, of course, handle them all, but there's a small hope she'll be willing to stay in the room with us and maybe even add what she knows.

The two Citizen Patrollers assigned to guard the women and children ask Deputy Shaw if they can be dismissed. Shaw scoffs and tells them to stay put and stay quiet.

Since Shaw doesn't really know the women and the major has only seen them in passing, they'll stay out front with the Patrollers, Leo, and the remaining med students while Merissa, Captain Williams, Lieutenant Paul, and I visit with Kemeera. Paul carries a couple of kitchen chairs. Leo offers to take one back for me, but I shake my head and tell him I'll be fine.

The captain has me go to the bedroom door first, just so Kemeera knows we met her request. She greets me with a smile. As we file into the room, she says, "I didn't expect things to happen so quickly. Does this mean you'll be moving us soon?"

I glance at the captain, who gestures toward Lieutenant Paul.

Paul clears his throat. "Those arrangements are being made as we speak. Is there any place specific you'd like to end up?"

Before she answers, Stella steps forward. "Perhaps I should take the children? Maybe read them a story?"

Kemeera nods her agreement and tells her daughter to go with Dr. Stella. She keeps hold of her newborn son. Mindy, sitting in the rocking chair with her baby Zach, makes no effort to move. When Stella and the older children have left, it's Mindy who speaks first.

"Neither of us have any family. My boyfriend's family lives in Denver, but I can't imagine it'd be smart to go there."

I take a step toward the usually silent woman. "Your boyfriend?" I move into a squat near her, my injured hip protesting with the motion.

"He's dead. Died before I even knew I was pregnant."

I glance toward Merissa, who's sitting on the edge of the twin bed next to Kemeera. She lost her husband shortly after discovering her own pregnancy. She gives me a barely perceptible nod, a hand resting on her swollen belly. "You're probably right about Denver. They've started the rebuilding process and even have power in some areas, but we've heard some reports of trouble that has stalled the efforts. For now, it's probably best to avoid it. Plus, with the weather . . ." She tilts her head to the side.

Keeping her eyes on Merissa, Mindy asks, "When's your baby due?"

"About two months."

"Your man?"

"Also dead."

"Mine too," Kemeera adds. "Only he knew about Caleb. He was excited. I already had Shawna, and he treated her like his own. When Danny died— "

"Kemeera," Mindy snaps. "I'm sure they don't need all the details."

I glance at Kemeera, then return my attention to Mindy. "You can tell us anything you wish."

She shoots a look toward Mindy that basically says, *I told you so.* She takes a breath and launches into her story. "When Danny died, I didn't know what to do. I was pregnant. We were both working our jobs in the Main Street District. I was in the bakery, and he was part of the cleanup crew. Shawna went to a nice daycare that was part of the bakery. We'd gone to a few of Preacher's services in the different parks. Mindy was there. We started talking since we were both pregnant."

Mindy stares at the floor, her big toe drawing shapes on the carpet.

"Anyway," Kemeera continues, "when Danny died, Mindy and the others helped me. I started living at, uh, the house with the others."

She's silent for several beats. I'm thinking about asking her what happened next when she starts again. "I didn't know about the other plans, neither did Mindy. We were just trying to get by. I wanted to keep Shawna safe, keep my unborn child safe. Same with Mindy."

"How many of you lived in the house?" Merissa asks.

Mindy's eyebrows furrow. "Why does that matter?"

"I'm sure they're just wanting to know so they can count the number they captured," Kemeera says. She turns toward the men. "Right? But, as I mentioned earlier, you didn't get everyone. See, not everyone lived at the house. The night you showed up— "

"The raid," Mindy interrupts. "That's what you call it, right? A raid?"

"The night you showed up," Kemeera repeats, "we were having a service. I guess you probably knew that. Only Mindy, me, and a few other women lived there. Everyone else was just there to hear Preacher. He's an amazing speaker. His voice is just . . . just mesmerizing." She gets a dreamy look on her face.

I've seen the preacher in action a couple of times before. Once at the church during the harvest festival, right before the explosions went off and chaos ensued. Then, when we were escorting Kemeera and the kids from the house, he began reciting scripture. Even with the knowledge of the murders he and his cult were responsible for, I couldn't help but feel drawn to his compelling voice, wanting to pause and listen despite everything that had happened.

"She told you earlier that only select people were involved in the other activities," Mindy says.

"She did," the captain says with a nod. "We'd like to know more about that."

The women share a look. Mindy gestures toward Kemeera in a go-ahead motion.

She takes a deep breath and recounts everything she witnessed and overheard during her time with Preacher and his followers. Her voice trembles with fear and determination as she reveals the homes they used, their resources, and their prior activities. "You have to understand, Mindy and me, we weren't told about things before they happened. It wasn't until afterward. I wouldn't have ever . . ." She vigorously shakes her head.

Mindy sighs. "I was already living with them after the first attack."

"The church festival?" I ask.

"Black Canyon," Merissa whispers.

I snap my head in her direction.

"That's right," Mindy says.

Captain Williams leans forward in his straight-back chair. "Hold on a minute. Are you saying your group was behind the attack on the town of Black Canyon?"

Mindy lifts a shoulder. "Do you know what they did in that town? They ordered the slaughter of all the pets—cats, dogs, even fish and birds. That kind of evil shouldn't be allowed to exist. Preacher did the rest of the Black Hills a favor."

I swallow hard and think about what she's saying. While it's true the town had a terrible edict, many of the people who were killed when the town was attacked were innocents. The man behind the rule, Dr. Eugene Newsome, escaped the carnage and went on to practice at the Guard District Hospital under Captain Williams. With the realization of this attack, it becomes clear that the cult is more organized and dangerous than we initially thought.

"Black Canyon happened before Danny died," Kemeera says. "Before I moved in with them. We'd already been listening to Preacher's sermons, but we had no idea. I knew something was being planned but didn't know what it was. There was a lot of whispering and private meetings. The day after the attack at the festival, we moved to a new house. I didn't think much about it then, but soon started to wonder. I asked Mindy, who told me to mind my own business." She shoots her friend a nasty look.

"I think, if the people I'm living with are murderers, it is my business. When we moved again after the ration centers blew up, I knew. I was going to leave, just slip away. But where could I go? I was pregnant and had Shawna. Mindy had Zach the day after we moved that time. And with Nico's parents dead, I didn't want to leave him."

"How'd Nico's parents die?" I ask, my curiosity about the little boy we brought from the cult house piqued. It always struck me as odd that none of the cult members claimed him or the two girls.

"They were killed in the explosions. Didn't get out in time," Kemeera replies.

"What about the girls?" I gesture to the room next door, where Stella is with the children. "Are they orphans too?"

Kemeera nods. "Yes, but they had been for some time. They were found in the early days of the trouble. Mindy knows more about them."

Mindy nods but remains silent.

"Preacher was behind the hospital attacks?" Captain Williams interjects, a sharp edge to his voice.

Kemeera's gaze drops, and she lets out a heavy sigh. "He was. We lost a few more people then."

Williams crosses his arms but refrains from commenting. I recall our hospital being targeted, and the attackers were stopped, resulting in their deaths. Not much information was released about their identities, but rumors circulated that no one seemed to recognize them.

After several beats of uncomfortable silence, the captain asks, "And Camp Rapid?"

Both of them shake their heads. "We had a prayer service afterward," Kemeera explains. "But it didn't seem like the others. And we didn't move to a different house."

Lieutenant Paul and Captain Williams exchange a glance before Paul inquires, "Do you believe there's another target?"

"At least one." Kemeera nods. "Something to attract attention and then something . . . significant."

Merissa and I exchange worried glances. It's clear that our struggle for survival is far from over.

Chapter 18

Katie

Kemeera and Mindy provide additional information about the preacher and his most devoted followers. Similar to the military, they maintain a hierarchy and ranking system. Most, including Kemeera and Mindy, are simply referred to as disciples. The individuals sent on missions to "cleanse the area of any return to progress" are known as the warriors. According to the women, there appear to be at least two separate groups of warriors, each on a distinct mission.

When asked to explain their reasoning for this belief, especially given their lack of knowledge about other attacks until after the fact, Mindy speaks up, "Because of the midwife."

"Addison?" I ask.

Mindy nods, while Kemeera adds, "Yes, the one I mentioned earlier. She assisted Mindy with Zach and was supposed to help me with Caleb. However, when the flu hit, she disappeared."

"Was she one of Preacher's followers? His disciples?"

Kemeera shrugs. "Yes and no. She attended services occasionally, but her primary role was in the medical field. Preacher knew her from before. They were friends."

"*Were* friends," Mindy emphasizes. "Something happened right around the time the flu got serious. I overheard them arguing. She called him a fool, and he told her to leave and never come back. We weren't even supposed to visit her, but I needed Zach to be checked since he was so small, and Kemeera was due any day. One of the guys took us to her house, but it was empty. He suggested we visit a friend of his, a doctor, but she didn't answer the door."

The captain perks up immediately. "What was the doctor's name?"

Mindy shrugs while Kemeera says, "We didn't know her name, but there was another doctor—Dr. Loving."

"Dr. Loving?" Captain Williams clarifies.

When Kemeera's water broke the night of the raid, she'd told me Addison had a friend who worked at the hospital, a female doctor. I'd discreetly shared the information with Captain Williams after she gave birth. There was no mention made of Dr. Loving.

"Do you know where the house is?" I ask. "The one you went to where she didn't answer?"

Kemeera says she wasn't paying attention, but Mindy provides a street name and describes it as a beige house with white trim and a large front porch.

Chastity's house.

The captain's breath is much louder, a combination of a sigh and a groan. "But you never met her, the female doctor?"

"Not the lady doc. Dr. Loving, though, he sometimes comes to services. Seems a little young to be a doctor." Mindy glances at me. "I saw him with Addison a few times. That was before Zach was born. I haven't seen him recently. Have you, Kemeera?"

"Last time was right before Christmas. I went to an appointment with Addison, and I was early. I think I interrupted something." Kemeera shrugs.

"Describe him," Captain Williams orders.

"Um . . . young, like I said. Probably in his early twenties? He was skinny, like most people these days, but it seemed like he'd always been that way. He had blond hair and was cute, but kind of conceited. He rolled his eyes a lot and made snide remarks."

Sounds exactly like Geoff Landers.

Captain Williams appears visibly angry. He straightens his back and lowers his shoulders. "Did you speak with him?"

"Not that day, not really. He said something like he'd see her tomorrow, and she said she'd have everything ready."

"Did you see Addison again? Before she argued with the preacher?"

"No, and I didn't see her that day either. I didn't hear the argument. Mindy told me about it later."

"Is there anything else you can tell us about Addison, the man calling himself Dr. Loving, or the doctor you didn't meet?"

Both women shrug and shake their heads.

"What about the plans of the warriors? What do you think their intentions are?"

"I'd tell you if I knew," Kemeera says. "All I want is to get out of here and find a place where my children can grow up without violence. I understand it may not be entirely possible in today's world, but at least we can go somewhere where people don't know us. I'd like to keep Nico too."

"And the girls?" I ask.

She drops her gaze and shakes her head.

I turn to Mindy, who responds, "Not me. I can barely take care of myself and Zach."

"I'm sorry," Kemeera whispers. "They're not bad girls, but they've had a rough time and need more than I can offer. Like Mindy, I'll have my hands full."

"You could work together to take care of all the children," I suggest.

Mindy purses her lips and gives Kemeera a sidelong glance. "You're not sending us to the same place, are you?"

I look back at Lieutenant Paul, who shrugs. "That was the initial plan."

"No," the women answer in unison. Kemeera adds, "I've watched enough detective shows to know they'll be looking for us together. We need to go to different places, and . . . and the other can't know where. That way, we can't talk. And the girls should go somewhere else too. Don't tell either of us where, and don't tell them where we've gone."

I suppress a giggle at the intricacy of their plan. When Leo showed up at the Williamses' house and briefed me on the situation, my first thought was that we were reenacting a government-style witness protection program. It appears the two of them have thought about this as well and devised a detailed plan to ensure their safety. I force myself to maintain a serious demeanor, given the gravity of the situation.

Lieutenant Paul stands. "Excuse me a moment. I need to alert the major of this new development." He swiftly exits the room.

Once he's gone, the captain asks if there's anything else they believe we should know. The women exchange glances before shaking their heads. "Then, if you'll excuse me, I'll join the lieutenant in updating the arrangements. Weaver, Burnett, please accompany me."

Back in the kitchen, only Leo and the major remain. When I give my husband a quizzical look, he says, "Shaw had Trooper Schroeder come over. He took the guards, along with Jeff and Matt. Once the guards are, uh, comfortable, Shaw will return."

The captain sinks heavily into a chair and rubs the thigh of his injured foot as he speaks. "It seems the fewer people who are aware of exactly what's happening, the better."

Leo nods in agreement, his expression serious. "I understand the need for caution, Captain. The fewer people involved, the lower the risk of leaks or complications."

Merissa and I take our seats at the kitchen table, the weight of the situation sinking in. Captain Williams leans forward, his voice filled with urgency. "This could be a mess. It's hard enough to relocate the group as a whole. But to find places to send them individually . . . what's the plan?"

The major is the first to speak. "The original plan was to send them all east to Sioux Falls. The general has contacts there who are willing to help. His friend was especially interested in the children—the girls."

"Interested in the children?" I blurt. "What does that mean?"

He gives me a stern look. "Well, *Sergeant*, it means they'd give them a good home. The couple lost their daughter early in the collapse. The wife has had a hard time of it, and her husband thinks adopting the girls would be good for her."

"But— " I start to protest.

Leo places his hand on my arm, and I shake it off. I realize I'm on the verge of insubordination, but if Kemeera asked me to be here for this, there must be a reason. The details they shared earlier weren't something I was needed for. Maybe she knows I only want the best for her and the others.

I paste on a smile. "Thank you, sir. I appreciate the explanation. I'm sure it'd be wonderful if the girls could find a loving home. But what if they get there, and the couple doesn't like them? Or they like one and not the other? The girls are going to be all on their own, and they're so young, only six and nine. They have . . . difficulties."

"They're not sisters," Merissa adds. "Plus, they've already been through a lot. Orphaned and then living with Preacher's group. Like many, they're malnourished, and they barely speak. We don't even know their names."

"Do you two have a better idea?" he demands.

"No, sir," Merissa says. "It's just crucial to understand how . . ."

"Damaged," I offer. "How damaged the girls are. All of them, really. They have nightmares." I look at Leo, who nods in confirmation. Even though I haven't been directly involved in their treatment since they left the hospital, I know from Leo and the captain just how difficult their experiences have been.

"The girls, the women, all of them have had a rough time," Captain Williams says. "I'm surprised they didn't share more about the difficulties they faced in the cult. There's been no mention of it, and the women deny it when asked. But I suspect they endured corporal punishment. Both the women and the older children had suspicious bruises. Mindy spoke more today than she has in the entire two weeks they've been under our care. The older girls have hardly said a word. Nico, the boy, speaks occasionally, but then he acts like he's done something wrong. At least the toddler seems to have normal development and behavior."

"So, what do you suggest, Captain?" the major counters.

The captain raises his hands. "I'm just ensuring you have all the facts. I've included this in my reports to the general, and I'm sure he's considered it in his arrangements. I share the concerns of Sergeant Burnett and Mrs. Weaver. Those girls have been through a lot. If the family they're placed with expects them to be immediately loving and affectionate, they might be disappointed. I believe they could flourish in the right environment, but that environment might not exist in today's world."

The major rubs his hand across the back of his neck and seems to release some built-up stress. "All right. I'll contact them and make sure they're aware of the situation. We'll leave the choice up to them. Now, what about the women? Any ideas where we can send them to ensure at least some safety?"

I glance at my husband and raise my eyebrows. After a brief moment of confusion, he furrows his brow and gives a slight shrug.

"Uh, sirs," I interject, "I might have an idea."

The three officers turn their attention toward me. "Go ahead," Williams urges.

"I'm not sure it'd be possible with winter and everything, but Kemeera may be able to go to Bakerville, where we used to live." I gesture toward my husband.

"Bakerville?" the major furrows his brow. "Where's that?"

"Wyoming," Lieutenant Paul responds. "Western Wyoming."

"Humph," the major scoffs. "Impossible."

I purse my lips as heat rises to my cheeks. "Perhaps so, sir. It was just a thought."

"It's actually not a bad idea," Captain Williams chimes in. "No one there would know her history, and according to the Burnetts, it's a relatively safe location. They've been working together and providing for themselves."

The major groans. "Impossible. It's on the other side of Wyoming. It's the dead of winter. And how can we even be sure they'd accept a woman and two children?"

"Three children," Merissa corrects. "She's taking the boy, Nico, with her."

"They have a radio," I offer. "We could try contacting them and ask if they'd be willing."

"I know the radio protocols, or at least what they had when we were there," Leo says. "I think I can secure a channel if we can reach them directly."

"Can you manage that?" Merissa asks. "Aren't the Black Hills and the Bighorn Mountains between here and there?"

I'm impressed Merissa remembers where I used to live. Bakerville is situated in the high desert near the Beartooth Mountains. During the winter, they move up the mountain to a former ski resort and dude ranch, which is easier to secure than the sprawling open spaces of the high desert.

The major sighs. "We can try to contact them. If they're willing to take them, we'll figure out a way to get them there. What about the other woman?"

We spend another ten minutes brainstorming ideas. Lieutenant Paul eventually suggests checking with a friend of his at Custer State Park. It turns out they've formed a somewhat thriving community at the State Game Lodge. With our plan coming together, we exchange nods and reassuring glances. By the time Deputy Shaw returns, we have a solid plan in place and are ready to take action.

Chapter 19

Katie

Leo and I stride in unison toward the radio room at Camp Rapid, our shoulders almost brushing as we move forward. With the guards dismissed, Merissa, Deputy Shaw, and Captain Williams protect the women and children.

Stella, who calls herself a conscientious observer due to her gun-free stance, also remains at the house. To ensure today's information doesn't leak out, the two female guards, along with med students Jeff and Matt, are kept at an undisclosed location with Trooper Schroeder of the South Dakota Highway Patrol, whom Shaw trusts.

Lieutenant Paul and the major walk with us. Paul will try his contact from Custer State Park, while the major updates the general on the situation and determines how to proceed with the girls. Will the general's friend still want the children after their difficulties are brought to light?

There's a flurry of activity when we reach the radio room. I'm immediately struck by the similarity between this radio room and the one we had at the Bakerville winter retreat. I'm not sure what this space was like before the EMP, but now it has only two radios and two operators, a sergeant and a corporal who were probably plenty bored until the major enters the room and they pop to attention.

The major relays the need to use the room and dismisses the men, telling them to take a break. He tells Paul he'll confer with the general and return soon.

Lieutenant Paul makes his call first. From the first greetings, it's apparent Paul has spoken to his friend recently. Her voice starts off very friendly, almost intimate.

When his next words alert her to the audience in the room and that he has a situation, her tone becomes professional. He asks her to switch to a different channel, one she seems to know without needing any details or prompting. On the new channel, Paul quickly and succinctly relays his need without divulging unnecessary details.

"A woman and an infant?" I can hear the dismay in her voice. "How old?"

Paul glances in my direction. "Zach was born at the end of November," I say.

He tells his friend, who responds with, "The woman. How old is she?"

I shrug. "She won't say, but we think around twenty."

I should've asked Mindy her age when she was so chatty earlier. I wonder what changed to make her suddenly want to talk, to make her and Kemeera realize they need to leave and find forever hideouts. Could one of the guards have said something? Threatened them in some way?

It's no secret there's a lot of blame and hatred directed toward the women, even the children. Poppy Gardner didn't want them at her care centers because she was afraid of what could happen, that someone would find out and target them.

While we tried to keep their existence quiet, everyone talks. Even the once-a-month newspaper, printed with an old press on handmade rough paper, had an article about the capture of Preacher and his followers, detailing how one of the women went into labor during the raid.

Thankfully, the newspaper implied the woman and child were being held with the others. There was no mention of Nico, Shawna, or the other children, and no mention of Mindy and Zach. But there's little doubt they haven't been kept a full secret. Even though the guards have been instructed to tell no one, not even their family, people talk. It's just a normal thing.

It takes only a few more minutes of discussion for Paul's friend to say she'll speak with the others about Mindy and Zach. "When do you need an answer?" she asks.

"Now. Today. This is a life-and-death situation."

"Give me twenty minutes to get a consensus. She'll have to pull her weight. Will that be an issue?"

I try and keep my face even as I glance at Leo. He, too, is staring straight ahead, looking passive. From what Leo's told me, Mindy seems to be a bit on the lazy side. Kemeera is the one handling all the children and making sure the house is functioning, and that's after recently giving birth.

Paul doesn't look at us, just says he's sure she'll do what's needed. His friend huffs a response, leading me to believe she's less than convinced. Before they sign off, Paul tells her to call back on the main channel, but to immediately switch to their nighttime channel and he'll meet her there.

I hold back my smile, realizing my first instincts about Lieutenant David Paul and his "friend" are on target. I'm glad for him. When we first arrived in the Black Hills, he was dating Dr. Wolff, but that didn't go anywhere.

Leo said Paul was praying for a woman to spend his life with and believed God would provide the right person. Is this lady the one? And if so, how can they make it work with the distance between them? Custer State Park, which was an easy drive from Rapid City before everything fell apart, might as well be on the other side of the country now. Travel for pleasure just doesn't exist.

As he signs off, a wide, infectious grin spreads across his face, transforming his expression into one of pure joy. He pivots toward us, his eyes sparkling with delight. "Your turn."

Knowing how to work the radio and dial in the frequencies, Paul asks Leo for the details.

"If nothing's changed, it'll work," Leo says after Paul has adjusted the calling frequency.

My heart pounds in anticipation. It's too much to hope my sister Calley will be the one monitoring the transmissions today. If not her, whoever it is can at least pass on a message to my family.

Part of me wishes we had the opportunity Paul has and can call and chat whenever we wish. That'd sure make the duty of staying in Rapid City and putting in our time with the National Guard easier to bear.

While we're able to send letters through the provisional mail system, I'd love to be able to chat, to call up one of my sisters or my stepdad and just talk. A wave of grief passes over me; I wish I could do the same with my mom. To have just one more conversation with her, to be able to tell her how much I love her.

Leo clears his throat. "This is Rapid City One for Bakerville Winter, over."

Before the apocalypse, the amateur radio owned by one of the men in Bakerville had its unique call sign, as required. Now many of those using the radios across the country have adapted new call signs, often utilizing their location or a nickname.

In her last letter, Calley mentioned a guy out of California who calls himself Five O'Clock Charlie and often talks about the terrible things our government is doing by forcing people to move out of the Wastelands. He insists many of the areas are still habitable and the damage from the ground strikes was not as extensive as we've been led to believe.

"This is Bakerville Winter. Go ahead, Rapid City," the voice on the radio says. I blink away my tears. It's not my sister, but it's still a voice from home.

While I don't recognize the voice, Leo must. "Grant? Is that you?"

I smile and nod. Of course! Grant Cameron. He, his wife, and extended family, along with several others, moved to Bakerville after the trouble in nearby Prospect. The Cameron family was a welcome addition and was instrumental in our survival.

Grant's brother Dax married my friend Kelley Hudson's daughter. Last winter, tragedy struck the family when Grant's wife Shelby was kidnapped, along with her friend Milena. Thankfully, we were able to get them back when Prospect was liberated.

There's a delay in response from Bakerville, so Leo adds, "This is Leo Burnett."

"Leo! Wow. Great to hear from you."

"You too, buddy. Hey, I don't know the protocols now, but can you switch to Index Peak?"

"Index? Uh . . . give me a minute. I'll meet you there."

When we lived in Bakerville, the different radio frequencies were given names of popular mountains in the Absaroka and Beartooth Ranges, along with Gannet Peak from the Wind River Range. Naming the channels after mountain peaks allowed us to change frequency without others knowing which one we'd be using.

Leo directs Paul on the change to make. Once that's done, he waits a full minute before reaching for the mic. Just as his fingers graze it, Grant's voice comes through loud and clear. "Are you there, Leo?"

"Yep. Glad my code worked."

"Barely. I had to grab an old book. Hey, I sent someone to find your family. You just missed Calley. I relieved her only about five minutes ago."

I glance at my watch to see it's 1835 hours. If she's still in the same cabin as last year, she hasn't had time to get home yet, and whoever he sent could easily catch up to her and send her back to the radio room.

"I don't know if we have time to stay on for them to arrive," Leo says, his voice tinged with sadness. He casts a wistful glance my way. "Katie's here with me, so be sure to let them know we're fine and we miss them." He leans forward, his tone inquisitive. "We have a request. Who's making the decisions around there now?"

"The usual. Belinda Bosco, Evan Snyder, Bill Shane, Phil Hudson, my grandpa, your father-in-law . . . a few others."

My tears well at the mention of Jake. I'm mildly surprised to hear him mention Belinda first. While she was certainly an important component of our survival as the leader of the medical team, I never really considered her one of the decision-makers.

In the days following the EMP, there'd been an election and we formed a town council. Evan Snyder and Bill Shane were part of it. When one of the councilmembers tried to overthrow the system, resulting in several deaths, things were revamped. When we left, there wasn't an official form of government for Bakerville, but maybe things have changed since then.

Leo asks if anyone who can make a decision is nearby. Grant says he's already sent for someone when he sent for our family. "I figured you weren't calling to chat," he adds.

Even though Grant says we didn't call to chat, that's what happens while we wait. Grant info dumps as quickly as he can about life on the mountain. He tells us Shelby is doing okay and is recovering from her time as a hostage, and their baby Hannah is running all over the place. She often plays with my nephew Tate, who's only two months younger.

He says Mollie, Calley's baby, my niece, is crawling. And Grant's going to be an uncle. Dax and Sylvia are expecting their baby in June. He fills us in on bits and pieces of other gossip before abruptly saying, "Evan and Jake are here. I'll turn you over to them."

Leo motions me to join him at the mic.

"Katie? Leo?" Jake's voice trembles with emotion as he says our names.

As soon as Leo keys the mic, my words rush out. "Jake! I can't believe we get to talk to you."

"Me neither. Calley's here too."

"Hi, Katie! Hi, Leo!" Calley's bubbly voice comes through. "We're trying to get Sarah, Angela, and Malcolm, too . . . well, everyone, but I don't know. Evan's here."

"Yep. I'm here," Evan's gravelly voice responds. "Good to hear from you."

Leo glances toward Lieutenant Paul, who lifts his hand to show five fingers. Leo nods. "I'm told I only have five minutes, so let me get to the point of this call and then maybe we'll have time afterward."

"Go ahead," Jake urges.

Leo quickly lays out the situation, without detailing why we have the issue.

"So, you're asking if this woman and her children can stay with us?" Jake clarifies.

"Correct," Leo answers.

"Well, sure. That's fine, but how will they get here?"

"We'll figure that part out as long as you're willing to house them and care for them."

"Make the arrangements to get them here, and we'll take care of the rest."

Paul gives Leo a nod and tells him to let them know we'll contact them again when the arrangements are made so they have an idea of when to expect them.

"Will you want us to meet them in the valley?" Evan asks. "Or will they be brought all the way to us?"

We again look to Paul, who shrugs.

"Can we let you know next time we speak?" Leo asks. "Those details will need to be ironed out."

"No problem," Evan agrees.

"Two minutes," Lieutenant Paul says with a nod.

"We've got to start wrapping things up," Leo declares. "Here's Katie again."

"I'm so glad to be able to hear your voices," I gush. "The letters have been great. And, Jake, thanks for sending all the papers Mom had. They're still considering what to do with us, but I'm sure, at some point, it'll help."

"Sure, Katie. Lieutenant Katie Burnett does have a nice ring to it. I hope the school records and the information on Leo's graduation help. How's your work at the hospital?"

"It's good. Fine." I choose not to tell him about the attack and how I've been off work recovering from the frostbite. "The med school's going good too. Leo enjoys teaching, and I'm still helping with some of the classes. They're going to be starting a nursing school in a few weeks."

"That's great. We've been working on letters. Maybe we can send them with the troop that delivers your friends."

"We'll send letters with them too." I glance at Paul, who motions for me to wrap it up. "I have to go. I don't know if we'll be here when they call you with the details. I'll try, but . . . I don't know. I love you. Please tell everyone we're fine and we love them all. Give Malcolm a big hug for me. Gavin and the others too. I can't even imagine how big everyone's getting."

"We love you too," Jake says.

"I love you!" Calley practically yells. "You too, Leo."

Chapter 20

Merissa

The crisp morning sun bathes the cozy living room as I sit in the rocking chair, my hands cradling my ever-growing belly. Mother Pearl insisted on the new piece of furniture. She said the ability to rock and soothe the baby will make our lives much easier.

Jesse Talbot carried the heavy wooden chair from the furniture depot to my house while I walked alongside him. Like everything else needed for our day-to-day living, I used a ration chip to buy the piece. As an expectant mother, I receive extra rations compared to others. My food rations exceed Pearl's, and I have specific ration chips for baby furniture and clothes.

The rocking chair didn't qualify as baby furniture, which caused Pearl to raise a fuss when we originally went looking for one. I'm sure the poor woman in the store didn't know what to do when Pearl started talking. My mother-in-law has a way of making her point known with a serene smile on her face while being less than kind.

The weird thing is, unless you really know the woman, you may not even realize what just happened. I've been on the receiving end of Pearl's tongue enough times to know exactly what she was saying. In the end, the woman gave a weary sigh and told us to take whatever we needed.

I glance at my watch and release a quiet breath. Today is a rare morning off for me. I'm expected at the hospital at 1330 hours to join Dr. Wolff on her rounds, which will include visiting Kemeera, Mindy, and the children. I have some time before I need to get going.

I lean back, my thoughts continuing to wander, exploring the intricacies of my relationship with Pearl. We're forever bound by our shared love for her son and the anticipation of my unborn child. Living together has been a challenge. Living during this time in history has made the challenge even more difficult.

I open one eye and glance around the room. Pearl is at the kitchen table, working on her mending, the tip of her tongue showing between her lips. She has two pots of water on the stove to boil and sanitize as part of her water crew job. Sewing and water sanitation are common jobs for the elderly. They do the work they're able to do in order to contribute to our struggling society.

Not that there's a large population of elderly remaining. Many were lost in the early days of the attacks, even before the EMP. In the last eighteen months, the population of those over the age of sixty has plummeted.

Pearl lifts her head, a smile softening her weathered features. "It's nice to see you relaxing."

I lean forward in the rocker and return her smile. "It feels weird to just sit."

"You need it. The doctors are sure you're not overdoing it? Today's, what, February 2nd? Only two months and he should be born."

I silently add "or she" as I give a nod.

"When did you say they'll get the new medic trained?" Pearl asks.

"A week, maybe two."

"Then you'll not have those shifts."

"Only if they're shorthanded. But the school and shadow shifts will continue. I'll keep with med school as long as I'm able."

Pearl waves a hand dismissively. "Oh, I'm sure. Just think, soon you'll be a doctor."

"Not that soon. Captain Williams thinks it'll be two, maybe three years, before we're trained enough to act on our own. Speaking of, I should get dressed."

Glancing out the frost-covered window, Pearl tuts. "Think it'll ever warm up?"

"It's better than it was." The severe cold we had the night Katie was attacked ended after a few days. It's still been cold, especially at night, but not deadly cold. Even though we only had Katie affected with hypothermia during that frigid spell, other districts had several cases of frostbite, and there were even a few deaths throughout the Black Hills. "Besides," I continue, "it is February. We should expect a little winter weather."

"I s'pose you're right." Pearl sighs as she continues to look out the window. "And I guess it's not as bad as last winter. Why, I can even see a few patches of brown grass poking through the white stuff.

Wouldn't take much of a warm-up for it to melt." She frowns. "Then we'd have a heap of mud. Not sure that'd be any better."

I hide my smile at her antics. Soon, it'll be spring, and we'll have plenty of mud and rain. Her complaining will continue, as it will when the heat of summer arrives. Pearl doesn't care much for any of the seasons other than autumn. She's always said that's her favorite.

As I get up from the rocking chair, Pearl glances over at me, her eyes filled with warmth and concern. "You take care of yourself, now," she reminds me, her voice gentle but firm. "No pushing too hard at the hospital. You're carrying precious cargo, and we don't need any mishaps."

I bite back a retort and nod in agreement. I know I should be grateful for her care. In the time since I've told her about the pregnancy, she's been a pillar of support, offering wisdom and guidance whenever needed. She's often reminisced about her own experiences during her pregnancies with Braedon and Tomas. Truthfully, I've learned more about Pearl Weaver in the past month than the entire time I've known her. She's shared much of her heart with me recently. I know I'm lucky to have her by my side. Not lucky, blessed.

As I make my way to my bedroom to get dressed, I again find myself reflecting on the challenges we've faced since the attacks. The world we once knew has been turned upside down, and every day is a battle for survival. Yet, amid the chaos, we find moments of solace and happiness, like the one I just had in the rocking chair, talking about nothing special with Pearl. It's these times I force myself to hold on to. To remember.

I let out a long breath as other memories threaten to take over. Finding Braedon and Tomas dead after the battle. The way the brothers were together, the younger Braedon seeming to protect his older sibling. Pearl said it'd always been that way. Even though he was eighteen months younger, Braedon had always been the leader of the two. When Braedon chose to join the Army instead of the family's construction business, no one was really surprised. That was just who he was.

When he made it a career, it caused some ripples in the family, especially with their dad, who didn't understand why Braedon was doing his own thing. Eventually, Braedon returned home to

Livingston, Montana, but he still didn't work with his dad and brother, instead opening a private security firm.

His choosing to marry me, a brash and awkward tomboy who prefers horses and firefighting to fancy dinners, didn't go over well. While Braedon's dad verbally made his feelings about me known, Pearl said little. She didn't need to speak; her thoughts of me were clear in the narrowing of her eyes and the downturn of her lips.

But now, here we are. Pearl and I are the only two remaining of the Weaver family. Well, that's not exactly true. My sister-in-law Courtney, Tomas's widow, is still alive—as far as we know. She joined her family near the Western Wastelands demarcation line. Pearl has sent letters to her. With the mail system what it is, we don't know if she's received them. Pearl didn't even have an address for Courtney, just addressed the letter to *Courtney Weaver, Sandpoint, Idaho*, in hopes it'd reach her. We both know the chances of her receiving it are low. The chances of us receiving a return letter are even less likely.

I shake my head and turn my attention to my clothing. Dressing for the cold takes some time. I start with a base layer of long woolen undergarments. The bottoms are long enough to pull up over my stomach, while the top ends up a little short. I wasn't able to get a matching set, so I wear a pair of white bottoms with a soft pink top. I have a second pair of black bottoms, but only the one top.

After the base layer, I add a pair of leggings and a turtleneck. Before putting on a button-up shirt, I fasten on an underarm holster Opal gave me. The holster holds a dainty .380 that was also part of the gift. Once it's in place, I add my street clothes and hip holster, then take a moment to check myself in the mirror.

Becoming a doctor wasn't something I ever imagined possible. It wasn't even something I wanted. At least, not before the EMP. I'll admit, helping at the clinic we set up in our Livingston community was something I enjoyed. Being able to help and to know I was helping was very fulfilling. Now that this opportunity is here, and despite the hardships and long hours, I'm determined to see it through. My desire to help others and make a difference in this shattered world propels me forward.

As I head back to the living room, I notice Pearl has put her sewing aside and is now carefully tending to the pots on the stove. The rhythm of her actions reflects a lifetime of experience, and I'm reminded of the importance of these small tasks that contribute to the survival of our community. We all have a role to play, no matter our age or abilities.

I move to the bench by the woodstove to put on my boots. Once I'm dressed for the cold, I grab my backpack and move toward the door. "I'll see you later," I say to Pearl.

"Take care, dear," she replies with a smile. "Think you'll be home for supper? I'll heat up the stew."

I shrug. "I should be. It's only supposed to be rounds with Dr. Wolff. But, you know . . ." I raise my hands.

Pearl groans. "Yes, I know. I'll not bother waiting for you if I get hungry."

As I step outside, I feel the chill in the air, but there's also an unfamiliar sense of hope in my heart. Somehow, the morning off and time spent with Pearl seems to have lightened my load. We've endured so much, and yet we press on, each day bringing us closer to the future we strive for. I let out a snicker. It's not like me to be so optimistic.

"Hello, Merissa." Bowski gives me a nod.

"Oh, Bowski. Hey." I feel the warmth climb up my cheeks. "Is it . . . are you the escort today?"

"Yep. Deputy Shaw added me to the rotation. We'll pick up Stella next."

I pull my lips tight, trying to tamp down the silly smile that seems to want to take over my face. As a memory of my husband's face flashes, the urge to smile disappears.

What am I doing? Here I am, only a widow for four months, and pregnant at that. Bowski has been kind and supportive since I first met him, but I can't shake the feeling of guilt for even allowing myself to feel a hint of joy. It's too soon, and I should be grieving properly.

But life doesn't always wait for grief to run its course, and it certainly hasn't paused for me.

As we walk silently toward Stella's home, I try to focus on the present moment. The world outside is still scarred from the attacks, with buildings standing as silent witnesses to the horrors we've endured. But amid the ruins, there are signs of life and rebuilding.

Stella waits for us outside her small home, bundled up against the cold. Unlike many in the area, she still lives in the same home she had before the EMP. The house and gardens, even in the dead of winter, show her love of plants and herbs. She has bundles of herbs in the front window, hanging like curtains.

In her midforties, Stella is the oldest of the med school students. She's already spent many years honing her craft as an herbalist and natural healer. As she lifts her hand in greeting, her eyes meet mine with a knowing glint. She's seen enough life to understand the complexities of the human heart.

I drop my gaze, embarrassed at my transparency. If Stella can see my inappropriate interest in Bowski, does he see it too?

Chapter 21

Merissa

As we reach the hospital, Stella touches Bowski's arm to express her gratitude for walking us to work.

"Any time, Ms. Stella. In fact, I'll accompany you home." His gaze meets mine. "I'll be back around 1800 hours." He gives me a smile before turning back to her. "If you aren't ready, I'll wait."

"There's no need," I reply. "We do the care center rounds and then just walk by our houses, dropping people off as we go. It's fine."

Stella glances at me, then back to Bowski. "Merissa's right. That's how we've done it before. The only times it's different is if we have classes or for some reason need to end up back at the hospital. Did Shaw not give you the schedule?"

Bowski lets out a low chuckle. "I heard the schedule is subject to change."

Stella agrees. "It changes regularly. Too regularly. If they'd stick to a schedule, it'd be much smoother."

I hold my tongue. Stella's frustration with the lack of organization is well known, but emergencies disrupt even the best schedules, like our recent rounds with Kemeera, Mindy, and the children.

Kemeera and Mindy sharing crucial information about Preacher's group forced us to alter our plans. Stella seemed fine at the time and entertained the children while we talked. But afterward, it was clear she was upset. Captain Williams either didn't notice or chose to ignore it.

She was still in a funk during yesterday's classes but seems back to normal today. Truthfully, I'm surprised the women and children haven't already been moved out of the area. Yesterday, the captain quietly told us the arrangements were taking longer than expected. Stella shook her head and commented under her breath about how there'd probably be more issues affecting us before they finally left town.

"See you later, Merissa," Bowski says.

"Uh, okay," I mutter, while Stella says, "See you later."

Inside the hospital, we stop at the bench by the backdoor to remove our snow boots and heavy winter jackets. Normally, we'd change into scrubs in the break room, but today's rounds take us outside again. I retrieve my tennis shoes from a high bin on the wall. Kerry Hendricks suggested these bins to avoid walking barefoot through the hospital, a wise suggestion.

All three doctors—Williams, Wolff, and Murphy—are assembled by the nurse's station. The new arrival, Dr. Murphy, is soon to be taking shifts on his own. Captain Williams feels he's oriented enough to how our hospital works. Standing next to Williams is Leo, no surprise there.

Alice Williams is sitting in a chair behind the desk. She greets both of us in her usual welcoming way. Fellow students Matt, Jeff, and Kerry are also waiting, as is Katie. I crinkle my brow when I see her.

Noticing my reaction, she gives a slight lift of her shoulders and shakes her head.

"Good afternoon, ladies," Captain Williams says.

"Are we late?" Stella asks, sounding bewildered. "Did you change the time for rounds?"

Williams waves his hand. "Not at all. We've just assembled."

Stella sighs in exasperation.

I sympathize with Stella's frustration. The ever-changing schedules and our unpredictable work can be exhausting. But in our current world, structure is a luxury we can't always afford.

"Let's get started," Dr. Wolff chimes in, sounding irritated. "We have a lot to cover today."

"Indeed," Captain Williams adds. "You'll join Dr. Wolff on rounds here at the hospital and then at the care centers. I'll join you before you finish. Dr. Murphy will handle the hospital during that time. I'm also delighted to announce Sergeants Katie and Leo Burnett will accompany you on rounds today."

He lets out a low chuckle. "As your shadows. I've asked the Burnetts to consider new roles in our med school. You're all well aware they have assisted me as instructors. They'll continue in this capacity while also, should they agree, joining us as students. With the changes in our numbers, I feel adding the Burnetts makes sense. I'm sure you all know Leo has been studying right alongside you so he'd be ready for the classroom discussions. While Katie hasn't had the exact lessons, I've been giving her extra reading materials for the past couple of months."

All eyes turn to Katie as the captain continues, "Both Burnetts are well-versed in what's involved with attending our school. Joining you on rounds will give them another glimpse into what's expected of them . . . though I dare say Leo's made these rounds more often than most of you. Today, his job is to attend as a potential med student and future physician rather than as my aide. I trust you'll all make the Burnetts feel welcome as they consider their new roles."

I can't actually say I'm surprised. It makes sense to add Katie and Leo to the med school. Frankly, I was surprised Katie wasn't part of the school when it started. I think the main reason was her lack of formal training. Even though she functions as a more-than-competent nurse, her medical knowledge didn't really start until after the attacks rocked our world. Even then, it was only because her sister was injured that she was enlisted as an almost unwilling participant in her hometown's makeshift medical team.

Leo, too, was part of the newly formed healthcare crew. Katie insists it made sense for Leo to be on that crew since he'd had EMT training, but all she had were a few first aid classes. Either way, I'm confident both will be an asset to our med school.

Stella slowly raises her hand. When the captain nods at her, she almost reluctantly asks, "What about Leo's arm? How will he take rotation with his handicap?"

I watch Leo's face as he struggles to maintain composure. Her concern about his broken arm, though not a handicap, is valid. It limits his capacity, much like my growing belly. I'm truly grateful the captain has added Austin Chambers to our staff, and I won't be expected to function as a medic for much longer. Not that I'd admit it to Mother Pearl or my fellow med students, not even to Captain Williams, but it's getting difficult to do what's needed in my current condition.

"In a few days, Leo will travel to the main hospital to meet with Dr. Bollinger," Captain Williams says. "We anticipate the fixation device has done its job and the bones have properly healed. Leo's likely to be in a splint for several weeks, but we do expect a full recovery." He directs a smile and a nod at Leo.

"When Leo goes to see Bollinger, we'll also transfer Private Tillman to the main hospital for intensive physical therapy. Katie will ride along to act as a nurse for Tillman. Our new medic, Austin Chambers, will be their driver. Now, unless there are additional questions, get your rounds out of the way."

A chorus of "thank you, sir" follows as we trail after Dr. Wolff to the first patient room. After visiting the patients in the hospital and discharging two, we don our winter gear to head to the care centers. Poppy Gardner is there, tending to her tasks. While she's competent, something about her rubs me the wrong way, though I can't pinpoint exactly what it is.

Captain Williams mentioned she has been conducting interviews for the new nursing school. She has narrowed her choices down to eight candidates, in addition to one former medical student who'll now be attending the nursing school. The captain intends to personally interview each candidate to ensure they align with their shared vision.

I believe the captain will trust his instincts fully this time, unlike his past decision regarding Geoff Landers. It's rumored that Landers was admitted as a favor to his uncle, Sheriff Melvin Cabal. Jacquie suggests it was more like blackmail, claiming the sheriff holds something over the captain.

Perhaps, over the decades, something occurred between Williams and Cabal that he's embarrassed about and wishes to keep hidden. I believe it would need to be a significant secret for Williams to tolerate Geoff Landers. Now, Landers has even threatened Captain Williams. I can't help but wonder if Cabal is somehow involved in that as well.

My mind shifts back to Poppy Gardner, and I can't help but wonder if my feelings about her are warranted or merely a result of the stress and uncertainty we all face daily. It's possible, based on recent events, that my instincts are heightened, causing me to be more cautious about the people we bring into our close-knit group.

Captain Williams meets us as we're finishing up at the last of the care centers. Mrs. Williams is with him, pushing his snow-adapted wheelchair. After he takes our reports, which includes Dr. Wolff relaying Elliot Tillman's excitement to get his physical therapy underway, he dismisses Dr. Wolff to return to the hospital while the rest of us make our final evaluation of Kemeera, Mindy, and the children.

Captain Williams assures us the final arrangements have been made and the group will be relocating tomorrow. The women have yet to be informed. The plan is for us to give them a medical checkup to ensure all is well, without notifying them of the plans.

"Will you be returning to the hospital?" Dr. Wolff asks Williams.

"I'll dismiss everyone when we're finished. We'll have regular classes in the morning."

"Thank you, sir." She gives him a nod. If Dr. Wolff is upset at being dismissed, she hides it well.

Alice walks back to the hospital with Dr. Wolff, while Leo takes over pushing Williams. As Kemeera and Mindy's safe house comes into view, in a hushed voice, Captain Williams orders, "Stop." He points toward a couple scurrying down the walkway.

The smaller of the two turns her head in our direction before whipping it the other way and grabbing her partner's elbow. They break into a fast walk and go in the other direction.

Chapter 22

Katie

"Leo!" My fingers tighten around my husband's arm, my voice hushed but urgent. "I think that was— "

"Landers," Leo interrupts.

Almost simultaneously, Captain Williams narrows his eyes. "Why is Geoff Landers here? And who was that with him?"

"It's Addison," Stella says. "At least, I think it was. Hard to tell from this distance."

Geoff Landers and his companion take a right turn and disappear from sight.

Leo's brows furrow with concern. "Why were they here?" He clears his throat. "Sir?"

"I'm right with you, Leo. Why are Landers and Addison together? And even more importantly, why were they here? Nobody should be at the safe house. Something's going on. We need to proceed with caution. Who has the radio?"

Kerry Hendricks produces the radio.

Williams fiddles with the channel to change it to the agreed-upon frequency for the safe house operation.

The final arrangements to move Kemeera, Mindy, and the children were made late yesterday. I was disappointed not to talk to Jake, Calley, or anyone from home again, but am pleased they've agreed to house Kemeera and the three children.

Lieutenant Paul's friend at the State Game Lodge also agreed to take Mindy and her son. The general's contact in eastern South Dakota confirmed they understood the older girls might have difficulties from their recent experiences and would do their best to help them cope.

Using the handheld radio, Williams quickly reaches someone from the general's team. He's told they'll contact the guards in the safe house—replacements who were hand-chosen—and we should remain where we are until one of the guards comes for us.

"Um, sir?" Leo's voice is cautious. "If there's a problem . . ."

The captain lets out a weary sigh. "Exactly what I'm thinking. Why would the guards let Landers inside? We'll give it three minutes." He glances at the group. "Besides the Burnetts, have any of you been trained to clear a house?"

Merissa and Kerry both say they have, but Kerry specifies she was trained when she was an Army MP. Jeff and Matt shake their heads but indicate they'll do what they can to help. Stella cowers, saying she'll hang back with the captain.

Captain Williams shakes his head and asks Jeff to get him to the line of winter-weary foliage and trees at the bottom of the walkway. "I'll be going in with the rest. Jeff, I want you and Matt to go around to the back door. Find someplace with a view of the door and yard. If anyone comes out, let them leave, but observe as many details about them as you can. Ms. Swenson, you wait in the front, behind that big tree." He points to a deciduous tree with a good-sized trunk.

"We'll holler at you when it's clear or we need you. Jeff, Matt, you listen for us too. We're going to start with knocking on the door. If they answer, and everything seems fine, then we'll quickly check the house. If they don't answer, we'll breach. Katie, Leo, and I will go in first. Katie has the right side, Leo has the center, and I'll take the left. Weaver and Hendricks are right behind us—Weaver right, Hendricks left. Go in quiet. Questions?"

"When do we go?" Kerry asks.

"Another minute," Leo says. "We should see the guard or have a call by then, I'd expect."

"Agreed," the captain confirms.

With her face pale and her lips tight, Stella shakes her head. "I think we should wait."

"Not if they're hurt, we shouldn't," Merissa says.

The captain's fingers deftly manipulate the radio, his voice determined and unwavering. He listens intently to his contact on the other end, his brow furrowing in concern as the man conveys his inability to reach the guards.

Without missing a beat, the captain makes a decisive call. He delivers crisp, no-nonsense instructions, his voice laced with urgency. "Jeff, Matt. Go now. We're fifteen seconds behind you. Go. Everyone else, check your weapons and make them ready."

Those fifteen seconds stretch into an eternity, each heartbeat echoing in my chest. I methodically inspect my 9-millimeter semi-automatic, ensuring it's primed for action. A second magazine rests on my belt, ready for a swift reload.

"Okay, let's go!" Williams starts moving, his gait as stealthy as his walking boot and cane allow.

I take my position at the front door, my heart thundering so loudly that I wonder if I'll even hear the captain's impending knock. The memory of the last time I faced a similar situation floods my mind—a house breach at Chastity Morrow's place. We found her dead. Apprehension consumes my thoughts. What will we find today?

Williams silently gestures to each of us, seeking confirmation of readiness. I respond with a firm nod, mirroring the resolve in the eyes of my fellow team members. My gaze briefly shifts to the spot where we left Stella; she's concealed from view, positioned behind a tree that offers shelter from potential gunfire.

If I allowed myself a moment of contemplation, I might find amusement in the sight before me—Leo with his arm in a sling, the captain nursing an injured foot encased in a walking boot, Merissa visibly pregnant, and myself bearing the signs of frostbite on my ears, cheek, nose, and fingers. Our motley crew must appear as quite the spectacle. Fortunately, Kerry stands as the lone member unscathed and whole.

Captain Williams delivers a sharp knock on the door. Surprisingly, even with my pounding heart, he uses such force I hear the noise clearly.

A second later, Kemeera's soft voice says, "Just a minute."

I let out a breath of relief. My first instinct is to reholster my weapon, but no one else does, so I leave it along my thigh, consciously making sure my finger is well away from the trigger and indexed alongside. A quick glance shows Captain Williams and Leo using the same caution.

When the door opens, Kemeera smiles. "I was wondering— " Her voice stops abruptly, and her smile fades. "What's wrong?"

"Is everything okay?" Williams asks.

"Y-yes. Fine. Oh . . . you must have seen Addison and Dr. Loving as they were leaving."

Captain Williams's voice tightens with a hint of disdain. "Dr. Loving, huh?"

"Uh, yes." She tilts her head. "Do you have news?"

"Where are your guards?"

She shrugs. "They were called away."

His lips form a firm line as he nods, the gesture deliberate. With measured movements, he holsters his sidearm and turns slightly toward Kerry. "Mrs. Hendricks, please relay this information to the major via the radio, then gather the rest of our team." He turns back toward Kemeera. "May we come in?"

"Please, do so."

Within a few minutes, the entire team is gathered in the house. Kerry says the major will have new guards at the house shortly. Williams has Jeff keep an eye on the front walkway, waiting for whoever is sent from Camp Rapid. Captain Williams nonchalantly asks why they had a visit from Addison and Loving. I notice he doesn't use *doctor* in front of Loving's name.

"She said she just wanted to check on us. Heard I had my baby and wanted to see him. I was surprised when she arrived. I didn't realize she knew where we were. I thought it was a secret?"

"When did the guards leave?" the captain asks.

Kemeera shrugs. "About an hour ago. Said the protection detail had been removed. We thought maybe it meant we'd be leaving."

Captain Williams shakes his head but refrains from commenting.

"Did she see the baby?" I ask. "Did you show her Caleb?"

She gives a slight smile. "Well, yeah. She said he was adorable and absolutely perfect."

I step closer to Kemeera. "Did she examine him? Or any of you?"

"Not really. Mindy mentioned she's been having trouble sleeping. Addison said she had something for that, something we could all use. It's even safe for the children."

The pounding in my chest is immediate. I work to keep my face even. "She did? Something she gave you?"

She narrows her eyes. "Is that not allowed?"

I purposefully widen my smile. "We just need to make sure it's not something contraindicated with, um, other things." I glance around at the other med students and the captain.

He gives me a brief nod as Stella steps forward. Clearing her throat, Stella adds, "Some of the herbs are very powerful. Can you show me what she gave you?"

Kemeera rolls her eyes and motions toward the back of the house. "I packed my vial. I'll grab it."

"Where's Mindy?" Merissa asks.

"She went to lie down. I'll wake her."

As Kemeera steps back, Merissa reaches for her elbow. "Why don't you let me do that? Kerry, can you come with me? Stella and Katie can go with you to get the herbs."

"Tincture. Addison gave me a tincture."

I dip my chin, understanding she has a concentrated herbal extract. Whatever the herb was—or possibly a bark or dried berry—it was dissolved in alcohol or vinegar and is now taken as a liquid. Tinctures are sometimes taken by the dropperful and other times added to a different beverage or medium so it tastes better. Many of the remedies turned into a tincture don't have the most pleasant flavor.

As we follow Kemeera down the dim hallway, the captain's hushed directives reach my ears. The others are cautioned to stay prepared for any eventuality. A knot forms in my stomach, and my throat feels parched and scratchy, aligning perfectly with the captain's unspoken evaluation of the situation.

A flurry of unanswered questions swirl within me, each one adding to my mounting unease: What had driven Addison to this place? And why in the company of Landers? How had they managed to uncover the whereabouts of these women? What was the purpose behind the medication she'd left behind? Despite my fervent hope for a benign explanation, an unsettling premonition tugs at my gut, refusing to be ignored.

Kemeera deftly dips her hand into a small exterior pocket of her backpack, the very one provided to her after Caleb's birth. She was brought from Preacher's house with nothing but the clothes on her back, and in the days that followed, while she recuperated from childbirth, the house had been emptied by the National Guard and law enforcement.

They unearthed clothing to fit her toddler, Shawna, along with a dresser containing women's attire—much of it maternity wear or sufficiently stretchy for maternity clothes. These garments had been gathered for Kemeera, and suitable clothing was also located for Mindy and Zach, as well as the other children. Over time, we've managed to find additional clothing for Kemeera to accommodate her rapidly changing body.

With a few fidgety moments, Kemeera retrieves a small, dark vial from the pocket. Stella extends her hand, taking the vial and uncapping it. She proceeds to take a cautious sniff, then shrugs. "Could be just about anything. The alcohol masks much of the . . ." Stella pauses momentarily and inhales again. "But it's a little musky. I think— " Without finishing her sentence, she hastily exits the room, the vial still grasped in her hand. "Merissa? How's Mindy?"

Chapter 23

Merissa

Mindy lies in her bed. Her face glistens with a layer of sweat as she gasps for air. "I . . . I don't . . . feel . . . well. Why is . . . there pain?"

I call over my shoulder to Kerry, "Get the captain." The words leave my mouth just as Stella calls out, asking about Mindy.

Kerry rushes out of the bedroom and collides with Stella as she enters. Stella utters salty words, followed by, "Did it get on you?"

Kerry points to her unzipped winter coat. "My shirt. What is it?"

"Don't touch it!" Stella barks. "I've got it all over my hands now. I've got to wash. Get your shirt off. If either of us has a cut, it could get into our systems." Stella's in a near panic. "Merissa, how is she?"

"Perspiring and breathing rapidly." I rest my fingers against her wrist. "Pulse is thready."

"I don't . . . feel well," Mindy mutters. "I think— " She turns her head just in time to vomit, splattering it all over the floor and barely missing my boots.

"And vomiting," I add to my assessment.

"Captain!" Stella calls out. "We need you."

As Stella's urgent call reverberates through the house, Kerry again asks what it is.

Stella's voice is shaky as she replies, "I can't be sure, but I think it's hemlock. Probably the root turned into a tincture."

"Hemlock?" Kerry exclaims. "That's deadly."

The captain quickly appears with Leo at his side. Stella relays what she thinks was in the tincture, saying she assumes Mindy took some since her symptoms fit, and they need to get her to the hospital immediately. "I spilled the second vial—the one Kemeera had. Thankfully, she didn't take any. I need to get it off my skin and clothes, and so does Kerry."

"Go," the captain orders. "Leo, radio the hospital. Tell Jesse to bring the truck." Neither Stella nor Kerry have moved. He dips his chin at them. "There's water in both the bathroom and kitchen."

"Yes, sir," Kerry mutters.

Stella takes a moment to put the lid back on the vial. "We should keep this. Put it in a baggie or something after I wash off the outside. Find Mindy's vial too."

I turn toward Mindy and ask her if she took the medicine Addison left.

She opens her mouth and quickly slams it shut. Her hands clench into fists and her eyes go wide as her entire body begins to shake.

"She's seizing." I glance at my watch.

The captain groans. "Not good."

I feel completely helpless as Mindy's arms and legs lock, the convulsions overtaking her body.

"Where's the baby?" the captain asks as he hobbles to my side. "You're okay, Mindy. You're having a seizure, but it'll be over soon."

I look over my shoulder at the bassinet. Zach appears to be sleeping soundly. I step toward him and rest my hand on his chest, reassured by the gentle rise and fall. I use the back of my hand to check his forehead. He feels completely normal, not sweaty or having any of the difficulties of his mom. I send up a quick prayer of thankfulness that she didn't give him the medicine to help him sleep too.

"Jesse's on his way," Leo says. "I checked on the rest of the children. They're in the third bedroom and seem fine. Kemeera and her baby are in the living room, and she's asking about Mindy."

"Tell her to get the children dressed and ready. We're taking everyone to the hospital," the captain says. "Looks like she might be coming out of it."

With Stella and Kerry still cleaning up, and Leo instructing Kemeera to get everyone ready to leave, I remain at Mindy's side and continue to pray, this time for her to come through the seizure safely.

As the convulsions gradually subside, Mindy's body starts to relax, but she remains unconscious. Her breaths come in ragged gasps, and her glistening face has turned pale, a stark contrast to the sheen of sweat that was there just moments ago.

"It's going to be okay, Mindy." I gently wipe the sweat from her forehead with a burp rag I grabbed from nearby. "We'll get you to the hospital, get you taken care of."

Even though I speak calmly and with assurance, I question if that's actually the reality. I know little about hemlock poisoning. But from the little I do know, I don't believe there's an antidote to counteract the effects, nor is there a cure. I check my watch. The seizure has mostly subsided after lasting for over two and a half minutes.

Mindy's still twitching occasionally as I say, "You're okay, Mindy. You had a seizure. I want you to just relax."

"Let's move her to the recovery position," Captain Williams instructs. "I'll take her legs. Can you handle her shoulders?"

"I can handle both." I bend her knee and roll her on her side with her head facing toward me.

"Good, good. Keep talking to her as she comes around. I'm going to make sure we're ready to go and check on Ms. Swenson and Mrs. Hendricks." He gives me a final nod before slipping out of the room.

After a minute or so, Mindy takes a deep breath. She moves her head and exhales.

"You're okay, Mindy. You're okay. You had a seizure."

She groans and throws up again, this time covering the bed and my insulated pants in the process. With a shiver, she whispers, "Sorry."

"It's fine, Mindy. We're going to take you to the hospital. See what we can do to help you feel better."

She shakes her head. "Why do I hurt so much? It's not supposed to be like this?"

"What's not, Mindy?"

"Addison. She said . . ." She lets out a sigh as tears run down her cheeks. "Kemeera . . ." Her voice fades away.

"Kemeera's fine. She's fine." I move toward the bassinet and look over the sleeping infant. He seems perfectly well. "Where's the medicine Addison gave you?"

Mindy motions to the drawer of the nightstand. I slide it open and see the small dropper vial tucked along the edge of the drawer. "Did you give any to anyone else? The children?" I use a T-shirt to pick it up, carefully wrapping it as I avoid contact with the glass canister.

"I couldn't. I know . . . I just couldn't."

I furrow my brow. "You couldn't? You were supposed to, but you didn't?"

"Kemeera . . ."

A ruckus sounds from the front of the house. Seconds later, Jesse appears with a spine board and fellow med student Jeff.

"She stopped seizing?"

"For now." The stretcher is one of our few factory-made versions. This one is bright orange and was salvaged from a local swimming pool. The open slots along the edge allow the use of a head immobilizer and a series of belt splints to keep Mindy from slipping off. With careful coordination, they gently move Mindy onto a stretcher.

I grab a throw blanket from the foot of her bed and follow behind as they carry her down the hallway. In the living room, Katie is with Kemeera and the children. All are dressed and ready to leave.

I meet Katie's gaze and motion toward the bedroom. "Zach's asleep in the bassinet. He's fine."

Katie lets out a relieved sigh. "I'll get him." She turns back to Kemeera. "Be right back."

"Put Mindy in the bed of the truck," Captain Williams says. "Merissa, you ride with her. Jeff, you too. The rest of us will follow on foot."

Stella calls from the kitchen, "Kerry and I need new shirts. We'll see what we can find here and be right behind you guys."

"Matt will wait and walk with you. Catch up to us," Captain orders. "Let's move, people."

With Mindy in the bed of the pickup and me sitting by her side, Jeff perches on the raised wheel well. Williams must have instructed him to act as a lookout, based on the pistol in his hand and the way his eyes keep darting around.

When he catches me looking at him, he says, "The National Guard guy called back. He said there was an issue at the jail and help would be delayed. We're to keep the women and children safe."

My eyebrows shoot up. "An issue at the jail? With Preacher and his people?"

His shoulders lift. "Didn't say. I'm sure that's what Williams thinks. I think so too. Makes sense."

The acceleration of my heartbeat leads me to agree with Matt. I turn my attention back to Mindy and place my fingers alongside her neck. Her pulse is still beating wildly. I haven't taken the time to check her temperature or blood pressure, but from the way she looks, I'd be surprised if they're anywhere near normal. The cool air does little to help her symptoms. Even though she's bundled under the blanket and sweating, she's also shivering.

When we arrive at the hospital, both Dr. Wolff and Dr. Murphy meet us in the driveway. "Leo said she's been poisoned?"

"Stella thinks it's hemlock. I brought it with me, but I don't know how we'll tell."

"Where's Stella?"

"Some of it spilled on her and Kerry. They needed to get it off. They'll follow on foot. Same with the captain and everyone else."

They move Mindy from the bed of the pickup. Dr. Murphy has one end of the spine board, while Jeff has the other. We're almost to the front door when Mindy's arms and legs jerk tight.

"She's seizing," I say, as Dr. Wolff orders, "Get her inside and set her on the floor."

She's barely on the ground, and the doctor is undoing the straps that held her to the board. "So she doesn't hurt herself," she says as she releases the chest strap. "We'll leave the headblock in place."

I time this second seizure at over three minutes. As her body begins to relax, Dr. Wolff instructs Jeff and Dr. Murphy to get a room ready for her. "Don't bother with the exam room. Let's get her in a patient room. I want a wider bed in case she seizes again."

As I'm talking softly to Mindy, she opens her eyes. "Make sure Zach is taken care of." Her voice is weak and raspy. "He's innocent. Just a baby. Promise me you'll find him a good home? Maybe the nurse and her husband?"

"Of course, Mindy." I wipe her forehead. "He'll be fine."

"Promise me. You understand, right? Your baby . . . you already love him? You know how important it is. I couldn't . . . I couldn't do what I was supposed to do. Zach, the other children, even Kemeera . . . they can be free now."

"Free?" I crinkle my brow as I try to follow the conversation.

"Zach . . . he's innocent. The things I did . . . he's just a baby."

"The things you did?"

She closes her eyes and lets out a breath. "Black Canyon. I was with them. Kemeera . . ."

"I'll make sure Zach has someone who loves him," I say, not letting the shock show on my face. "What about Kemeera?"

"Katie, the nurse, she could love him. Love my baby." Mindy's eyes flutter closed. A trembling breath escapes her lips, and a shiver courses through her frame.

Dr. Wolff rests a hand against Mindy's throat. After a moment, she shakes her head. "Probably for the best. If it was really hemlock, there's nothing we could've done for her."

I blink back tears and reach into the pocket of my coat to pull out the vial still wrapped in a T-shirt. "Here it is."

The doctor takes the wrapped poison. "Do we know how she got it?"

"When we got there, Addison and Geoff Landers were leaving."

"You think they gave it to her?"

"Seems so. Kemeera was given a vial too. She didn't take any. That's the vial Stella spilled."

"They poisoned them. Why?"

I tilt my head to the side. "Someone from the National Guard was supposed to meet us there. They called back and said there was a problem at the jail, and we were to keep the women and children safe. Did you hear about this?"

The surprise on her face is evident. "No. Another jailbreak?"

"I'm not sure." I hoist myself to my feet. "Should I call Hugo?"

"Let's wait until the captain arrives." She turns to Dr. Murphy and Jeff, who are walking toward us. "She's passed. Time of death 1432. Please take her to the room until we can make arrangements."

Chapter 24

Katie

We tread down the street with Leo pushing Captain Williams in his wheelchair, Kemeera cradling her infant, and me holding Mindy's baby. The weight of our situation presses heavily upon us.

It takes Stella and Kerry mere minutes to change into clean, poison-free shirts. The women and Matt catch up to us before we reach the end of the block. Stella maintains a firm grip on the older children, while Matt's watchful eyes scan the surroundings, searching for any signs of danger.

Even the usually composed Captain Williams appears on edge. His head swivels back and forth, and he clutches his pistol with a visible tension. The unsettling circumstances surrounding the jail's trouble, which prevented the National Guard from assisting us, have clearly rattled the captain.

Zach is still too light in my arms. He's gained weight in the time he and the rest of them have been under our care, but he's still underweight for his age and not thriving as he should be. I bundle him tighter, wanting to protect him from the cold and any lurking danger.

Leo walks beside me with his sling-free hand on the captain's wheelchair. He glances down at the baby and offers a cautious smile. "How are you holding up?"

"Are doctor rounds always this exciting?"

Captain Williams snorts. "Too often, they are. I hope that doesn't dissuade you from wanting to become a doctor. As I said when I approached you about it, I think you have a real aptitude for medicine. Leo too."

"There's rarely a dull moment in our apocalyptic hospital," Leo agrees. "No matter what the position." He looks at me intently. "Is the baby asleep?"

"Soundly."

"His mom . . ." He shakes his head. "Hemlock poisoning isn't survivable."

I give a brief nod. "What will we do?"

"We'll figure it out," the captain adds. "The child will be well cared for."

Tears well in my eyes, and a profound warmth engulfs my heart. I have every confidence that Captain Williams will ensure this baby finds a loving home.

As we round a corner, the remnants of a burned-out building loom ahead, a grim testament to the devastation that has befallen Rapid City. The acrid scent of scorched wood and metal has long dissipated, but it lingers in the back of my mind, a constant reminder of the world's upheaval. My hold on the baby tightens instinctively.

I can't help but wonder about the world baby Zach will grow up in and the stories he'll hear about our vanished life. The same uncertainty awaits my nephews and nieces. Tate and Mollie, born in the post-EMP era, will have no knowledge of the world that existed before. My nephew Gavin was only two when everything fell apart, and my sister Sarah's adopted son, Andy, was roughly the same age. They're too young to hold any memories of the world as it once was.

I steal a glance at Nico, walking hand in hand with Stella. Does he remember what life was like before the lights went out?

"Captain." Matt's low voice breaks through my reverie and pulls me back to the present. His tone puts me on high alert.

Williams must hear it too. He responds with a tentative, "Yes?"

"I think we're being followed. I caught a glimpse of someone before they stepped behind a building."

Williams audibly exhales, the sound laden with fatigue. "Katie, can you pass the baby to Kemeera? She'll need to carry both of them. Ready your sidearm. Stella, get up here with us."

After a brief pause, he continues, his voice firm. "Katie, you'll take the lead. Stella, Kemeera, and the children will follow you and stand in front of the three of us." He gestures to Leo, Matt, and himself. "Leo, use the radio. Call the hospital and the guard station. Inform them of our situation. Tell everyone to be on high alert and see if they can send someone to us. We may need backup."

I step to the front, my pistol drawn and ready. My gaze sweeps in all directions. My heart thumps loudly, nearly drowning out the surrounding sounds. To regain focus, I take a few deep breaths.

My ribs and hip ache, along with my knee, a reminder of the recent beating. The cold air stings my frostbitten face, making the injured spots burn. I pull up my neck gaiter for added protection against the chill.

Why are we being followed? And who could it be? That answer seems evident. Geoff Landers . . . Addison . . . maybe even Geoff's friend with the brown beanie I met a few weeks ago when Landers threatened the captain.

As we walk along the frozen, empty street, my mind fills with worries about the potential dangers lurking nearby. Landers and Addison have a history of deceit and wrongdoing. I can't forget the unsettling encounter I had with Landers, where he made menacing threats against Captain Williams and the rest of us. It's a stark reminder of his intense hatred for our group. It wouldn't be surprising if he's the one following us, waiting for the right moment to seek revenge.

Addison giving poison to Kemeera and Mindy is proof of her wickedness. Why would she want these women dead? And the children? Just thinking about it sends chills down my spine.

Furthermore, Addison's connection to Preacher and his group becomes increasingly apparent. Landers, whom Kemeera knows as Dr. Loving, seems to be part of their strange cult too. Even Chastity Morrow may have been involved.

I wonder if Addison gave the poison on Preacher's orders? Was it to silence the women, to stop them from revealing important information? Or was it a desperate attempt to prevent them from leaving the Black Hills and finding safety elsewhere? And the bigger question: how did Preacher know they were talking?

And what exactly is happening at the jail? It's a rare occurrence for the facility to be used. It's typically reserved for the most extreme cases like Preacher and his followers. Whatever is happening at the jail surely must involve the preacher.

I grip the pistol tightly and glance back at Kemeera. She's holding both Caleb and Zach in her arms. She looks determined, like a protective mom. Stella is keeping the older kids in line, urging them forward.

Matt is at the back, behind Leo and Captain Williams. He's watching for any dangers around us. He may not have official defender training, but like all of us in this world, he's learned to be flexible and deal with tough situations. I really hope we don't have to fight. Our goal is to reach the guard shack and find safety at the hospital.

I snort out a breath. At least I hope the hospital is safe. The building has been attacked before, so it's certainly plausible something terrible could happen there again. I quicken my pace. Better there than out here in the open. Half a block before we turn the corner, the guard station will be in view.

With our slightly quickened pace, we reach the corner and make our turn in mere minutes. My breath is heavy from the exertion, as are those behind me. Nico asks Stella if we're almost there. As she's about to answer, a low voice says my name.

I spin in the direction.

Josiah Talbot peers out from behind a tree. "It's just me," he says. "I'm assigned to the guard station today. Figured I'd meet you all here. Watch your back as you make it the rest of the way. Deputy Shaw and a team are on their way."

"Good thinking," Captain Williams says as he approaches. "Let's keep moving."

I give Josiah a nod and do as commanded. With the hospital in view, my breathing seems to come easier, and the pounding in my chest is decreasing. Even though we're close, I know better than to lose my focus. My training in Bakerville and with the United Volunteers has drilled into me to stay alert until the mission is over. Not for the first time, I wonder if there will ever be a time in this apocalyptic world where we won't be on edge, where we won't be running from danger. I'm beginning to think the answer is no.

Jeff and Dr. Murphy step out of the building; both have their sidearms. Jesse Talbot is with them, holding one of the rifles we keep at the hospital. For reasons I can't explain, the idea of armed hospital personnel causes a giggle to bubble up from within me. Gone are the days of metal detectors at hospitals and other buildings to prevent weapons from being brought in. Now carrying is part of our everyday life.

Soon, though, this will likely change. Ammunition is dwindling. Even the reloaded cartridges are becoming scarce as the items needed are no longer available. It won't be long until we're melting lead in the woodstove and making bullets like Pa Ingalls did in the *Little*

House books. That and using bows and arrows not only for gathering food, as we did last fall, but for defense too.

"Are you still being followed?" Dr. Murphy asks.

"Haven't seen anyone," Williams responds. "That doesn't mean they aren't there."

In the warm hospital, I pull down my neck gaiter. My face and nose sting, thanks to the frostbite from weeks ago. Once we get everyone settled, I'll apply the aloe vera lotion Stella gave me. I'll also take a dose of willow bark, a natural aspirin substitute. I thought I was ready to come back to work and start med school, but now I'm wondering if staying home in bed might have been the smarter option.

After getting myself situated, I open my arms to take both babies from Kemeera so she can unbutton her jacket. Merissa has already changed into her hospital clothes and shoes and offers to take one of the infants. I raise my eyebrows at her in question. The barely there shake of her head tells me Mindy has already passed or is expected to do so soon. Poor Zach.

"Let's get everyone into the break room," Stella suggests.

"Yes, good idea," Captain Williams agrees, rising from his wheelchair. "I'm going to use the radio and see if we can get an answer as to when we'll have backup."

Chapter 25

Katie

Captain Williams heads straight to the radio, his expression serious as he attempts to contact his National Guard connection. The radio crackles as we pass by. As usual, Leo is by the captain's side. Our eyes lock, and his warm gaze brings me comfort. My heart flutters as I silently acknowledge our love with a slight nod.

While Jeff and Matt stay behind, to be available should the captain need them, Dr. Murphy follows the rest of us into the break room. He asks if he can examine Kemeera and the children to make sure they're all right.

Kemeera gives him a hard look. "I don't know you. I'll wait until Dr. Williams is available." She looks at me. "Or Katie or Merissa can check us." She shoots Murphy a dirty look. "Not you."

He lifts his hands in surrender and backs up toward the door. "Fair enough. I'll let the captain know."

After he's gone, I whisper to Merissa, "Where's Dr. Wolff?"

"She was with Mindy last I saw her. We lost her shortly after we got here. There was nothing we could do. Dr. Wolff wanted to get her ready for Hugo."

"What'd you say?" Kemeera steps toward us.

Merissa and I share a look. I clear my throat. "Mindy didn't make it."

Kemeera's entire body seems to collapse. I quickly pass Caleb to Merissa and guide Kemeera toward the couch. With her sitting, I settle in beside her. "I'm very sorry. I know you and Mindy were friends."

She snorts. "Not really. I mean, I guess. But not good friends, you know? She was young and . . . and I don't think she was always truthful. What will happen to Zach? Will someone take care of him?"

"I'm sure they will. We'll talk with the captain."

She sinks back on the sofa as her baby lets out a cry. "He's ready to eat. Zach will be hungry soon too."

Merissa takes Caleb to his mom while the rest of us move to the other side of the room to give them some privacy. As anticipated, Zach soon awakens.

"I'm almost done feeding Caleb," Kemeera says. "Guess I can feed Zach too."

I burp and walk Caleb as Kemeera feeds the now-orphaned infant. I can't help but notice her gazing and cooing at Zach, telling him everything will be okay and how loved he is.

As my eyes fill and my heart swells, it occurs to me Zach should stay with Kemeera. She may not be able to care for four children on her own, but with the help of my family and friends in Bakerville, they'll thrive. That's certainly the logical solution, considering Zach's feeding needs.

Captain Williams informed Leo and me last night the transportation plans came together beautifully. A contingent from the guard will take the horse and wagon that the hospital uses to Beulah, Wyoming, on Interstate 90, at the Wyoming-South Dakota state line. From there, another horse-drawn wagon, which operates as public transportation, will take them to Gillette, Wyoming.

Similar arrangements have been made using private and military transport to Buffalo, then south on Interstate 25 to Casper, across Highway 20/26 to the small town of Shoshoni, and through Wind River Canyon to Thermopolis. From there, they'll continue making their way north until they reach Bakerville near the Montana state line.

Understanding my concern for the safety of a woman with children, Williams assured me there should be little danger. Interstates 90 and 25 have been cleared and are considered under military control. Unlike South Dakota, which eschewed assistance from the federal military in favor of the South Dakota National Guard, Wyoming has taken all the help it can get, using the Army, Marines, and United Volunteers, along with the Wyoming National Guard.

I agree that our experience of traveling across Wyoming to reach South Dakota was also relatively safe. While we encountered some minor issues during the trip last summer, it wasn't overtly dangerous. I hope this holds true on Kemeera's journey.

Williams estimates they'll be on the road for around two weeks, depending on the weather. Everyone contacted about the trip commented on how much easier it'd be to wait a couple of months until spring arrives, but their safety requires them to go now.

Mindy's death and the attempt on Kemeera's life drive this home. They'll be sent with a supply of food, hopefully enough to last the entire trip, but Williams received assurances no one will let the children and new mother go hungry.

A loud knock on the door is immediately followed by Dr. Wolff and Captain Williams entering. I expect to see my husband, too, but he isn't with them.

"How is everyone?" Williams asks. "Warming up from the walk?" He peers at me and motions to his own cheek. "Better get some lotion on that."

"I did, sir," I say.

He gives me a nod before addressing the entire group. "Deputy Shaw is on site. He and his patrollers are roaming the area, making sure all is well." He clears his throat before looking at Kemeera. She's still on the couch, holding Zach while she burps him. "I'm sorry to inform you Mindy has passed."

She grimaces. "I overheard Merissa telling Katie."

I glance toward Merissa to see the embarrassed look covering her face. Talking about a patient where another patient can hear is a cardinal sin in a hospital setting. Even in an apocalyptic hospital, we try to keep private matters private. This oversight on her part could earn her a tongue-lashing from either Williams or Wolff . . . possibly both. Rather than saying anything, both doctors give Merissa a look that I translate as, "We'll be discussing this later."

Captain Williams takes a deep breath, his face a mixture of sorrow and determination. "I'm sorry for the loss of your friend, Kemeera. But right now, we need to discuss the next steps."

Kemeera looks up, her eyes reflecting a combination of grief and worry. "What about Zach? What will happen to him?"

Dr. Wolff rests a hand on her shoulder. "We've been discussing that, and we have a proposition for you. We believe Zach should stay with you."

Kemeera's eyes widen in surprise. "But how will that work? I can't— "

Dr. Wolff interrupts her. "We understand you may not be able to care for four children on your own, especially with a newborn, but you won't be alone in this, Kemeera. While I haven't been told the final plans, as I know you haven't either, Captain Williams assures me you'll have plenty of support."

I do my best to keep my face even. While the captain and his wife, along with Leo, me, and a handful of others, know Kemeera will be going to my family, we haven't told her or any of the med students. The fewer people who know, the safer she'll be. The safer *my family* will be. We didn't even tell Jake why she and the children needed to go to Bakerville, only that it was for their safety.

"It's obvious you care for him," Captain Williams says. "And you've already bonded. He needs love and care, and we believe you're the best person to give it to him. I'm confident you'll have the help you need."

Kemeera hesitates, clearly torn. "I want what's best for Zach, but I'm scared. What if I can't handle it all? I've got Caleb and Shawna. And I've already planned to take Nico."

"I'll help with baby Zach," Nico speaks up proudly. "With Shawna and Caleb too. I can be the older brother."

"I'll help too," the oldest girl, whom we've taken to calling Ivy, surprises us when she speaks. The younger one, who we call Daisy, agrees with a nod.

Kemeera's head drops as she whispers, "I haven't told them yet. They don't know we're not staying together."

"Understood." Captain Williams nods. He directs his attention toward Nico and the girls. "I'm sure all of you will help as best you can." He gives them a warm smile. "Now . . . we've had some developments that require a change in plans. Ms. Swenson, I'd like you and Merissa to take the older children with you. Dr. Wolff is going to give everyone a quick checkup in one of the exam rooms. We'll join you soon."

"Me too, sir?" I ask as the others prepare to leave.

"Please stay with us, Sergeant. Leo should be joining us too."

As the group leaves for the exam room, Leo steps into the break room. His eyes travel to baby Caleb snuggled in my arms. He raises his brows and gives me a brief smile. Captain Williams motions for Leo to take a seat as he hobbles to a molded plastic chair, pulling it closer to Kemeera.

With all of us sitting near each other, Captain Williams keeps his voice low. "Kemeera, I'm afraid I have more disturbing news."

She collapses within herself. Her voice comes out in a sigh. "The plans fell apart. You don't have someplace for me to go."

"No, that's not it." The captain offers her a slight smile. "Everything is still set. You're leaving in the morning. The only thing to decide is what you wish to do about Zach."

She gestures for me to trade babies with her.

I carefully hand Caleb to her while I take Zach.

Kemeera shakes her head. "It's not really my decision to make. I know— " She clears her throat. "Mindy told you Zach's dad is dead, but that's not true." She gazes at her baby, the love she feels for him evident. "Mindy said a lot of things that weren't true."

Captain Williams interjects, his voice calm and measured. "I've been informed of some of it."

My eyes dart first to the captain and then to my husband, who cocks an eyebrow at me. Whatever it is Mindy lied about, Leo also knows.

Kemeera sighs. "She wasn't innocent in the . . . the events. She was part of the team that attacked Black Canyon. I swear, I didn't know. Not when we told you the other day. I didn't find out until Addison was there this morning."

I lean back in my chair and tighten my arms around Zach. He lets out a soft sigh as his lips make sucking motions.

"Was Addison part of the group that attacked Black Canyon? Attacked the ration centers and other places?"

Kemeera shrugs. "She didn't come out and say she was, but I think maybe. Maybe Dr. Loving too."

Captain Williams's face goes hard.

"I don't know for sure," Kemeera says. "Just the things they said. I guess Addison figured it didn't matter since I'd be dead soon too. I've been thinking about that. Maybe Mindy knew what it was—the poison."

Captain Williams nods. "Why do you think that?"

"She told me not to take mine. To put it up and ignore it because I needed to take care of the children. I think maybe she planned on giving it to Zach too. He didn't get any, though, right?"

"I don't believe so." Captain Williams opens his arms to take the baby from me. "He seems fine. Had she given him hemlock, he would've had the same reactions she did. Vomiting, seizures, and— "

"Death," Kemeera interrupts.

The way Captain Williams recites the symptoms Mindy experienced reminds me of something. A memory or thought I can't quite place.

"Correct," the captain says, his voice soft. "Zach appears to be just fine. She must have decided to only take it herself and spare her son." He hands the baby back to me before returning his attention to Kemeera. "Did you know anything about a suicide pact?"

"Suicide pact?" Her eyes go wide. "No. No. We didn't . . . I would never."

"Did you hear the others talk about it?"

"The others? From the house? No, never."

"You said Zach's dad isn't dead?"

She drops her gaze to her infant. "Zach's dad is Preacher."

"Ah . . ." Captain nods. "I must admit, I wondered about that." He leans forward to look her in the eye. When he speaks, his voice is soft, almost apologetic. "Preacher is deceased. Most of the people taken to the jail have passed."

My chin snaps toward Leo, who gives me a nod.

The captain continues, "They had a visit late yesterday from Addison and Landers. At least we believe it was them, based on the descriptions provided. They were fine at lunchtime today. The discovery happened minutes after I called for assistance at your safe house."

Kemeera says nothing. Her jaw is tight, and her eyes glisten with tears. After several beats, she whispers, "All of them?"

"I'm very sorry. It seems they all took the poison. A few have yet to pass, but if it's hemlock, like we believe, there's no antidote. They'll be kept as comfortable as possible."

"So, Mindy knew about it. She was supposed to . . . what? Make sure the children and I also took it?"

Captain Williams shrugs. "We don't know for sure, but it seems plausible."

Kemeera drops a kiss on her baby's forehead. "She changed her mind. Why'd they do this? Why'd Mindy? We were going someplace safe."

Captain Williams places a reassuring hand on Kemeera's. "You're not responsible for her choices. The important thing now is to focus on the future, on keeping yourself and the children safe."

She nods, her voice choked with emotion. "Okay. I'll do what I can to protect them. I just hope I can be strong enough."

"You already are." Captain Williams gives her a small smile. "The arrangements have been made for the girls to go to their new home. And for you, your children, and Nico to go to a safe place. The remaining question is Zach. It needs to be your choice to take him or not."

"I understand. I need time to think. To rest. Can you take me home?"

"We're going to have you stay here, where we can keep you safe until it's time to leave. You can rest on the sofa. There are a few more things I want to discuss, then we'll give you some time alone."

Chapter 26

Merissa

After exiting the break room, Dr. Wolff instructs Stella and me to set the children up in exam room two. "Bring in a few extra chairs to ensure everyone has a seat," she says. "But first, secure this poison. Lock it in the medicine cart in the recovery room." She hands me an envelope with the vials. The envelope is clearly marked "Hemlock. Poison. Do NOT touch."

After locking up the poison and arranging the exam room, we examine the four children, and all appear unchanged from their last checkup.

"Ms. Swenson, would you please stay with the children?" Dr. Wolff asks.

Stella shrugs. "Sure. I think Nico has a book in his pack."

The older girl sighs. "Nico has a baby book. I have a better book you can read to us."

As we reach the door, Dr. Wolff turns back toward Stella, who has Shawna nestled on her lap and the others close by her side. A gentle smile plays on Dr. Wolff's lips. "Ms. Swenson, you have a special gift with children. They adore you, and you bring so much joy into their lives."

Stella blushes, attempting to conceal her emotions, but her eyes sparkle with appreciation. "Thank you, Dr. Wolff. Sometimes, I think about what it may have been like to have my own children. Especially in times like these." She tightens her grip on Shawna and plants a gentle kiss on the top of her forehead.

Although Stella is often uptight and struggles with disruptions to her schedule or anything out of the ordinary, her demeanor completely transforms when she's with the children. She mentioned always wanting her own, but never finding the right partner to have them with. Instead, she became an honorary auntie to neighborhood kids, many of whom now have children of their own.

Sadly, she lost many others she cared about in the days following the EMP or during the brutal winter that followed. Few, if any of us, were spared the grief of losing a loved one. Soon, Stella will part with these children she has obviously grown fond of as they move on to their new, hopefully safe homes.

Even though we've been informed that arrangements have been made, none of us know the exact details. Based on the little I've pieced together, I assumed the plan was for the women to be separated. Mindy, of course, would keep her son and maybe the older girls, while Kemeera takes custody of her daughter, her newborn, and Nico.

Now, with Mindy deceased, what will happen to the older girls and Zach? Will Kemeera care for them all? I have a suspicion, based on what I overheard the other day, that Kemeera may head to Katie's hometown, where her family will take them in.

How they will make the journey during the harsh winter remains a mystery. With winter upon us, we're mostly confined to short trips between our homes and the hospital, occasionally using a horse and wagon to reach Opal's ranch. This leaves us with little to do in our daily lives, not that there's much time for leisure activities. Work and school currently consume our attention.

With biodiesel in short supply, Kemeera and the children cannot undertake the several-hundred-mile trip by vehicle. They'll need to make it the old-fashioned way, by horse and buggy. This winter has been relatively mild, except for the few days of arctic cold that nearly claimed Katie's life when she was injured and left for dead. It's nothing short of a miracle she didn't suffer worse frostbite damage than she did.

If Kemeera and the children travel by wagon, we must ensure they're well-equipped with winter clothing and warm blankets.

Mrs. Williams sits at the nurse's station, offering me a kind smile before inquiring about my well-being. I confidently reply that I'm fine, to which she tilts her head and asks, "Truly?"

Dr. Wolff also gazes at me, awaiting my response.

"Yes, I feel fine. A little tired and wishing I could sleep through the night, but nothing serious." I gesture toward the exam room with Stella and the children. "This has me on edge, of course."

"All of us, dear." Mrs. Williams nods. "We're all on edge about this. I can't fathom how anyone managed to access the prisoners at the jail, let alone sneak in poison like that."

I crinkle my forehead. "What happened?"

Dr. Wolff takes a moment to brief me on the situation at the jail and the death of most of the prisoners. "It's unlikely there will be any survivors," she says quietly before turning back to Mrs. Williams. "Any updates?"

"Lieutenant Paul called." Mrs. Williams gestures to the radio. "He's on his way here and should arrive in a couple of hours. In the meantime, we're on partial lockdown. Keep the patients in their rooms, and staff can perform their duties. Shaw's team is patrolling the hospital, and anyone seeking treatment will be thoroughly screened before entry."

I run my hand along the nape of my neck and shake my head. "Are we allowed to leave?"

The women shrug. "We'll see what Deputy Shaw and the captain decide," Dr. Wolff says. "That probably won't happen until David Paul arrives with updated information."

I understand the need to secure the hospital, but I regret not being able to inform Pearl of the situation. I have no way to convey that I won't be home until . . . well, who knows when?

She's aware that my shifts can sometimes stretch out longer than expected, but today was supposed to be a brief, four-hour round with Dr. Wolff. I know she'll hold off on the stew she planned for supper, postponing her own meal in anticipation of our rare dinner together. I suppress the sigh that threatens to escape.

"Where's everyone else?" I ask.

"Dr. Murphy has Matt, Jeff, Kerry, and Jesse in Captain Williams's office." Dr. Wolff gestures down the hallway. "They're poring over the books, researching hemlock and making sure we're accurate in our assessment. Captain Williams and the Burnetts are still in with Kemeera. Jacquie's in the patient room."

"I'll go see if I can assist Jacquie," I offer.

Dr. Wolff nods in response. "I'm going to the call room to see if I can get a nap in."

After more than a month of intense activity, beginning with the Christmas Day explosion at Camp Rapid and escalating with the virus sweeping through the Black Hills—and across much of the Midwest and Rocky Mountain States, according to reports—it feels strange to have the hospital so quiet.

The beds and clinic we set up in the adjacent office building, now transformed into a medical school, remain in place. Although we only utilize a few of the office suites for the medical school, Captain Williams had always planned to use the entire space for medical and nursing education, along with a clinic. He even managed to enlist workers from another crew to help bring his vision to life.

Obviously, none of us are happy to find ourselves in the midst of an apocalypse, but the disaster has revealed people's true nature. Individuals like Preacher, Addison, and Landers, who choose to perpetuate chaos and inflict more death and destruction, clearly expose their true intentions.

On the other hand, Captain Williams is doing everything he can to create a fully functional medical community by training doctors and nurses. And not only for the Guard District but also for the entire Black Hills and the state. He even hopes that his experiment of training lay people as doctors and nurses will spread across the country.

What's left of the country.

At the hospital, we rarely discuss what's happening in other places since there's too much here that demands our attention. However, Pearl and I sometimes ponder it. Does the United States of America still exist as a nation?

There hasn't been an address from the president in weeks. In his last address, he sounded ill and claimed to have the flu. We've hypothesized he didn't survive the flu. If he was even the real president to begin with. There's been ongoing speculation that the president is an impostor, someone pretending to be the duly elected leader. With radios serving as our primary means of communication, it'd be relatively easy to fabricate his identity. We cannot see him, and the connections are often unreliable.

If it is our president addressing us, when will he begin orchestrating a more effective rebuilding plan? Does he believe that relocating people from the Eastern and Western Wastelands is the sole solution? Last winter and spring, he often cited Billings, Montana, as a prime example of the rebuilding efforts. The Black Hills and Cleveland, Ohio, were also included in his updates. The talk of rebuilding persisted into the summer but waned as autumn arrived.

I didn't even notice he had ceased mentioning it in his radio addresses. It was Pearl who brought it up, and that wasn't until we were en route here, sitting side by side on one of the makeshift transports, passing the time as the road seemed to stretch on indefinitely.

Since she mentioned it, I've paid closer attention and realized that the president seldom acknowledges the progress made by local organizations. Considering the trouble that erupted in Billings just before Christmas, it makes sense he stopped mentioning them. But it seems he should've continued touting the positive developments until the trouble arose, rather than ceasing several months prior.

Unless he knew.

If this entire apocalypse was an inside job, and the president was complicit, it stands to reason that he was aware of sinister elements in Billings that planned to seize control of the military. Or if the person addressing us isn't the actual president but an impostor, they also might have been aware.

I furrow my brow as I recall the fake Deputy Garcia from the nearby Main Street District. We never uncovered the identity of the prankster or the reason behind such a deception. Captain Williams suspected it was Landers or someone acting on his behalf. But why? What would drive someone to impersonate an authority figure like that? Could it have been an individual who stumbled upon a radio and decided to play around with it, perhaps testing its capabilities? Once again, the question remains—why?

I release a weary sigh and lightly rap on the patient's room door. Jacquie occupies the chair next to the woman undergoing monitoring as she recovers from a slip on the ice that occurred yesterday during her walk home from work. We considered discharging her today, but her head injury necessitates an additional twenty-four hours of observation.

Jacquie acknowledges me with a nod and leans toward the patient, offering soothing and reassuring words in her warm tone. "I'll swing by to see how you're doing a bit later. Just give that bell a ring if you need anything, all right?"

The bell, an old cowbell repurposed as a nurse call, hangs within easy reach. When struck, it emits a jarring and noisy clang, a stark contrast to the tranquility enveloping the room. Undoubtedly, the bell's noise won't do anything to alleviate the woman's pounding headache.

In the hallway, Jacquie whispers, "Has this mess been sorted out yet?"

"The mess with the lockdown? No."

Jacquie rolls her eyes. "Of course not. Will we have a shift change at our regular time?"

"I don't know."

"Probably not. Whatever they can do to make things more difficult for us. I'm sure they'll just have us wait until . . . who knows when? Send the new shift home and tell them to take the night off while we toil and . . ." She sighs. "Are the children okay?"

"They seem fine. Kemeera too."

"Did you hear about the jail? A suicide pact, can you believe it?"

I shrug my shoulders and keep my thoughts to myself. In these tumultuous times, I've learned to entertain almost any possibility. The world has become a swirling vortex of madness, where nothing seems too far-fetched.

Dr. Wolff's words still linger in my mind. She said the individuals who paid a visit to the jail yesterday matched the descriptions of Addison and Geoff Landers. Could they have been part of the cult's suicide pact, their lifeless bodies waiting to be discovered? That doesn't align with my impression of Landers. He doesn't strike me as the type to take his own life, even if it were for a cause he believed in.

Speaking of causes, I remain utterly clueless about what could drive an entire sect—or as many label them, a cult—to commit mass suicide. It's baffling. Mindy appeared to be privy to their plans, yet Kemeera, who shared the same house with her, was left in the dark. It's puzzling.

Of course, it also appears Mindy was involved in the attack on Black Canyon that resulted in the town's destruction and the deaths of hundreds. Kemeera claims complete ignorance of that attack and the others.

My mind grapples with a central question: How did Addison and Geoff Landers manage to enter that jail? Were Preacher and his group even allowed visitors? My thoughts scatter when the main radio at the nurse's station squawks, drawing Jacquie and me toward the source of the commotion.

Chapter 27

Merissa

"Roving patrol to hospital base, come in, over."

Even from the distance of the hallway, it's easy to identify Deputy Shaw's voice from the radio. Jacquie and I walk toward the desk where Mrs. Williams is now alone.

"Go ahead, patrol, over," Mrs. Williams says.

"Captain Williams has a visitor. I'm bringing him in, over."

"A visitor," Mrs. Williams says, without pressing the talk button. She looks at Jacquie and me. "Perhaps the lieutenant arrived earlier than expected?"

I respond with a shrug, while Jacquie suggests, "Ask him who it is?"

With a shake of her head, she replies, "I'm sure Deputy Shaw wouldn't allow anyone in that he didn't personally vet. He understands the situation." She bobs her head and gives us a smile before pressing the talk button. "Understood, Deputy. We'll unlock the front door."

I tell the women I'm going to open the door for the deputy. After what feels like an eternity, the deputy finally emerges from the distance, accompanied by not one visitor but three. They all look like men from how they walk and their body shapes. All are bundled up against the biting cold, their forms slightly trailing behind the deputy instead of walking alongside, preventing me from getting a clear glimpse of their faces.

I unlock the door and hold it open for the men. When the deputy is within a few feet of the front door, he pauses. As I make eye contact with him, he wrinkles his face and flares his eyes before taking a stuttering step.

A tight knot clenches in my stomach, a gut feeling that screams danger. My fingers tremble as I edge closer to the door, ready to throw it shut and relock it.

But before I can act, a low, ominous voice slices through the air. It's the man directly behind Shaw, his words chillingly quiet.

"Not so fast there, missy," he murmurs. His voice is a menacing whisper, dripping with malevolence. "I've got a gun in the middle of Shaw's back. I'm sure I don't need to tell you what a shot at this distance will do, not only to him but possibly to you too. Be a shame for it to go straight through him and into you. *Into your baby.*"

"It's okay, Merissa," Shaw's voice soothes, but his eyes betray an underlying tension. "The sheriff just needs to talk with Williams. It'll be fine."

"That's right," the man Shaw called the sheriff chimes in, his words coated with a veneer of false reassurance. "It'll all be just fine. In the meantime, you keep your mouth shut, and you'll be home with your feet up soon enough."

As his words hit me, my heart pounds like a warning drum. I struggle to stay calm, not wanting to make things worse. I've seen Sheriff Melvin Cabal at the hospital before, but today, with his hat pulled low and his coat buttoned up, I can only guess he's the person Shaw mentioned. What's confusing is why the sheriff is pointing a gun at his own deputy, especially the head deputy for our area.

I glance at the two men standing behind Shaw and Cabal, their faces hidden beneath the brims of their hats. Despite the obscured view, a creeping suspicion settles in my gut that one of them might be Geoff Landers.

The sheriff keeps the gun pointed at Shaw's back, a constant reminder of the danger we're suddenly in.

Deputy Shaw looks uncomfortable, his eyes boring into mine, silently urging me not to do anything rash.

Even though I'm armed, with a pistol tucked in a holster in the small of my back—kidney carry—and a second hidden in an armpit holster, I'm not stupid enough to think I can draw and take out the sheriff, plus two other men who are likely armed, before Deputy Shaw is killed. I'm also not stupid enough to think I'd survive the ordeal.

"I won't cause any trouble," I say, trying to keep my voice steady. "Just let Shaw go, and we can sort this out peacefully."

Sheriff Cabal smirks and takes a step forward, pushing Shaw closer to me. "That's a smart decision. Now let's remember what the situation here is. Keep your hands where I can see them. No sudden moves, and no alerting any of your little nurse friends. I'll have my chat with Captain Williams . . . and we'll see what happens. Continue to be smart, and, like I said, you'll be able to go home and get off those swollen ankles."

I can't help but glance down at my feet to see if they really do appear swollen. I take a slow step backward, my eyes remaining on the men.

Deputy Shaw lifts his chin and straightens his back. With Shaw and the sheriff inside, the other two men follow. The first thing I notice about them is both have their sidearms out and at the ready.

As my eyes drift from the pistols to their faces, I'm rewarded with a sneer from Geoff Landers. Yep. No surprise there. I glance to the left and take in a gasping breath.

"Trooper Schroeder?" The name doesn't want to form around my suddenly dry mouth. "I-I don't understand."

"Merissa." He nods, greeting me like it's any other day, any other situation. His clean-shaven face even has a slight smile. "Let's get the door shut. We're letting all the heat out."

As I close the door behind them, the seriousness of the situation grows more pronounced. Trooper Schroeder is now standing with Sheriff Cabal and Geoff Landers. I can't comprehend why he would be part of this menacing group. My mind races to figure out their motives, but I'm too overwhelmed to make sense of it all.

Jacquie is leaning against the desk of the nurse's station, taking in the situation. Mrs. Williams, now standing, looks at me with concern, but I can't bring myself to meet her gaze. I fear that any slip in my composure could lead to catastrophic consequences.

As I struggle to remain calm, Trooper Schroeder's presence in the group only deepens my confusion. When I was with him the day Geoff Landers threatened Captain Williams, I found him to be helpful and courteous. A little naive and terribly optimistic, for sure. But I never would've imagined this. That he could be tangled up with Geoff Landers and his deadly schemes . . . my mind races, trying to connect the dots, but it's like assembling a jigsaw puzzle with pieces missing.

Sheriff Cabal keeps his eyes fixed on me, a smug grin etched on his face as he revels in the control he holds over the situation. I can feel his power over us, his authority making it difficult to breathe.

Meanwhile, Geoff Landers continues to glower, the embodiment of malice and hostility. His unrelenting hatred toward me—toward everyone from the med school and hospital—is baffling. Certainly, I can see how he may have some anger toward Captain Williams. I can even understand him questioning Chastity Morrow's death. But to find out he was also involved with Addison and assisted her with the mass suicide of Preacher and his followers is something else.

Jacquie is no stranger to tense situations, having seen just about everything possible in a hospital. She's very adept at keeping her cool, but she now seems on edge, and rightly so. She exchanges a concerned look with me, silently asking if there's anything she can do to help. But with Cabal's gun still in Deputy Shaw's back, along with Landers and Schroeder brandishing their own weapons, we can't risk it. Not at the moment. For now, we're at the mercy of these individuals.

Sheriff Cabal motions to the chairs around the nurse's station. "Why don't you sit back down, Mrs. Williams? I must admit, I'm surprised to see you here. I thought you killing two people in the name of medicine, the name of *compassion*, would've been enough for you."

Alice Williams's face pales as she sinks into the chair. The tension in the room intensifies as Sheriff Cabal's chilling revelation hangs in the air. Mrs. Williams, the always dignified and composed wife of Captain Williams, now appears shaken to her core.

"Oops," Cabal says with a sinister smile. "I guess the cat's out of the bag now. I've been keeping a close eye on you, Alice. Your little secret was never really a secret to me, though, was it? Your nervousness. The way it was staged. How could it be anything but murder? Worked out well for me, though. Made it possible to get your husband to cooperate." He gives her a wink. "I knew he'd do anything to keep you out of hot water. To keep you from being brandished a murderer."

Alice's gaze drops to her trembling hands, and it becomes clear there's more to her story than I ever imagined. In many ways, it makes sense. She wanted nothing to do with the hospital until recently. I found it odd she used to work as Captain Williams's nurse but wasn't working here. She insisted it was because she didn't have the formal training she felt was necessary to care for the people we see, but that excuse didn't really make sense.

Many of our staff and med students, including myself, have very limited training. It's only been the previous few weeks Alice has been working here, and she mostly just does paperwork or acts more in the capacity of an aide, helping people to the bathroom and providing comfort but making herself scarce when difficult cases arise.

Jacquie glances at me, silently asking if I knew anything about this, but I can only shake my head in confusion.

With his gun still pressed firmly into Deputy Shaw's back, Cabal leans in closer. "Don't think I'm finished yet. I'm positive the information will continue to come in handy, just like it did before." Sheriff Cabal lifts his chin toward Geoff Landers. "How else do you think my nephew got into the medical school? You didn't think your husband admitted the boy on his own merits, did you? I mean, really?"

"Hey," Landers says. "I have merits. I was premed, you know."

"You had one year of college." Cabal shoots him a look. "And your grades were dismal. You're no more doctor material than I am." Sheriff Cabal straightens. "Now, enough chitchat. Who's all in this hospital, and where are they?"

Deputy Shaw shuffles uneasily, and Landers's lips curl into a malicious grin, evidently savoring the power he and his uncle hold over us.

My heart pounds, its rhythm echoing in my throat, and I silently yearn for a swift end to this harrowing ordeal. However, with Cabal's gun unwaveringly trained on Shaw's back, and the two other men gripping their weapons with intent, any notion of escape would be impulsive and put everyone's lives at risk.

When none of us respond, Cabal lifts his chin in Schroeder's direction. "Perhaps you can entice the pregnant one to talk?"

"Oh, I'm sure Merissa will tell us what we need to know." Landers shifts his pistol toward me, lining up perfectly with my belly button.

"The med students, Jesse Talbot, and all the doctors," Mrs. Williams says, her words coming out in a rush.

"Well, thank you for that, Alice," Cabal says in a congenial tone. "I sincerely appreciate your cooperation. Now where is everyone?"

"Jesse, Dr. Murphy, and three of the med students are in Chris's office. They're doing some research."

"Not your husband?"

"He's in the break room with, um, a patient and two other med students. The final med student is in the exam room." She motions to the room with Stella and the children. "We have one room with two overnight patients. Dr. Wolff just went to the call room to take a nap while it was quiet."

I notice Mrs. Williams doesn't mention Rand Hendricks, the janitor on duty today. Funny thing, I haven't seen him since we brought Mindy back to the hospital. The hospital was put on lockdown at about that same time. Did he go home? Is he in the med school building?

Cabal chuckles. "Quiet, huh? Geoff, station yourself by the office door. Assume they are armed."

"They are. Talbot always carries. So do the med students." He motions toward me with his gun.

Sheriff Cabal furrows his brow. "You're just telling me this now?"

"Well . . . I figured you knew. Everyone carries a gun now."

"Not in a hospital," Cabal growls. "What kind of idiot would think a doctor would be armed? Schroeder, get her gun." He gestures toward me.

My hands rise and extend out to my sides as Schroeder inquires about the location of my waistband gun. With a measured tone, I disclose its position. He retrieves it and secures the paddle holster onto his own pants.

He doesn't ask about any other firearms or attempt to pat me down, so I keep quiet about my concealed backup weapon. I can't help but question his professionalism, but I refrain from voicing any concerns about his oversight. My hope is this oversight can benefit us later.

"How about you two?" Shroeder motions toward Jacquie and Mrs. Williams.

Mrs. Williams shakes her head, while Jacquie says, "I hate guns. Like the sheriff said, we're a hospital. It's weird to me how there are so many people wearing guns."

"Check them anyway," Cabal says.

Jacquie raises an eyebrow. "Oh, please. You think I'm going to lie to you when you're waving guns around? Look." She lifts the hem of her scrub top to show the waistband of her pants as she turns to let them see her back. "Happy?"

Cabal nods. "Now you, Alice."

Mrs. Williams stands and does a similar movement as Jacquie. After ensuring that Mrs. Williams and Jacquie are unarmed, Cabal motions for Landers to go to Williams's office door.

"Should I barricade it or something?" Landers asks. "So they can't get out?"

"How you planning on doing that?" His uncle rolls his eyes. "It opens inward."

With a perplexed look, Landers shrugs. "Tie it to another door? There's some old twine hanging off a nail in the wood storage room."

"Why?"

"We keep it on hand in case we have a combative patient we need to restrain. There're some zip ties in the med carts, too, for the same use."

"Fine. Tie the door shut. You're still stationed there. Shoot anyone that tries to get out."

"I can tie the office door to the call room door," Landers sniggers. "Two for one."

"What about the med student in the exam room?" Schroeder asks.

"Who's she in with?" Cabal lifts the muzzle of his gun toward Mrs. Williams.

She swallows before answering, "Children. Just children."

"Which one?" Landers asks.

"Which med student? Stella Swenson."

He chuckles. "She's nothing. A wallflower. We won't have to worry about her. She's the only med student who doesn't carry a gun. Plus, she must be in her sixties."

I keep quiet, though I know Stella's in her late forties, and while she does have some interesting habits, I wouldn't describe her as a wallflower. He's right, though. She doesn't carry a gun. Doesn't even like them.

"Figure out a way to secure that door too," Cabal says. "Bring some extra twine and those zip ties. We'll tie these women up while you work on the doors. Except for this one." He gestures in my direction. "The little momma is going to be our special helper."

Chapter 28

Katie

Captain Williams leans in, his eyes fixed on Kemeera. "Any more questions?" He pauses, then adds, "Does it sound like a good plan?"

She offers a small smile in my direction. "Katie's been very nice to me. I'm sure her family is just as nice."

I suppress a chuckle. My siblings, though generally kind, have their moments of unkindness, like any siblings. Over the years, we've had our share of disagreements.

Despite our occasional clashes, I'm confident they'll treat Kemeera and her children with kindness and care. My Grandma Dodie will be thrilled to have more little ones around. She was in her element with Gavin and my adopted nephew Andy, both toddlers. When baby Tate arrived, Dodie was almost in awe of him, just as she was with baby Mollie. There's no doubt Kemeera and her children will receive a warm welcome at my family's home.

"I'm sure they'll make you and the children feel welcome," I say with a smile.

"Are you sure you won't be able to go back home anytime soon?" she asks with apprehension.

Maintaining my smile, I shake my head slightly. "Leo and I are currently part of the United Volunteers, but soon, when his arm heals, we'll be joining the South Dakota National Guard, like Captain Williams." I gesture toward Williams, dressed in his combat uniform with captain's bars and a prominent medical insignia. Similarly, Leo and I are in our makeshift Volunteer Unit uniforms, handsewn stripes on our arms.

"And you'll stay here?"

"That's correct. We'll serve out our commitment either here in Rapid City or possibly somewhere else in South Dakota." I'm not sure why I added that last part. While it's possible we could be transferred elsewhere in the state, it seems unlikely, especially now that both Leo and I are becoming medical students. Excitement courses through me at the prospect of becoming a doctor. Being a doctor was a childhood dream, initially chosen for its perceived financial stability.

When I realized how much I loved art, thoughts of becoming a doctor faded away. Instead, I pursued a college education with dreams of becoming a successful artist, fully aware of the stereotype of a "starving artist." I cherished art in all its forms—graphic design, sketching, and most of all, working with oils. The textures achievable with oils are truly remarkable.

Yet, my path led me to nursing, and it feels like the right fit. I'm drawn to the sense of purpose it provides, even though it's far from perfect. Dealing with death is heart-wrenching, and severe injuries are nothing short of devastating. Nevertheless, I sense that I'm fulfilling the calling God intended for me.

As I contemplate the possibility of making it through the demanding classes and becoming a doctor, I can't help but stifle a sigh of longing. I'm aware that I might be getting ahead of myself.

"Um, so, we'll be here and ready to help the community for as long as needed," I conclude, hoping Kemeera doesn't notice my momentary distraction.

"I was in the radio room when Katie's town called to let us know they'd welcome you and the children,"

My head turns toward the captain. How I wish I could've been there, even for a few more minutes of conversation with someone from home. It was a wonderful but too brief first call. My throat tightens with longing for my family.

Kemeera gives a grateful smile to all of us in the room. "Thank you. It's just, it seems lately I've needed to rely on myself. I thought I was safe with Preacher, but . . ." Her eyes well with tears. "I still just can't believe it."

She shakes her head as a knock sounds on the door. "Captain?" Merissa calls out, her voice quivering. "Um . . . okay if I-I come in?"

Merissa's usual confidence seems absent in her hesitant tone, which strikes me as strangely strained. The captain appears to notice too.

"Merissa, is everything all right?" he asks, his voice laced with concern as he gestures for Leo to approach the door.

Her response comes after a moment's pause. "Yeah, everything's fine. Just wanted to check in." She hesitates again. "I mean, we just got a call from the jail. There's been a new development."

Kemeera's worried glance shifts from the door to us. "What's happening?"

Captain Williams's eyebrows shoot up. "Let her in," he directs Leo with a nod.

Leo opens the door. "Come on in."

Merissa suddenly rushes toward him. He extends his good arm to stop her forward motion.

In that split second, Sheriff Cabal materializes behind Merissa, his voice dripping with mockery. "Good to see you, Williams."

Caught off guard, Captain Williams stammers awkwardly as he attempts to get to his feet, his walking boot slipping on the slick tile. "Melvin?"

"No reason to get up." Cabal waves a gun in Williams's direction.

Kemeera shrieks, causing her baby to jump and cry. I pull Zach closer to me, covering one ear with my hand and pressing the other against my chest. Kemeera's frightened cry ripples through the room, mingling with her baby's wails, creating a mess of fear and confusion.

Leo's grip on Merissa tightens as he steps back, his expression a mixture of surprise and dread. Captain Williams regains his balance and settles back into the plastic chair, though his hands instinctively lift in a gesture of surrender.

"Melvin, what's the meaning of this?" Captain Williams's voice is strained as he assesses the situation.

Sheriff Cabal's lips curl into a malicious smile. "Seems like I'm here to settle up, Williams."

Merissa's face pales, her eyes darting between Sheriff Cabal and Captain Williams. "I didn't . . . I didn't have a choice," she stammers, her voice trembling. "They're holding Mrs. Williams and Jacquie at the nurse's station."

"They?" Williams asks. "Who's with him?"

"Don't you worry about that," Cabal interrupts before Merissa can respond. He carelessly waves his gun. "You two get over here with everyone else. Keep your hands where I can see them. We'll get rid of the guns one by one. Don't worry, Ms. Preggo already surrendered hers."

"Joseph?" Kemeera says quietly. "What are you doing here?"

Cabal's gaze shifts to her. "Well, well. I heard there was a survivor. Didn't know it was you. Though, I guess I shouldn't be surprised."

Kemeera shakes her head. "I thought you went— "

"Enough!" Cabal bellows.

Kemeera shrinks down, and I'm left confused, but one thing is clear: Kemeera knows Sheriff Melvin Cabal but believes him to have a different name, Joseph. My mind quickly replays the information we have. Geoff Landers is known as Dr. Loving, and Sheriff Cabal as Joseph. Just how deeply are they involved in this situation?

"Get rid of the guns," Cabal orders. "Now!"

With Leo and Merissa standing by the captain's chair, Cabal has Merissa remove Leo's gun from his hip holster. "Be smart about it," Cabal warns. "I'm not opposed to shooting pregnant women." He shifts the gun slightly to aim it toward Kemeera. "Or women holding babies."

Kemeera whimpers as tears flow down her cheeks.

After Leo's pistol is placed on the break room table, Cabal has Merissa disarm the captain and then me. There's no mention of checking for weapons elsewhere, which means both Leo and I are still carrying our backup 9-millimeters in ankle holsters.

When all the weapons are on the table, he instructs Merissa to move them to the counter against the back wall.

When she's finished, he positions her close to Leo again. "Not too close," he warns. "There. Good." He tilts his head and points his gun toward the captain. "Now, where's the vial?"

"The vial?" Captain Williams looks confused as he shakes his head. "I'm not— "

"The poison."

"The hemlock? Why would you want that?"

"Oh . . . multiple reasons." His grin takes on a wicked twist, and his mustache wiggles like a cartoon character.

As I stare at him, it suddenly clicks in my mind. "You murdered Chastity." The words blurt out before I can hold them back.

All eyes dart toward me. The memory of finding Chastity in her home, her head in a pool of dried vomit, comes rushing back. The symptoms of hemlock poisoning we witnessed in Mindy were similar to how we found Chastity. It makes sense now how she died.

She'd had the flu, but not severe enough to cause death. We thought it might have been an overdose of Ploy, a new drug that has been floating around since early December and has caused several deaths or near deaths.

The sheriff snorts and shakes his head. "Wasn't me. Chastity was useful in our operation. Or she would've been once she got off her moral high horse."

"Your operation?" I ask. "You mean . . ." The puzzle pieces continue to shift in my head. "Ploy? You're behind the drug Ploy? You got her addicted? She and Geoff? Isn't he your nephew?"

Cabal throws back his head in laughter. "I didn't get him addicted. His use of Ploy is purely recreational. I keep telling him not to sample the product, but . . ." He lifts his hands. "Can't tell the kid anything. He's still at the age he thinks he knows it all. Remind me, which little mouse are you?"

I crinkle my nose, wondering why in the world he's referring to me as a little mouse.

"Never mind, it doesn't matter." He turns his head slightly to call over his shoulder. "Geoff? You and Schroeder get in here."

My eyes shoot toward Merissa as I mouth *Schroeder.* She flares her eyes and gives a slight nod.

A frightening tension fills the hospital break room. This room, usually a spot for doctors and nurses to relax, now seems like a dangerous trap, a stage for looming peril.

Leo's mouth tightens, and his eyes dart around the room before his gaze rests on mine. He gives me a brief nod and lightly lifts the toe of his boot from the floor.

Captain Williams, though visibly concerned, maintains a level of composure, likely honed through years of military training and medical practice. He keeps his gaze locked on Cabal. "Where's my wife?"

"Don't worry none about her. She's fine . . . for now. I don't know if I can say the same for the rest of you."

Kemeera clutches her baby tightly, her eyes wide with fear as she shifts slightly to put herself between her child and the menacing figure of Sheriff Cabal. The baby's cries have lessened to the occasional hiccup to punctuate the tense silence.

I adjust baby Zach in my arms, feeling the need to have my hands free. Leo again lifts his boot slightly, signaling that he's ready to use his ankle gun if he needs to. I want to do the same, but I can't with Zach in my arms.

Is Merissa carrying a backup weapon? Opal recently gave her an underarm holster with a small pistol.

As Landers and Schroeder enter the room, their presence only amplifies the feeling of unease. Kemeera whispers something, but I can't make out what it is. The fact Landers is involved in the distribution of Ploy and likely played a role in Chastity's death underscores his ruthless nature. Cabal said he didn't kill her, but did Landers?

I turn toward Kemeera. "Perhaps you holding Zach, too, would help calm your baby? I've noticed they seem to relax when they're near each other."

She gives a slight shrug as I pass off the second infant. When my ear is near her face, she whispers, "They're all part of Preacher's group. Joseph, Dr. Loving, and the other one."

"Good thinking, mouse," Cabal says. "I like things quiet. Quiet and calm." He waves the gun again. "Let's make sure that happens."

I step back from Kemeera and give a nod. Luckily, Caleb does seem to settle when Zach comes near. He lets out another hiccup before nestling into his mom, his little hand moving toward Zach's arm.

Captain Williams speaks up, his voice measured yet resolute. "Melvin, whatever you're seeking, we can find a way to resolve this peacefully. We don't need to resort to violence."

Cabal's laugh is mocking and cold. "Peacefully? Williams, you've always been an optimist. You think I'd walk in here like this if I wanted a peaceful resolution? We'll start with the vial of poison and go from there. Where is it?"

"I'm not sure." Williams lifts his hands. "I gave it to Dr. Wolff to lock up. We didn't want it floating around."

"And where is she now?"

Merissa fidgets slightly. My gaze meets hers before she quickly looks away.

Williams shrugs. "Did you not see her in the hallway?"

"Nope. Just your wife and a sassy nurse."

"Dr. Wolff," Landers interrupts, "she's the one taking a nap. I've secured the door of the call room so she can't get out."

Sheriff Cabal rolls his eyes. "Then I guess you'd better go unsecure the door and bring her in here. Another one for the party seems like a good idea." He shifts his gaze back to Captain Williams. "Don't you agree, Chris? That is, unless you want to rethink not knowing where the poison is."

Captain Williams pinches his lips. "I truly don't know. I asked her to take care of it, assuming she'd inform me the next time I saw her."

"Fine, then. If that's how you want to play it . . ."

Merissa adjusts her stance. "I know where it is," she says quietly. She turns toward Geoff Landers. "It's in the recovery room. Locked in the medical cabinet. You know where the key is."

Chapter 29

Katie

With the revelation of the poison's location, an uneasy tension grips the room. Merissa's admission has shifted the balance of power, and Cabal's sinister grin widens as he contemplates his options. Geoff Landers, his eyes gleaming with anticipation, steps forward and looks at Cabal for approval.

"Smart girl," Cabal purrs, his voice dripping with a mixture of condescension and amusement. "Seems like you're finally playing along." He motions for Landers to retrieve the vials.

As Landers leaves the room, Leo's gaze searches out mine once more. Our eyes meet, and he dips his chin slightly and raises the toe of his boot. I shift my attention to Merissa as she scratches her armpit. My heart races, hoping it's not just a scratch but a signal. She flicks her eyebrows and scratches again.

Do we have an opportunity to regain control of the situation? To take out Cabal and Schroeder while Landers is out of the room?

I survey the room. Leo and Merissa have a straight line to the door and Trooper Schroeder. My location is much too near Cabal to pull my weapon and use it before he shoots me . . . or worse, shoots Kemeera and the babies.

I let out a deep breath and consider my options. When I have a rough plan in mind, I lift my chin toward my husband. He gives me a small smile.

Leo steps back and seems to accidentally catch one of the plastic chairs. It flips over and clatters on the tile.

Cabal spins toward him. "Watch your step, you idiot. I told you, I like quiet."

"S-sorry." Leo stutters as he bends down to pick it up.

The captain clears his throat, drawing Cabal's attention. Everything seems to slow as Leo's hand goes to his ankle. Merissa's also moving, catching Trooper Schroeder's awareness. "Hey!" the former highway patrolman calls. "Hold still."

I seize the moment, capitalizing on the chaos unfolding around me. In one fluid motion, I hurl myself toward Cabal, my elbow extending like a missile aimed at his nose. The satisfying crunch of bone on bone is instantaneous, echoing through the air. His hands instinctively clutch his face, but I don't relent. My knee swiftly finds its mark and delivers a crippling blow to his sensitive area, as my injured leg protests.

Behind me, the sudden assault prompts Kemeera to let out a startled cry as the captain throws himself over her and the crying babies, shielding them from danger.

Cabal's agonizing scream fills the room as he bends at the waist in excruciating pain. Gathering my strength and ignoring my pain, I clasp my hands together, bend my arms at the elbows, and thrust my double fists upward, targeting his chin. A gunshot sounds, then another, followed by a third. The deafening noise leaves my ears ringing, while the cries of the babies and Kemeera's terrified screams fill the room.

"Schroeder's down," Merissa declares.

Adrenaline courses through my veins as the aftermath of the attack settles in. My final blow to Cabal propels him in a backward arc until he crashes onto the break room table, causing it to creak and groan under his weight until he collapses to the floor. His pistol lies inches from my feet.

I bend down and snatch up the weapon in my trembling hand. In the same instant, the break room door swings open, unleashing a rush of tension into the room.

At the doorway, Landers freezes, clutching the gun tightly in his hand. Kemeera's screams subside, but the wailing of the babies continues, a heart-wrenching chorus of fear and distress.

Williams shifts his position, moving himself away from the trio. Now, he places himself between them and Landers, a human shield of sorts, his tense posture revealing his readiness to protect them.

"Drop it, Geoff," Leo says with a bite to his voice.

Sighing, Landers shakes his head. "And then what? You're going to haul me off to jail? I'm pretty sure once it gets out what my uncle and I . . ." He tilts his head toward Shroeder. "*Both* uncles and I were involved in, things won't end up good for me."

"Both uncles?" Merissa says. "Is Schroeder your uncle?"

He shrugs. "He's married to my aunt, so yeah."

"Put the gun down, Geoff," Leo repeats.

"Don't you want to know? Know all the dirty details? Isn't it just eating you up, as you wonder just what exactly went down with my uncles, the preacher's group, and Chastity?"

"Why'd you kill Mindy?" Kemeera asks, poking her head around Captain Williams's shoulder.

"Shut up, Geoff," Cabal growls from the floor.

"It's over, Uncle Melvin," Landers says. "They killed Uncle Carter. I'm making a deal. Buying my way out of here."

Cabal mutters something about us being murderers and going to prison. The response strikes me as funny, but I don't laugh.

"Katie?" Captain Williams says. "Why don't you pass me Melvin's gun. You can collect the other weapons too. Leo, Merissa—if Landers moves, shoot him. I plan to do the same if Melvin moves."

Leo and Merissa, each with their backup weapon trained on Landers, nod in agreement.

When Leo, the captain, and I each have our full-sized guns in our hands, the captain orders Cabal to get off the floor and move to a chair. Landers is still standing at the doorway, his pistol against his thigh. I'm not sure why he's refusing to give it up or why the captain isn't forcing the issue.

I've done my best to avoid looking at the pool of blood surrounding Trooper Carter Schroeder's head. Merissa told me a little about the man from the day they ended up as unlikely partners at one of the neighborhood houses. She also said his wife was expecting their first child. His wife must be Melvin Cabal's sister. What a mess.

With Cabal in a chair and me holding my gun on him, Captain Williams instructs Landers to move away from the door and against the wall. When the doorway is clear, Williams has Merissa take Kemeera and the babies out and asks her to untie and release anyone who is a hostage.

"Send Deputy Shaw in here, please," he adds as she moves toward the door. "Only Shaw. Inform everyone else to remain where they are. Please tell my wife I'll be right out." He directs his attention back toward Landers. "Now, Geoff, you were saying? All the dirty details?"

Landers sneers. "Figured it was eating you up. I guess that's something you and my uncle have in common, isn't it? His nosiness is what bought me a ticket into your med school. It really was the perfect addition to his . . . his plans."

"Geoff," Cabal warns, his voice more nasally than earlier when he spoke. With the amount of blood and the way he sounds, I suspect I broke his nose.

"Oh, what does it matter?" Geoff says. "You thought his wife killed her neighbors, so you blackmailed him into putting me in the med school."

My eyes quickly dart to Captain Williams to see if there's any truth to what Geoff is saying. Williams's face is blank and without response.

"Having me in this district allowed you to resume the drug business." Geoff looks toward Williams. "You did hear the rumors about someone in the police department being part of the drug trade before the EMP, right?" Landers looks around the room.

"When my dear uncle ended up in charge of the county, he contacted the dealers and whatnot he knew from before. The ones he was in cahoots with. Ploy isn't that much different from the drugs that were around before the EMP. Other than the recipe keeps changing based on what's available . . . often with deadly results. Not that old Uncle Melvin wants people dying from it. Nope. He needs them alive and buying, keeping his version of the black market going."

Cabal grunts and mutters, but Geoff waves him off. "The truth shall set you free, Uncle. How do you think those robbers . . . what were their names? The ones who took Burnett hostage?"

"Bryson Young and RJ Kittleson," I whisper as the memory of that day comes rushing back.

"Right. They and the rest of the gang that was captured and escaped on the way to the main jail. Who do you think arranged that? The almighty sheriff, that's who."

Landers points at me. "You're a bit of a mess, you know. The scab on your cheek is bleeding. Heard about the beating you took and how they left you for dead. You know who did it?"

"Enough from you," Leo orders.

"Hey, I said I'd tell all. How about I start with who beat up your wife? You interested? *Julius MacAllister.* Does that name sound familiar?"

The air whooshes out of me. One of the others had called the man Julius.

Landers smiles. "Yep. That's right. He was the ringleader. It wasn't supposed to be you. He had it in for your neighbor. A rogue act that my uncle didn't approve of and couldn't ignore. Isn't that right?" His gun wavers slightly as he directs his attention to the sheriff. "Don't worry, Katie," he says, keeping his gaze on his uncle. "Julius can't hurt you again. Uncle Melvin made sure of that."

A knock on the door interrupts Geoff's revelations. "It's Shaw. May I come in?"

"Please do," Williams responds.

Shaw's eyes take in the room and then travel to the floor and Schroeder's body. Captain Williams asks if everyone's okay.

"No one was injured. I've asked everyone to stay in the different rooms. Your wife and Jacquie are now with Stella and the children. Kemeera too. Merissa is in your office with the other students and Jesse. Believe it or not, Dr. Wolff went back to sleep. She asked about the shooting, and when told it was in hand, she said she was going to continue her nap."

Somehow, that doesn't surprise me about the ever-practical Nettie Wolff.

The captain asks Landers to repeat what he said before Shaw came in. Landers sighs before repeating everything he'd already told us.

"Doesn't surprise me about the jailbreak." Shaw glares at Cabal. "We suspected it was an inside job."

Cabal returns the dirty look.

Shaw pulls out a pair of handcuffs and less than gently puts them on Cabal. He flips him around several times, making a show of containing the sheriff. Or enjoying the sounds of pain the sheriff—or *former* sheriff*—is making.

Once Cabal is secured, Williams asks, "Did you know he was behind Ploy too?"

Shaw shakes his head. "Again, not surprised. Who else?" he asks, directing the question at Cabal, who's back to glaring.

"Who else, Geoff?" Williams asks.

"He's got one or two people in each district. Better distribution that way."

"Deputies? Citizen Patrol?"

"Some, yes. I'll give you a list so you can round 'em all up." He gives Shaw a wink. "'Course, all this information is going to cost you."

"No doubt," Shaw mutters.

"Here's the deal. I'll tell you everything I know, and you'll let me walk away. I give you my loving uncle and the rest of his cronies, but I ride off into the sunset with the girl."

"You mean Addison?" Williams asks.

"She and I had a little disagreement, but I think we'll work it out."

"Where is she?"

"Around. Safe."

"What disagreement?" Shaw asks.

"The disagreement over her using hemlock to kill Chastity."

"I knew it," I whisper.

Landers directs his gaze toward me. "When did you know? The day I saw you on the street?"

"No." I shake my head. "Just in the last little bit. When your uncle came in and I realized Mindy's symptoms were the same as how we found Chastity."

"Yeah. I guess Addison got tired of sharing me." He shrugs. "Too bad. Chastity and Addison together . . . whew! What a wild ride that was. Anyhow, Addison apologized, and we've agreed to start over. Somewhere else."

"Somewhere you can kill other unsuspecting people?" Shaw scoffs.

"Who said anyone—other than poor Chastity—was unsuspecting? You think Preacher didn't know exactly what was going to happen when Addison gave him the vials? It was always the plan. That's why she started making the hemlock tincture. It grows wild around here you know. Well . . . I didn't know, but Addison did. She discovered it in one of her books about wildcrafting." He motions to Cabal. "We were already attending Preacher's meetings."

"Kemeera called him Joseph," I say. "And she knew you as Dr. Loving. She even whispered to me that Deputy Schroeder was part of Preacher's group."

"That's true." Landers smiles. "Thick as thieves we were."

"You were behind the killings?" Williams asks, shaking his head.

"Behind, involved in, however you want to think of it. Although, I'll admit, I didn't actually participate in any. Neither did my uncles. They just didn't bother helping you all search for the perpetrators. Liked watching everyone run around in circles. I'll tell you, though, I thought Uncle Melvin was going to blow a gasket when he heard about the National Guard rounding up Preacher. You just missed us that night. We were there for the beginning of the meeting and then had to leave."

"Mindy said Preacher wasn't behind the National Guard explosion."

Landers gives a sloppy shrug. "As far as I know, he wasn't. But he had a way of only letting those who needed to know, know. I didn't know about the attacks that were planned on the hospitals until after the fact either. I was so mad when I found out our hospital was targeted. I could've been killed!"

"Tragic," Williams mutters.

"Preacher wanted a way out. Should they be captured, he needed assurances they'd be able to, as he put it, leave their bodily containers for the most high . . . or some such nonsense. Preacher was a nutjob, you know. He was a nutjob before the EMP, just hid it better. And since he had money from his IT company, people called him eccentric instead of crazy. But let me tell you, he was as crazy as they come. He did everyone a favor by arranging the mass suicide. The Black Hills is a safer place with him and his people gone."

"Who else is there?" Shaw asks.

Landers weaves slightly, the muzzle of his gun bouncing up and down. "You mean his followers? That I can't tell you. I'm sure there are some out there, but I doubt they'll move forward with anything once they learn Preacher's dead. You should get that newspaper gal to share the story. Spread the news far and wide. Whoever is left will fade away. I'm almost certain of it."

Cabal scoffs. "You're an idiot, Geoff."

"Oh, yeah?" He straightens his back and raises the gun in his uncle's direction. "Call me an idiot again. I'm buying my way out of here. I'm sure they won't much care if I cap you in the process."

Williams shrugs. "I'd rather not have to clean up the mess, Geoff. Could you at least wait until we get him outside?"

Landers seems to consider it before giving a thoughtful nod. "I suppose that's a good idea. Especially considering it'd probably be the nurse— " he shifts the gun toward me " —who would clean it up. Got to keep people in their proper places, right? Doctor, nurse . . . can't let the lines blur."

As Geoff rambles on, it's obvious something's very off with him. Not simply off as in "he's behind a mass murder" but off as in his words are beginning to slur and he's having trouble focusing. He blinks a few times before wavering enough that he needs to grab the wall with his free hand. I'm supposed to be focused on his uncle, but I can't help looking at Geoff.

I clear my throat. "Geoff?"

"Yesh, nursh?" he slurs.

"Are you okay?"

Melvin Cabal jerks his head in Landers's direction before letting out a ruthless cackle. "I don't think you're buying your way out of here after all. What'd she give you?"

Landers sways before muttering something I don't catch. His eyes roll up in his head, and he crumbles to the ground.

Cabal shakes his head. "I knew that ruthless broad would be the end of him."

Leo rushes to Landers's side and checks his vitals. "He's not breathing. Shaw, take care of Cabal. Katie, Captain, help me with Geoff."

Chapter 30

Merissa

Locked inside the captain's office with Dr. Murphy, Jesse, and most of my fellow med students isn't exactly my idea of a fun evening. Being held hostage by Landers and his unhinged uncle wasn't any better. I can't help but feel annoyed about being kicked out of the room after playing a role in resolving the situation. But I understand their concern, especially with my pregnancy.

I exhale sharply, aiming it toward my forehead where damp hair stubbornly clings. The room is stifling, especially for a February night. We've already cracked open the window and let the fire dwindle down to a mere bed of coals, but it's still unbearably hot.

And the unmistakable scent of someone in dire need of a shower wafts through the air. I tilt my head ever so slightly toward my armpit, wincing as the realization dawns that I might be the source. I pull my arms closer to my body and silently hope I'm the only one who notices.

Amid the simmering tension that fills the room, Dr. Murphy wearily props himself against the desk. His once-pristine lab coat now looks rumpled and disheveled, bearing witness to the ordeal we've endured. He adjusts his glasses, the left bow secured by a strip of black electrical tape, his gaze sweeping over our surroundings.

Kerry occupies a chair near the ajar window, her legs pulled up to her chest. The soft glow of moonlight filters through the partially opened blinds, casting gentle shadows on her face. She gazes into the night, her eyes distant and deep in thought. When Deputy Shaw ushered me into this room, Kerry's primary concern was for her husband, Rand Hendricks, the janitor on duty today. However, no one has seen him since before we brought Mindy in hours ago.

When Shaw instructed us to remain in the office until he came back for us, she asked if anyone had seen her husband. He promised to call on his radio and have them check once the situation in the hospital was under control.

After what feels like an eternity, a knock sounds from the door, followed by Captain Williams saying, "We've got a medical emergency."

Closest to the door, I reach it first.

"Wait," Matt says. "Didn't Shaw say to open it only for him?"

I'm sure the look I send him is less than kind. "You think the captain is in league with Cabal?"

"No, of course not. It's just— "

"Open the door," Dr. Murphy orders. "He said there's an emergency. Let's go."

After unlocking the deadbolt and removing the extra hasp lock, installed specifically in case of a lockdown situation, I'm the first one out of the room. The captain is already fast walking—or at least his version of it with his boot cast—down the hallway. "Mrs. Weaver, I want you and Dr. Murphy in the break room," he orders. "And bring me Ms. Swenson too."

"I'll get Stella," Matt says.

I follow the captain with Dr. Murphy by my side. "What's the issue?" the doctor asks.

"Not sure," the captain responds. "It may be another poisoning. That's why I want Swenson in here."

Inside the break room, Schroeder's body has been moved to allow better access inside, but nothing has been done about the blood. Cabal is in a chair, his hands cuffed and his boot laces tied together. Shaw is keeping his pistol trained on his former boss. Katie and Leo are on either side of Landers, who's on the ground.

"He still has a pulse, but he isn't breathing," Katie says.

"Are you thinking poison?" Dr. Murphy asks.

Directing his question toward Melvin Cabal, Captain Williams asks, "Do you know what she would've given him?"

Cabal chuckles. "I told you, that broad is crazy. Could've been anything."

"Not hemlock," I assert. "Not unless he took it within the past few minutes."

"He didn't take anything," Katie insists. "I think I lost his pulse." She moves her hand from his wrist to his neck. "Nothing."

"Start compressions," Dr. Murphy directs. "Mrs. Burnett, I'll spell you. Someone grab an Ambu bag so we don't have to give mouth-to-mouth."

As Leo begins chest compressions, the new doctor slides in on the opposite side.

I help Katie get the bag. Not that it takes two of us, but I'm not sure how else I can be useful.

We encounter Stella in the hallway. "What happened?" she asks, her expression etched with worry.

"Landers collapsed. They think it may be some sort of poison given to him by Addison," Katie says as we rush by her.

She clucks her tongue and shakes her head but keeps moving.

Inside the exam room, Katie grabs the Ambu bag. "What else do you think they'll need?"

"A stretcher," I suggest, grabbing one of the backboards.

"Good call," Katie agrees as she takes the other end.

Back in the break room, Leo and the doctor continue CPR as Williams quizzes Stella on what he could've been given. "I just don't know." She shakes her head. "There're things that would cause a delayed reaction, but most aren't so . . . so deadly. Is he allergic to anything?"

All eyes shift to his uncle.

With a noncaring look on his face, the man shrugs. "Don't look at me. I have zero idea about stuff like that."

"We had to fill out paperwork to get into med school," I suggest. "It asked about allergies."

"If it's anaphylactic, we don't have epinephrine." Stella shakes her head. "But I have a few things that may help. I'll be right back."

"Good." Williams nods. "Go. Merissa, personnel files are in the file cabinet on the left side under my desk. The key's hanging on a magnetic hook. Katie, help her."

Inside Williams's office, Katie pulls a flashlight from her pocket, a kind that has a squeeze thing on it instead of using batteries. She gives it a couple of squeezes, and it lights up the space enough for me to find the key and sort through the files. "I don't see it." I continue to flip through the documents.

"At the back. Look, there's a tab that says former. Try there."

"Okay, yep. Here it is." I pull out the folder and flip it open, quickly scanning for any helpful information. "There's nothing. See." I point to the spot where it asks about known allergies.

"Blank," Katie confirms. "No help. So, whatever she did . . . how will we know?"

"I don't know. Maybe Stella can come up with something?"

We meet Stella again in the hallway. "What do you have?" I ask.

"Osha root tincture used for anaphylactic shock. Also, cayenne pepper tincture for heart attacks, shock, and other things."

"Will they work?"

"They'd better. You two should be praying."

Katie and I share a look that I can only describe as horror. We should pray for someone who just held us at gunpoint? Someone who admitted to assisting in mass murder?

Katie takes a deep breath and whispers, "She's right. Love your enemies and pray for those who persecute you." Louder, she says, "Tell the captain the allergy information was blank. We'll be right in."

Katie first grasps my left hand and then my right. She bows her head without waiting for me to acknowledge what's happening. I consider protesting, but she's already speaking.

"Dear God, in the midst of confusion, we come before You. We're faced with a situation that challenges everything we believe in. Help us find the strength to rise above our fear and anger. We pray for Geoff. May Your light shine upon him. Please touch Stella, Leo, and the others who are doing all they can to save him. We know . . ." Katie clears her throat.

"Geoff has done some bad things. Terrible things. But You may have another purpose for him. A way he can redeem himself. If it's Your will, please, please help him survive. You teach love and forgiveness, even when it's difficult. Guide us toward understanding, not just for Geoff, but for ourselves as well. Give us the courage to open our hearts to the possibility of change, even in the face of unimaginable circumstances. Thank you for the strength to offer these prayers, and for the unyielding faith that sustains us. I pray these things in Jesus's mighty name."

As her prayer comes to an end, I find myself moved by the sincerity in her voice. The tension that had coiled within me begins to loosen, replaced by a tentative sense of compassion. If Katie can find it within herself to pray for our captor, then maybe, with God's help, I can too.

Katie gently squeezes my hands, indicating it's my turn. I let out a long breath and take a moment to gather my thoughts and emotions. Despite my skepticism and lingering anger, I let the teachings I've been learning from Shawn out at Opal's ranch guide me.

When I start to speak, my voice is steadier than I expect. "Father God, please give me the strength to replace any hatred with compassion. As Katie said, You may have plans for Geoff. Plans we can't even imagine. Plans of redemption and . . . and salvation. I don't pretend to understand why, or how, Geoff did the things he did. How he could so callously take lives and speak of it like . . ." I realize my voice is increasing not only in pitch but volume.

I take another breath and finish with, "I don't know much. But You do. May Your will be done. Amen."

As the last echoes of my words fade away, I open my eyes to find Katie looking at me, a mixture of surprise and gratitude in her expression. We share a moment of silent understanding before she says, "We'd better get back in there."

With the break room door ajar, we stop as we reach the entrance.

"He's breathing on his own," Dr. Murphy says, his voice full of awe. "Wipe his eyes. They're watering."

I let out a breath as Katie whispers, "Praise God."

"W-what happened?" I ask.

Leo looks up with a smile. "Stella's potions. She squirted some tincture in his mouth."

"Under his tongue. The cayenne. That's why his eyes are watering. When his heart started beating again, I gave him the osha root. Same delivery method, under the tongue. He may need it again, but at the moment . . ." She gives a wide smile. "We need to get a high dose of vitamin C in him. Rose hip and red raspberry to start."

Melvin Cabal lets out a low chuckle. "I can't believe the trouble you just went through. You do know he'll be executed, right? It's not like you'll just let him go."

Captain Williams turns his attention to Cabal, his eyes narrowing. "One would think you'd be pleased we just brought your nephew back from the dead. And we most certainly are willing to make a deal with him. I think you know I'm a man of my word."

Cabal's smug grin doesn't waver. "Oh, I know all about you, Chris Williams. I'm well aware of the lengths you'll go to in order to hide the truth. That is, after all, exactly how my dear nephew became a part of your little medical school experiment, isn't it?" Williams stiffens his spine as Cabal continues, "Do you know about that, Shaw? I'm guessing no."

"Let's get Landers on the stretcher and moved to the exam room," Dr. Murphy says. "He's not exactly stable. And this isn't the best— "

"Don't you want to hear the rest of the dirty details?" Cabal teases. "I mean, everyone was all ears when Geoff spilled the beans about me. How about I spill the beans about Williams and his dirty deeds?"

"We know you lie," Shaw says. "No matter what you say, it'll be contorted to your own benefit."

Cabal shrugs. "You've got me there. But his wife really did kill her neighbors. A mercy killing, she called it. I just happened to be in the right place at the right time to catch her red-handed, so to speak."

Melvin Cabal hinted at this when he first arrived, hinted that he held this over Alice Williams and that this information was how Geoff Landers became a student at the medical school. Now, as he publicly discloses this revelation, every set of eyes in the room darts toward Captain Williams.

He nervously runs his hand through his hair, and the room is filled with an unspoken tension. "It *was* a mercy killing. If you had anything resembling a heart, you'd agree and would've let it be, instead of trying to arrest my Alice for doing what she thought was best under the circumstances." He turns to Deputy Shaw. "We'll give you a full statement as soon as this is settled."

"Now can we move the patient?" Dr. Murphy requests, motioning Jesse Talbot to enter from the hallway.

Jesse and Dr. Murphy position themselves on either end of the stretcher, their actions synchronized without the need for words. In response to an unspoken command from the captain, Leo steps out alongside them.

Lying on the stretcher, Landers appears to be stable for the moment, but lingering questions cast a shadow over the scene. How had Addison managed to poison him? And who else might be in her crosshairs?

Chapter 31

Merissa

"Should I call Hugo?" I motion toward Trooper Schroeder's body.

"Please." Shaw nods. "Call Lieutenant Paul too."

"Paul is supposed to come here. He has updated information he was bringing directly to the captain."

"Ha! *Updated information*," Cabal says, mimicking my voice. For a moment, I wonder why I didn't shoot him when I had the chance. Choosing to ignore Cabal, I add, "Paul estimated he'd be here in two hours. I guess that was about two hours ago."

"Paul will want to handle the prisoner." Deputy Shaw lifts the muzzle of his pistol, still trained on Cabal. "Is there anyone else you want to have called?" Deputy Shaw directs the question toward Captain Williams.

"Not at this time." The captain's voice is hollow. "There'll be time for notifying command about— " he waves his hand " —everything, soon enough." He directs his attention toward Katie. "Please ask Alice if she'll wait for me in my office. Perhaps you can wait with her? Mrs. Weaver, join them after you notify Hugo."

"Absolutely, Captain," Katie responds.

Katie and I excuse ourselves from the room. When we're in the hallway, she touches my arm. "Cabal only told us about the situation with Mrs. Williams when you left with Kemeera. I didn't know until then."

"Okay? And?"

"I just didn't want you to think I was privy to that private information. You know, since we're staying at their place."

"I understand," I say, appreciating Katie's consideration but also finding it unnecessary. "Cabal had hinted about it when he first arrived. Do you want to get Mrs. Williams while I call Hugo?"

I key the radio and call for Hugo, but the voice that crackles through isn't his. Instead, Bowski's warm, familiar baritone responds, causing an unexpected rush of excitement to wash over me. He explains he's handling things while Hugo lends a hand over at the jail. Although each district has its own team for dealing with the deceased, they aren't strangers to working together in major emergencies like this.

Katie and Alice are leaving the exam room where Alice had been waiting with the children and Kemeera. A loud cry from one of the babies sounds as the door opens. Cradled in Katie's arms is Mindy's child, Zach. "Kemeera needs a break," she says with a shrug.

Seeing Katie holding the baby, I'm reminded of Mindy's final words . . . her last request. She wanted Katie to take care of Zach. She was sure Katie could love him.

"These babies are just the cutest." Mrs. Williams pats Zach on the arm. "All the children are. They're so well-behaved. I just can't . . ." She shakes her head. "I'm just glad it's over."

In the office, as we wait for the captain, the memories of the day seem to grow even more surreal. Cabal's mocking tone still echoes in my ears, as I consider half a dozen responses I could've given. I try to remind myself he isn't worth it.

"Well, I guess that's it," Mrs. Williams says. "Cabal and Landers were behind so many awful things. Working with the preacher and responsible for mass murders? Not to mention that terrible drug. I'm surprised about Deputy Schroeder. He always seemed so nice and professional."

I nod my agreement. I also thought he was nice and professional. Apparently, it was all an act.

"Do you know why Chris wants me to wait in here?" Alice asks, while glancing first at Katie and then at me. "I was fine with the children."

"I'm sure he'll be in shortly." I try to deliver a reassuring smile. Certainly, she must suspect Cabal would've told everyone about . . . well, everything. If she does, she isn't indicating anything. I can't help but wonder what happened. The captain referred to it as a mercy killing.

"Can you hold the baby for a minute?" Katie asks. "I need to find him a fresh diaper."

I wrinkle my face. "Is he wet?"

She tilts her head. "A little."

I take the squirming infant, trying to avoid the wet clothing. Alice's eyes are on me, a gentle smile covering her face. "Won't be long until you'll be holding your own little one."

As if on cue, my baby gives a solid kick. Does she know I'm holding Zach? Is she jealous?

Katie returns with a diaper and a change of clothes, along with a container to hold the soiled diaper and clothing. "I don't know how Kemeera will have enough diapers for the trip," she says. "It's going to take her weeks, and that's if the weather cooperates. She'll have to wash diapers every time she stops. Will they even have time to dry? Two babies may be too much for the journey. I think— " She slams her mouth shut. "I'm sorry. I forgot I'm not supposed to talk about the plans."

Alice waves her hand. "I'm not sure how much it matters now. Everyone is either dead or in custody, right?"

"Not Addison," I say.

"Oh, yes. You're absolutely right. They'll still need to be protected, of course. Keeping things quiet is the best."

"That and Landers suggested there may be others who weren't apprehended. Plus . . ." I crinkle my brow as I remember Kemeera and the way she called Cabal *Joseph*. She said she thought he went . . . went where? He interrupted her and told her to be quiet. Could she know more than she let on? She certainly seemed to think Cabal should've been somewhere else. Where could that somewhere have been?

A few minutes after Zach is changed into fresh clothes, Captain Williams arrives. "Sergeant, Mrs. Weaver. Thank you for keeping Alice company. I expect Hugo to be here shortly, along with Lieutenant Paul. I've signed the death certificate so Hugo may take the Trooper. Let me know when Paul arrives."

Since we are abruptly dismissed, I see no reason to tell the captain it'll be Bowski instead of Hugo. As I follow Katie out of the room and am pulling the door closed, Alice says, "What's this about, Chris?"

"Cabal told everything. We can't keep it quiet any longer."

As tempting as it is to put my ear to the door to listen to the conversation, I keep moving, walking behind Katie and baby Zach. As we reach the nurse's station, the radio squawks. It's the front guard declaring Bowski has arrived. I relay to the guard to let him through.

Waiting at the still-locked front door, my heart does that annoying little flutter when the pickup driven by Bowski comes into view. I take a deep breath and wait until he's parked and has exited his truck before I step outside to greet him.

"Hey." His eyes search my face. "I heard you were on lockdown. I didn't want to ask over the radio. Everything okay?"

I shake my head and blink away the tears threatening to overcome me. I lift my chin and will the emotions away. Bowski puts his hand on my shoulder. In that moment, all I want is to dissolve into his arms. I take a step back, wondering what's wrong with me. It must be the day—everything that's happened and the pregnancy hormones surging through my body.

Certainly, that must be it.

Braedon only recently died. It isn't right to have feelings for another man in such a short time. That would make me a . . . a hussy. A giggle bubbles up deep in my stomach. Yep. That's it. *I'm a hussy.* A loose woman. I snicker out loud. A second laugh escapes and I cover my mouth, which results in a snort. My laughter quickly turns to tears, and Bowski pulls me close.

As Bowski holds me in his arms, my emotions swirl within me like a chaotic storm. The events of the day, the weight of my responsibilities, and the conflicting feelings I have for him and my late husband create a tumultuous whirlwind of confusion. Bowski's comforting presence is a lifeline, grounding me in the midst of it all.

He lets me cry, offering silent support without pressuring me to explain my tears. It's as if he knows that, sometimes, letting the emotions flow freely is the best way to heal.

After a few minutes, my sobs subside. I pull away and wipe my tear-streaked face with the back of my hand. "I'm sorry," I manage to say, my voice still shaky.

Bowski gives me a gentle smile, his eyes warm and understanding. "You don't need to apologize, Merissa. It's okay to let it out."

I nod, trying to regain my composure. "Thank you, Bowski. I just . . . it's been a lot to handle."

He nods in agreement. "I understand. If there's anything I can do to help, please don't hesitate to ask."

I give him a smile as I let out a breath. In as professional a voice as I can muster, I say, "Follow me."

Inside the break room, Deputy Shaw is still in his familiar position, holding Cabal at gunpoint. Bowski takes in the scene but makes no comment about the dead trooper or the sheriff being in handcuffs.

Cabal chooses not to stay quiet. "Well, well. If it isn't Ritchie Kasubowski, troublemaker of Pennington County."

Bowski tilts his head. "Nice bracelets, Melvin. Good to know your less-than-savory actions have caught up with you." He glances at Trooper Schroeder's body. "Too bad you took your brother-in-law down with you. He was a good kid before you got your hooks into him."

"He was a weakling."

"Maybe so." Bowski shrugs. "Where's your nephew? He manage to get away?"

"Don't worry about it, Bowski," Deputy Shaw says. "Everyone's accounted for."

"You sure? I'm hearing scuttlebutt that may not be the case."

I glance toward the tall man, who seems to know more about our lockdown situation than he let on just a few minutes earlier.

Cabal lets out a throaty laugh, while Shaw sighs and shakes his head. "Just take Schroeder," Shaw says. "I'll check in with you later about the things you're hearing."

Jesse and I help Bowski load the trooper into the back of the truck. "Do you know his wife?" I ask as the tailgate slams shut.

"I know her." Bowski nods.

"Schroeder told me she's pregnant."

"I've heard that. They live in the Main Street District. I'll take him to the undertaker there. He'll notify her about Carter's death." As Bowski's gaze rests on my face, Jesse mumbles something about going back inside.

I acknowledge his words, promising I'll be right in.

Bowski clears his throat. "I was wondering, would you mind if I stopped by your place . . . um, maybe tomorrow?"

"My place? You mean my house?"

"Your house," he agrees with a nod. "Would that be okay? Are you working tomorrow?"

"Who knows? My days are crazy, to say the least."

He gives me an understanding smile. "It's just, I have a few things for you. For the baby."

"For *my* baby?" I crinkle my brow. "Why?"

"I thought you may need them. Tomorrow?"

"Um, before two o'clock? I'll have rounds and classes, for sure."

"Can I bring lunch? Say eleven thirty? For your mother-in-law, too, of course."

"She's working at the daycare tomorrow."

"Oh . . . would you prefer I wait until she's home to visit?"

I let out a laugh. "I'm sure it's fine for you to visit me when I'm home alone. Lunch is fine. In fact, I'd appreciate it. But, Bowski . . ." I pause as I consider my words. "I don't want you to think . . ." I shake my head.

"Don't worry." He smiles. "This is just lunch and a gift from one friend to another. That's all."

Chapter 32

Katie

"Thanks for volunteering to help with this, Katie," Kerry says, her expression carrying more than a hint of weariness.

"Sure." I nod. "It's . . ." I make a face to indicate my opinion of the necessary job. With Trooper Schroeder's body gone, we asked Shaw if he could move Cabal to another room so we could clean and sanitize the break room. Cabal and Shaw are now in exam room three, awaiting the arrival of Lieutenant David Paul. With our hospital still on lockdown, we're fortunate there have been no emergencies or illnesses requiring our services.

"Where do you think he may be?" Kerry's voice quivers slightly as she poses the question.

I know she's talking about her husband, who hasn't been seen since before the lockdown. We checked with the guards and asked if one of Shaw's men could search the med school. Kerry suggested he might have gone home, but there was little conviction in her words. We both know Rand Hendricks isn't the type to take off without informing someone, especially when he's working.

With the task of cleaning the break room complete, we make our way to the lobby. Mrs. Williams is sitting in one of the hard plastic chairs, her back straight and proper but her eyes vacant. She rouses herself slightly to offer us something that resembles a smile but turns out more like a grimace.

"Katie, may I speak with you for a moment?"

Kerry excuses herself as I take a chair next to Mrs. Williams. She's quiet for many minutes as her fingers fiddle with the hem of her scrub top. Finally, she releases her breath and drops her shoulders. "I guess I should've known the . . ." She pauses a moment. "I should've known what I did would come out eventually. Once Melvin Cabal found out, that was the end of any secrets."

I remain quiet, unsure of how to respond—even less sure of why Mrs. Williams is sharing this with me. Although we've become friendly during the time Leo and I have been staying with her, I wouldn't say we're friends. Not the type to share secrets, anyway.

"Hans and Diedre Niles were our neighbors. Had been our neighbors for years," Mrs. Williams says in a soft voice. "They already lived in their home when Chris and I bought ours. They were the first people to welcome us to the neighborhood. Even though they were almost forty years older than us, they seemed to go out of their way to be friendly. We used to play cards, have potlucks . . ." She raises her shoulders.

"All the things people used to do in years past. Not like how neighbors tended to be before the attacks, but the way they were years ago when they'd really try to get to know each other. They had a daughter, but she died before we met them, and Mrs. Niles often told me I reminded her of her daughter Jillian."

"Mrs. Niles was in hospice care when the attacks started," she adds softly. "She'd been fighting cancer for years and finally got to the point where there was nothing that could be done." Her gaze meets mine. "I know you understand."

I respond with a slight nod and whisper, "I do." Sometimes the memory of my mom's death, from what we assume was cancer, feels like yesterday, even though it's been almost nine months now.

"So, having gone through it yourself, I'm sure you can understand . . . at least, I hope you can understand. When the EMP happened and we knew there wouldn't be any more medicine for her, to help her with her pain, I-I did what Mr. Niles asked of me. What my dear elderly friends wanted." Mrs. Williams clears her throat.

"Hans wasn't well either. Even though she was the one in hospice, it was no secret he wouldn't survive long either. His heart had been bad for years, but he seemed to really go downhill after the EMP. I think it did something to his pacemaker. Chris said that was unlikely, but I believe it to be true. The hospice nurse had, of course, stopped coming in the early days of the attacks. I'd stepped in to help them. Chris, too, but he was spending so much time at the hospital, so it was really just me. He was able to bring more medicine home to help with her pain, so . . ."

"So, you helped them with a fatal overdose?" I inquire softly.

"That's what I did. I couldn't stand the idea of either of them suffering, and it was what they wanted. I truly believe they wanted to die together, just as they'd lived together. They were in their bed, side by side, holding hands. I stayed with them. Took care of them afterward to make sure everything was perfect. It was a fluke that Melvin Cabal happened to show up when he did. He'd come to the house to bother Chris about something and saw me as I was exiting the Niles home to go back to my house to get rid of the medicine bottles. The evidence." She raises her eyebrows at me.

"How'd he know?"

"I guess I'm a terrible liar," she snickers. "In those days, we were still reporting deaths to law enforcement. I figured, since he was there . . ." She shrugs. "I told him, and he wanted to see the bodies." She makes a face. "Can you believe that? He actually asked to see the bodies before he'd send someone to pick up their remains. I got flustered, and one of the pill bottles fell out of my pants pocket." She raises her hands.

"And here we are. I wanted to come clean then and face the consequences, but Cabal made it impossible. Instead of letting me admit to what I did, he blackmailed Chris. Me too, but he mainly used Chris to get his way with things. Not just bringing his nephew into the med school, but other things. Things of less consequence, at least we thought, but now I wonder if it wasn't all related to his drug trafficking and whatever else he's been involved in. I should've just come forward then. Surely, people would understand." She meets my gaze. "Wouldn't they? Do you understand, Katie?"

Tears well in my eyes as I nod, my throat constricting, rendering me unable to speak. The thought of my mother, her body ravaged by cancer, flashes through my mind. If it were her, racked by pain rather than miraculously paralyzed due to a freak accident, I'd have moved heaven and earth to alleviate her suffering.

Yet, even in the face of Alice Williams's actions, my beliefs remain steadfast: life and death should be left in God's hands. While I can empathize with what Mrs. Williams did, I find myself uncertain if I could—or would—make the same choice.

As we continue to sit quietly in the lobby, the radio at the nurse's station sounds. I can just make out the guard informing us Lieutenant David Paul has arrived and is requesting entry.

"Would you excuse me, Katie?" Mrs. Williams stands. "I'd like to go to the bathroom and freshen up before . . . before I need to repeat my story to the lieutenant."

Merissa heads toward us to open the front door for the lieutenant. She notices Mrs. Williams's puffy face and quickly averts her gaze. As the older woman makes her way down the hall, Merissa raises an eyebrow and tilts her head in my direction.

I pull my lips tight before mouthing, "It's not good."

Frowning, Merissa opens the door. "Lieutenant, Deputy Shaw is in exam room three. He'd like to update you on our situation."

"Do you still have a survivor from the cult?" he asks as he stomps the snow off his boots.

"Kemeera and all the children are in exam room two."

"Good." He glances in my direction. "Burnett, can I get your assistance after I meet with Shaw? I'd like a notetaker while I update Captain Williams on the situation." He furrows his brow. "Is he in his office?"

I glance toward Merissa, who gives a light shrug.

"I believe so," I answer, not really sure where the captain may be at the moment.

"Stay close," he says as he strides toward the exam room.

It takes Paul only a few minutes to learn what happened here today and how deeply Cabal and the others were entrenched in the situation with the preacher, Ploy, the burglary ring, the black market, and many deaths. If he's surprised by the revelation of Cabal, Schroeder, and Landers being involved, he hides it well when he exits the exam room. He catches my eye and lifts his chin before heading toward the captain's office. Grabbing a notebook and pen from the nurse's station, I start down the hallway.

At his brisk knock and the captain's offer for us to enter, I follow him into the room. The captain and Mrs. Williams are both seated on the sofa, their hands intertwined. When they see the lieutenant, they release their grasp as the captain says, "Thank you for coming, Paul. After you give me the update about the preacher, there's something additional I need to share with you."

Lieutenant Paul nods. "Melvin Cabal said as much. Shaw cut him off before he could give me the entire story." He glances toward Mrs. Williams. "Ma'am. Hope you weren't too caught up in things today."

"I wasn't in the room," she says softly.

Captain Williams looks in my direction. "Sergeant? Did you need something?"

"I've asked her to join us as our stenographer." Paul takes a seat and motions me to do the same. "I thought you might wish to have a copy of Preacher's suicide note."

Williams's eyebrows shoot up. "Really? He left a note?"

"Confessing everything. And clearing up what he didn't do. Specifically, he said he was not responsible for the explosion on our base." He pulls a piece of paper from his pocket and unfolds it. "I copied the original. A copy has already been sent to the general, the governor, and a few others who will need it."

Williams lets out a sigh. "Before you share anything additional with me, let's talk about what Cabal tried to tell you."

Lieutenant Paul glances in my direction, and Mrs. Williams says, "Katie already knows. I'd like her to stay."

"As you wish, ma'am." Paul sits back in his chair.

This time, the captain shares the story as Mrs. Williams stares at the floor. It's very similar to the way she told it, but it truly indicates his love for his wife as he takes most of the blame for the deaths as his own fault. "I brought home the medicine. I believe a part of me suspected what would happen, so I made sure to bring home what would . . . what would be the best option."

When the story is finished, Paul leans forward, his elbows on his knees. "We won't be able to sweep this under the rug."

"I'd expect not." The captain almost sounds insulted at the suggestion.

"Right. So, I'll give my report. It'll be up to the general how to handle it. The fact you wished to come clean about your actions, Mrs. Williams, but Melvin Cabal wouldn't allow it may help. I suppose, with this information, it'd be best not to give you full access to the confession. I can't say what the consequences will be, so . . ." He folds up the note and returns it to his pocket.

"Is Cabal still here?" Williams asks.

"I'm going to call for a transport to come and get him. Mind if I use your radio?"

"Not at all. Burnett, will you take him to the nurse's station? As soon as we're no longer on lockdown, I'm going to take my wife home. You'll be able to find us there should you need us this evening, Lieutenant Paul."

"Understood. My guess is this will wait until tomorrow. It's been a day . . . for everyone. The situation seems to be under control, so as soon as we can take Cabal, we can remove the lockdown. What about Landers? Think he's well enough to go too?"

"I checked on him shortly before you arrived. He's stable but still critical. Can you arrange for a guard? People you trust. The woman, Addison, is still out there somewhere."

As Paul and I stand to leave the office, the back doorbell sounds.

Paul jerks his thumb in that direction. "I thought you were on lockdown?"

Williams quickly gets to his feet. "We are. Wait here, Alice. Lock the door behind me."

"Chris?" she says with a quiver in her voice.

Since I wasn't told to wait in the office with Mrs. Williams, I follow the men out of the room. Merissa is in the hallway, quickly stepping toward us.

"Who went out?" the captain bellows.

"I don't know. I didn't see. Those who aren't in with Landers are in the break room now that . . ." She clears her throat instead of finishing her sentence. "I'll check on Stella. She's in with the children."

"I'll check on Dr. Wolff," I say. "I think she's still napping in the call room."

As Merissa opens the door to the exam room, one of the children lets out a cry.

"She won't wake up," a second child's voice says.

"Captain!" Merissa yells. "Stella's down."

Chapter 33

Katie

In the exam room, Ivy and Nico hover over Stella, their worried expressions etched in their furrowed brows. Daisy sits next to Stella with tears streaming down her cheeks as she wraps her arms tightly around her body, rocking back and forth. On the floor nearby, both babies are cradled in improvised nests of blankets, cocooned in warmth. Amid the commotion, it becomes evident that Kemeera and Shawna are absent from the scene.

I drop to Stella's side as she lets out a moan. "Stella? It's Katie."

"Mmm." She scrunches her eyes tight.

Merissa moves the older children. "Let's give Miss Stella some room."

"Why'd Kemeera hit her?" Nico asks, his voice quivering.

Ivy sends him a look as she moves her finger to her mouth. "Shh."

"No, I won't! I won't be quiet!" Nico yells. "Miss Stella is nice to us! She reads good stories."

His yelling startles Zach, who lets out a wail.

Captain Williams motions toward the screaming infant. "Katie, can you and Merissa get the children out of here? Lieutenant, please find my staff to help me with Ms. Swenson."

Merissa and I each pick up a baby. Caleb is also beginning to stir, thanks to the noise and ruckus. As we round up the older children, Leo enters the room. He takes in the scene before quickly going to the captain's side. "Sir?"

"Let's get her on the exam table. Where's Jesse?"

"I'm here." Jesse enters the room seconds behind Leo.

As Leo and the others care for Stella, Merissa and I move the children to the break room. The rest of the med students are now in the hallway, pondering how they can help while Dr. Murphy remains with Landers. I never did check on Dr. Wolff, but I assume she's still asleep in the call room; she can sleep through just about anything.

Nico is crying now, along with Daisy and the babies. Ivy crosses her arms and plops onto the couch. We call her Ivy, though she has never disclosed her name. Kemeera claimed to not know it, and Mindy refused to say. The same goes for the younger girl; she won't say her name, and we don't know it. Stella took to calling her Daisy, which she seems to like.

Both girls are older than Nico, and we've found it odd that he's more talkative and open than either of them. Not that he'll talk our ear off or anything. He often acts like he's done something wrong when he does speak, but it's more than the girls do. We can only assume their behavior is related to living in the cult. Nico, who had said he hadn't lived there long, must not have been exposed to the same conditioning as the girls.

With the older children sprawled on the couch while Merissa and I bounce the babies, I ask, "Do you know where Kemeera and Shawna are?"

Ivy stares at her shoes, and Daisy shakes her head.

"She told us to be good," Nico says. "She also said Katie should take care of the babies and me. You're Katie, right? Kemeera says you'll make a good mom."

My eyes go wide as my heart beats faster. "Where'd she go?"

Without looking up, Ivy says, "To finish the job."

After Ivy's announcement, Merissa says, "Go! Go and tell Paul."

Keeping hold of Zach, I find the lieutenant at the nurse's desk. I quickly relay what I know.

He runs his fingers through his hair. "She played us? I've already put out an alert on her. How she slipped out the backdoor without the rear guard seeing her is still unknown. I'd think he was part of it, but I know him and . . . well, I hope I know him, anyway. He's being taken to the base for questioning. We're getting the older girls out of here. Tonight. Now. Someone's on their way. They'll be safer away from here. I sure hope her child is safe with her."

I swallow my fears about the danger Shawna may be in. Kemeera seemed to be the doting mom, not only to Shawna but also to baby Caleb. Why'd she leave him behind? "What about Nico and the babies?" I choose not to relay Nico's declaration that I should take care of the babies and him.

He lowers his voice. "We can't send them to your family without an adult to accompany them. The babies . . . they need milk, right?"

"Right."

"I'm not sure what we can do. We'll figure something out. We'll make sure they're safe. But I'd think if they weren't, Kemeera would've . . ." He tilts his head to one side. "Don't you think?"

"I think the entire thing is nuts." Zach begins to fuss again, and I give him a bounce.

"Can't argue with you there."

I return to the break room and whisper to Merissa about the girls leaving soon.

She responds with a nod before snickering. When I raise my eyebrows, she says, "You would make a good mom. Mindy said so too."

"What do you mean?"

"She said she wanted you to take care of Zach."

"Let's not tell anyone about that, okay? This— " I lift Zach up slightly " —is not in my plans. Did you forget I'm joining the National Guard as soon as Leo is medically released?"

She puckers her mouth and raises her shoulders. "Are you, Katie? Are you really? Because I think, if you were as gung-ho about joining the Guard as you pretend to be, you wouldn't be waiting for Leo to be released to duty. You'd join on your own merits and on your own time. I think you're an amazing nurse and will be a fabulous doctor, but you can do those things without being in the Guard. You *should* do those things without being in the Guard."

I take a step back, almost feeling as if I've been slapped. "Y-you don't know," I sputter. "I've told you. I'm waiting so we can be finished with our commitment at the same time."

"Another reason I don't believe you should do it. When the commitment will end seems to be your focus, not what you'll do during the time you're serving. I know what it's like. The Coast Guard isn't the same. Just ask any of the guys who were in the military, and they'll make sure you know that. But at the same time, it is the same. When I joined, my focus was on how I could serve and what I could learn during that time. Not how quickly I could get out."

I give her a dirty look and move to stand next to the couch. Ivy is staring at us. Daisy has her head against Ivy's shoulder and is sleeping.

Nico is playing with the frayed hem of his pant leg. He doesn't look up when he says, "You don't want to be my mom?"

My heart clinches and my eyes fill with tears.

"Of course she doesn't, silly," Ivy says, shocking me again with her speaking. "Who'd want us? We're damaged goods. You heard Kemeera. She's damaged goods, too, and so are we. Besides, it doesn't matter. Preacher will find us and . . ." She shakes her head.

I grab one of the plastic chairs and slide it near the couch.

Merissa mimics my actions. Before she even sits, she says, "You're not damaged, Ivy. You're going to be just fine. You and Daisy are . . ." She tilts her head in my direction. "Tell them, Katie."

I clear my throat, buying a bit of time as I consider what to say. "I don't really know much, but I do know there's a nice family who can't wait to meet you."

Ivy snorts. "It won't matter. They'll find us and— "

"No. They won't. The family lives far, far away. They're going to keep you safe. Preacher can't hurt you."

"He will. He said if anyone ever tried to leave, he'd make them sorry. He whispered it all mean like, so I know he was serious."

In a soft voice, Merissa says, "He can't hurt you. Something happened, and he won't be able to hurt you."

Ivy lifts her gaze and tilts her head. "Is he dead?"

Merissa and I exchange a quick glance before returning our attention to the girl and nodding in unison. "He is," I say. As an afterthought, I add, "I'm sorry."

She shakes her head. "He isn't. Did you see his body? He can't die. He told us if anyone ever said he was dead, it's a lie."

I slide the chair back. "Give me a minute, okay, Ivy? I wasn't . . . I don't know everything but let me ask someone else."

Slipping back out to the hallway, I'm happy to find Paul still at the nurse's station. He lifts his gaze when he hears the door shut.

"We have a, uh, situation," I say.

"More information?"

"Well, the older girl, Ivy, is suddenly talking. We had to . . . she thinks the preacher will come after her. We had to tell her that she was safe, you know?" I realize my words are speeding up. I take a breath. "She said that he said he can't die and if anyone said he was dead, it was a lie."

Paul scoffs. "He looked pretty dead to me."

"You saw him? Saw his body?"

"I saw him. All of them." He shudders.

"We told Ivy they'll be safe. That there's someone who'll take care of them that lives far, far away." A look of concern crosses his face, and I add, "No details other than that. But she says she won't be safe anywhere because he can't die. See the problem?"

"You want me to tell her I saw his dead body?"

"Maybe in a gentler way?"

Paul sighs. "All right. I'll try. I just heard from the transport. They'll be here soon. Do you have the girls' bags?"

"Um . . . they're still in the exam room where Stella is being treated. Let me get them."

"Can you handle the bags and the baby?" He motions toward Zach.

"Good point." I thrust the baby in his direction.

He takes a step back and waves his hands. "I'll carry the bags. You keep the baby."

I give a soft knock on the exam room door. At Williams's terse "come in," I open it just enough to say, "May we grab the children's bags?"

"Go ahead," he agrees.

Stella is sitting up on the exam table. She doesn't look great, but not terrible either. "Are the children okay?" she asks. The way she cares about them, if anyone should become their mom, it's her.

"They're fine," I say.

"Good." She gives a weary smile. "I've already told the captain, but I want to announce to everyone that I'm done with this med school business. I'll continue to help with the medicines and in other ways, but this is too much for me."

The captain pats her arm. "I've suggested to Stella we create a position as a pharmacist. A position she can mainly work from home."

I can't say I'm surprised by this. While Stella has the potential to be a wonderful doctor, there are many parts of the job she despises.

Paul addresses the captain. "The transport is on its way, sir. The girls are leaving this evening."

"Leaving?" Stella's eyes go wide. "Ivy and Daisy are leaving?"

"Thank you, Lieutenant," the captain says as Paul picks up the bags. He hands one to me while he carries the other four. I hadn't noticed earlier, but there should've been two more bags, one for Kemeera and one for Shawna. Kemeera must have taken those when she left. I point this out to the lieutenant, who gives the captain a look.

We hadn't inspected the bags or anything. Just assumed it was the clothes and things they'd need to start their new lives. Now, with what Ivy said about Kemeera finishing what was started, I'm wondering if there could've been something else in those bags. Explosives or . . . who knows what she's planning to do.

As we leave the exam room, Stella asks if she can say goodbye to the girls. The door closes before I hear the captain's response.

Paul makes a beeline for the nurse's station. "Have you looked in these bags?" He plops them on the counter.

"No. I was just thinking about that."

He carefully opens the first one. "Clothes. The boy's, I think." He continues through each bag, filled with clothes for each child, including the babies. "I sure would've liked to have taken a look inside the woman's bags."

"Sorry. We didn't even think— "

"Understood. This is a mess. A complete and total mess."

Daisy is awake when we return to the break room. Lieutenant Paul speaks with Ivy to ease her fears. He's very convincing when he tells her she'll be safe. I'm still not sure she believes him, though.

Using a wheelchair, Stella is brought in to say goodbye to the girls. She hugs them and whispers how much she's enjoyed getting to know them.

Ivy whispers something in response.

With her arms on the girl's shoulders, Stella says, "It's very nice to meet you, Abigail." She turns to Daisy with a smile. "You too, Ella. I know you'll both be very happy and have a wonderful life."

Chapter 34

Katie

Shortly after the girls leave for their new homes on the other side of the state, another truck shows up to take Cabal somewhere. Exactly where is never said, at least not to me. Several soldiers—all officers— will be rotating guard duty for Geoff Landers until he is well enough to either make the deal he started to make earlier or join his uncle wherever he is being held.

With things stable for the moment, the hospital lockdown is lifted, and everyone who isn't currently on duty is allowed to go home. "Regular rounds tomorrow at 1400 hours," Dr. Wolff, finally up from her nap, reminds everyone. She glances at the captain. "Classes tomorrow?"

He shakes his head. "Not tomorrow. Rounds will suffice."

Faced with Rand Hendricks still missing, Jesse extends a helping hand to Kerry and offers to walk her home and assist in checking her house for her husband. She accepts his offer, her concern evident in the furrow of her brow.

Stella's head injury is severe enough to warrant spending the night in the hospital, with Dr. Murphy on as tonight's attending physician.

For tonight, the Williamses and us are taking the babies and Nico home. The babies are both making their hunger known. Mrs. Williams offers to get an emergency ration of goat's milk. Not ideal, but better than nothing. She seeks out her husband's gaze and assures him, "I'll go now and see you at home shortly."

"We'll be right there." His fingers brush her hand. "Tell Velda the situation. She'll help us. Get bone broth, too, if you can. And butter or cream . . . some kind of fat. Jeff? Matt? Would you be willing to help my wife?"

He intentionally fails to mention the National Guard will also escort Mrs. Williams. Lieutenant Paul said the Williamses' house would be guarded, and we'd have escorts on our way home. Kemeera might have left voluntarily, but we don't trust her or Addison, and we intend to ensure the children's safety.

"Of course, sir," Jeff replies as he fastens his jacket. "We'll see her home after we get the needed items."

Mrs. Williams offers her husband a slight smile before slipping out the back door.

My anger at Kemeera for leaving the infants simmers just below the surface. How she could leave her own child, I don't understand. And Zach . . . orphaned just hours ago and having struggled with his weight and growth so much before he came to live in our district. I pull my lips into a tight line and do my best to hold my tongue as Merissa, Leo, and I dress the babies and Nico for the cold walk to the captain's house.

With the babies bundled, Merissa asks if we'd like her to carry one of them. "Plop one of them on my lap," the captain says, moving to his wheelchair. "Leo can help me. Nico's a big enough lad he can walk alongside, isn't that right?"

Nico nods.

"Katie can carry the other one. Go on home and get some rest, Mrs. Weaver. See you tomorrow for rounds."

Merissa's eyes meet mine as she slides her coat on. I avert my gaze, conveying the weight of my lingering resentment regarding her unsolicited advice about my enlistment in the Guard. Who is she to assume she knows my feelings and decisions? My resolve to join the National Guard is unwavering; I've already mapped out my commitment to those eight years, and I'm determined to do my part. With a heavy sigh, I turn back to my friend.

"Can you hold Zach while I put my coat on?" I force a light tone into my voice.

"Sure," Merissa answers with a smile.

The captain has Caleb on his lap, talking to the baby. Nico is standing close, smiling and joining in the conversation.

Merissa walks with us until she needs to turn down her street. The captain informs her we'll wait until she reaches her house. Even though things have been better in the neighborhood around the hospital lately, we still avoid walking alone, especially after dark. It's almost 2300 hours and no moon, so it definitely qualifies as a time to not be walking the streets alone.

She gives me a smile and a small nod. I return both gestures. While I'm still angry at her, I suppose she does have a point. As she walks off, Zach lets out a whimper. I pull him closer to me and tug the blanket up around his ears. When Merissa waves from her front porch, we continue the rest of the way to the captain's house, the soldier assigned as our protection detail trailing behind.

Inside, Leo stokes the fire while the captain holds both babies and I get Nico out of his coat and boots.

He gives me a sweet smile. "Thanks, Katie." Then he wraps his little arms around my shoulders.

My eyes fill with tears as I consider what it might be like to be his mom. To take care of him, Caleb, and Zach.

As both babies let out bloodcurdling screams, I quickly tamp down those thoughts. Three boys? Two of them infants? How could I even manage? What would Leo think? I have yet to tell him what Nico said. And truthfully, I'm not sure I'm going to.

"Should we help the captain with the babies?" I ask as I release Nico.

I take Zach while the captain says he'll try to quiet Caleb.

Nico looks at Leo, who's still working on the fire. "Is Leo your husband?"

"He is," I say as Zach finds his thumb and begins to settle. The captain has also managed to quiet Caleb, though I think we all know it won't last. They need food and fresh diapers. Leo turns and gives us a smile.

"So, if Katie will be my mom . . . you'll be my dad?" Nico asks, his eyes wide.

So much for not telling Leo. I'll admit, the look on his face—shock—is priceless.

Captain Williams snorts out a laugh. "Do you want Katie to be your mom, Nico?"

"Kemeera does. She said Katie will be a good mom." He looks at me and tilts his head. "I like her, so I guess that'd be fine."

Leo's eyes are still wide in shock and, possibly, fright.

"It was not my idea," I murmur.

Leo gives a slight nod before turning back to the fire. "Just about have this going. I think there's leftover soup. I'll go check the cooler and see."

My husband hustles out to the garage we use as cold storage, keeping a variety of coolers with leftovers and other food. The key in the front lock draws my attention as Mrs. Williams thanks Jeff and Matt for walking her home.

"Can I bring in the box?" Jeff asks.

"Oh, no, I'll get it. See you tomorrow at work," she says, dismissing them. "Oh, good, you're already here. I was able to get the goat milk, butter, and beef broth. She also gave me bottles and nipples."

The captain has her melt a little butter into the goat's milk while it warms on the stove. "Don't get it too hot," he cautions.

"Yes, I know," she answers. Mrs. Williams is trying to act as she usually does, but it's obvious the revelations of today are weighing on her. Paul didn't say when someone would address the captain and Alice, or what the consequences may be.

"I'll change their diapers," I say. "Should I do that in my room?" I glance around at the nice furniture in the living room. None of them seem suitable for dirty diapers.

"Use the ottoman," Mrs. Williams suggests. "It's plenty big enough."

The captain keeps Caleb while I take Zach to the ottoman. Kneeling next to him, I take care of his needs. There're only three clean diapers left in his bag, plus a smaller bag full of dirties. The captain holds Zach while I repeat the process with Caleb, who has four clean diapers left.

With the bottles made, the captain and I take care of the feedings while Leo warms soup for us.

Mrs. Williams puts on a pot of water to boil the diapers. "I've never actually washed diapers before," she says. "But it must be the same as doing regular clothes, right?"

I shrug. I helped with washing my sister's baby diapers last winter. It was a much smellier process than regular clothes, but essentially the same.

There's a knock on the door, followed by a voice saying, "It's Jesse."

The captain motions Leo to answer.

Jesse briefly relays that Rand Hendricks isn't at his house. He said he let Deputy Shaw know and they'll continue to look for him.

By the time the babies and the rest of us are fed, and the diapers are hanging to dry, it's almost 0100 hours. Nico is sleeping on the couch in the living room. I offer to look after the babies for the night, indicating I'll sleep in the living room with them.

"Are you sure?" Leo asks. "Why don't we just take them into our room?"

"What if Nico wakes up? He may be afraid if he's all alone?"

Leo understands and says he'll sleep in the living room too.

We open up the sofa bed for us to sleep on. Mrs. Williams suggests we use dresser drawers as makeshift cribs for the babies.

"We'll go get the bassinets they were using at the safe house tomorrow," the captain says. "But the drawers will be fine for tonight. Hope you two can get some sleep." He chuckles as he and his wife retreat to their room.

I should've spoken up and said, "Tomorrow, we need to find homes for the children, not just bring bassinets over." But I'm too tired, much too tired to deal with it tonight.

"What a day," Leo whispers as we settle in. The babies are both asleep, but I wonder how long that'll last. Leo gently touches my jaw, just below the spot of frostbite. "Did you put the lotion on?"

"I did. On my nose too." I wiggle it to show off the salve. "And my ear. I think they're going to scar."

"You're still beautiful." He drops a gentle kiss on my lips.

"Do you think Landers was telling the truth about Julius? *Julius MacAllister.* The one who attacked me?"

He releases a sigh. "I suspect so. No reason for him to lie about it, especially because he really was trying to make a deal for his freedom. It sounds like Cabal killed him or had him killed. That means we can go home. So can Oscar and his family."

"That's good . . . I guess." I hear the lack of conviction in my voice.

"Let's get some sleep. We can sort out our housing and everything else tomorrow."

I snicker. "It is tomorrow. You know what Merissa said to me tonight?"

"Merissa? No . . ."

"She said she doesn't think I really want to join the National Guard. I think she thinks I should take the babies and Nico. Can you believe that?"

Leo raises up on his good arm to look at me. "We've talked about having a family."

My mouth drops open, and my eyes go wide. "We talked about having children, sure. But not anytime soon. And not . . . not three at once. Instantly."

"Your parents were willing to take in Tony and Lily when their mom died."

"They were older, more responsible. Besides, they had all of us to help. We can't . . . how could we?"

"I think this is something to pray about. Not something to decide when we've had the day we've had and we're both exhausted."

"Okay, yes. I guess you're right. But really, Leo. There's nothing to consider here. We just can't do it."

Leo nods in the dim light, his expression thoughtful. "We need to think this through. And we'll pray about it. It's not just about what we want, but what's best for these kids. And we can't make a decision like this when we're tired and everything's still uncertain."

I bob my head, grateful Leo understands the complexity of the situation. Leo gently kisses my forehead. "We'll tackle this step by step, together."

With a sense of relief, I let out a contented sigh. As we prepare to sleep, with the babies and Nico nearby, the uncertain future hovers. Yet, I'm confident that with God's guidance, Leo and I will find a way to navigate the challenges that lie ahead.

Chapter 35

Merissa

The knock at the door comes promptly at eleven thirty. One thing about Bowski is he's prompt. My heart quickens as I set aside the knife and wipe my hands on a dishtowel.

He mentioned bringing lunch, but it only seems right for me to contribute something. Our rations included a pair of forlorn-looking apples this week. Combining them with both wheat and zucchini flour, a lone egg, and a touch of honey, I attempted to create something akin to a cross between a crisp and a cake, or so I tell myself.

I make a brief stop at the hallway mirror and adjust a stray strand of hair escaping my barely contained bun.

As the door swings open, Bowski greets me with a wide smile, his eyes shining in a way that sends my stomach into somersaults. He cradles a package in his arms. Not just any package; it's a gift.

"You brought a present?"

"Well, it's . . ." He clears his throat. "It's for the baby." He gestures with a nod of his head, a hint of pink coloring his cheeks. "I wasn't sure what you needed, so it's just some basics."

"Really?" My voice emerges far squeakier than I intend. "I, uh . . . please, come in. It's freezing out there."

His warm smile flips my stomach again. "Let me bring this in. I've got lunch too." He motions to a utility wagon, then steps inside and casts a glance toward his boots.

"Here." I extend my arms to accept the package. Although not elegantly wrapped, it's still charming. Sheet material serves as the wrapping paper, secured with both pink and blue ribbons. Despite its size, it's not excessively heavy.

"All right. I'll be right back."

Within moments, lunch is on the table, and Bowski stands in his stocking-clad feet. "Do you want to open the package before we eat?"

I glide my fingers along the pink and blue ribbons. The days of ultrasounds and gender-revealing blood tests are long gone. "Will lunch get cold?"

He motions toward the thermos. "Just stew. I think it'll be fine."

I carefully untie the ribbons, my heart pounding in anticipation. Inside the package, I find a collection of baby essentials, meticulously arranged and packaged with care. Tears glisten in my eyes as I grasp the thoughtful gesture behind this gift. Bowski might be a rugged, stoic man on the outside, but he possesses a heart of gold. Clearing my throat, I take out a handcrafted quilt. "The Ebright sisters? Did they make this?"

"The blanket and the little dress things. Along with the diapers. They mentioned the dresses were what babies used to wear, for both boys and girls, to make it easier to change them. I was able to get the shirts with the snap closures . . . um, elsewhere. The socks as well."

"Onesies," I say, touching the adorable outfit bearing the words "Mommy Loves Me." It's not new, but it's still a perfect gift. "I think they're called onesies."

He tilts his head. "Do you like them?"

I meet his gaze. "I love them. Thank you. This means . . . it means so much to me."

Bowski rubs the back of his neck, a hint of embarrassment in his eyes. "I just thought . . . you know, with everything that's been happening, it might be good to have a few things ready."

His thoughtfulness for me and the baby resonates deeply. My life has seen such profound shifts in the past few months, and it's moments like these that affirm the existence of kindness in today's uncertain world. We take our seats to relish our basic stew, yet today, it feels like a feast, thanks to the warmth of Bowski's friendship.

As we continue our meal, conversation flows effortlessly between us. Bowski shares stories of the town's latest projects and the progress being made in rebuilding. We spend a fair amount of time speculating about the preacher and his group.

"I can't really say I'm surprised about the mass suicide." He shakes his head. "It seems historically fitting."

I let out a sigh. "Fitting, yet still tragic. Especially with Kemeera taking off too. She had us all fooled, I suppose."

"Somehow, I doubt she fooled you."

I lower my gaze to my bowl. "I wanted to believe her. But something didn't sit right. And when Mindy was dying, the things she said . . . I just didn't know what to think."

We delve deeper into discussions about Kemeera, Sheriff Cabal, and Geoff Landers.

"Will Landers make it?" he asks.

"It seemed that way last night. I wonder how he'll react when he learns it was Stella's magical potions that saved him. He used to mock her relentlessly."

"He made fun of her but dated Addison, who also brewed various herbs? Not that there's any comparison between Addison and Stella."

"No, certainly not. Deputy Shaw's making it a top priority to locate both Addison and Kemeera. Once Landers can finish giving his statement about whoever else is part of the preacher's crew, the ones who were not in the jail, they'll be added to the list. I hate to say it, but I don't think this mess is over yet."

Bowski tightens his lips. "I agree. In fact, I heard something recently that might interest you."

"Go on."

"Were you at the hospital the night a prank call came in over the radio?"

"I was. How'd you find out?"

He raises his brows, and I realize it's a silly question. Bowski seems privy to everything in the Black Hills. "Schroeder was on duty that night."

"Yes, he . . ." I sigh. "Don't tell me it wasn't a prank and is connected to Cabal and the whole debacle."

"I don't believe it was a prank. But I'm not entirely sure of its relevance. I've informed Shaw about what I heard, and he'll look into it further."

After lunch, Bowski insists on helping me clean up, and together we wash the dishes, sharing the work and the quiet moments in between. "Can I walk you to the hospital?" he asks as we put the last of the dishes away.

The silly flutter returns to my stomach. I swallow before replying, "If you'd like."

Our eyes lock, his expression a blend of uncertainty and sincerity. "Merissa," he begins, his voice gentle, "I've been thinking about something for a while now. With the baby on the way and the challenges we face, I want to be there for you. Help you however I can. Both you and your mother-in-law."

I gaze into his eyes and find a depth of understanding that mirrors my own feelings.

He gently touches my shoulder. "I know it might seem unconventional, given the circumstances, but I care about you, Merissa. And I want to be there for you and the baby any way I can."

Touched by his sincerity, I smile, my heart fluttering with a newfound hope. "I think I'd like that. We've already been through so much together, and I couldn't have asked for a better friend."

The tension between us eases as our hands briefly clasp, sealing an unspoken promise to face the challenges of this post-apocalyptic world side by side. In this moment, amid the ruins and the uncertainty, our connection deepens, and the prospect of a future together becomes more than just a possibility.

The adventure continues in Heightened Mayhem: Dakota Destruction Book 5.

With the Preacher gone, they thought they'd be safe...

While the Guard District is trying to figure out Preacher's final plans, they discover one of their own is missing.

Katie and Leo plan for an easy trip to the main hospital, but with evil lurking around every corner, things don't always go as planned.

Will the Black Hills finally find peace? And will Katie and Leo get the news they've been waiting for and become part of the South Dakota National Guard?

Thank you for spending your time on our new South Dakota adventure.

If you have five minutes, you'd make this writer very happy if you could write a short review on Amazon, Goodreads, Bookbub, or your favorite review site.

I appreciate you!

Join my reader's club!
As part of my reader's club, you'll be the first to know about new releases and specials. I also share info on books I'm reading, preparedness tips, and more.

Please sign up on my website:
MillieCopper.com

Also by Millie Copper

The Havoc in Wyoming Series

When a series of coordinated attacks devastate the United States, the people of Bakerville, Wyoming, must come together to survive. Unfortunately, not everyone has the town's best interest at heart. Some are striving for personal gain during the apocalypse.

The Montana Mayhem Series

A group from Bakerville, Wyoming strikes out on their own while searching for the desires of their heart. Unfortunately, the road will not be easy, and sometimes the heart is hardened and deceitful.

The Dakota Destruction Series

After a series of coordinated attacks devastate the United States, Katie and Leo sacrifice everything to help their country. But some things aren't as they seem. Is it time to go home and start fresh, or can something good come out of this terrible situation?

Wyoming Fall Series (In The October Fall World)

In the blink of an eye, an EMP changed everything for Lauren and her family. Now they are in a fight for survival, trying to keep their loved ones alive as society collapses around them.

Nonfiction Books

Millie has penned seven nonfiction, traditional food focused books, sharing how, with a little creativity, anyone can transition to a real foods diet without overwhelming their food budget. Many of her books also include preparedness and food storage tips.

Find these titles at: MillieCopper.com

Acknowledgments

Thanks to:

Ameryn Tucker, my editor, beta reader, and daughter wrapped in one. I had a story I wanted to tell, and Ameryn encouraged me and helped me bring it to life.

Dee from Dauntless Cover Design.

My husband, who gave me the time and space I needed to complete this dream and was very patient as I'd tell him the same plot ideas over and over and over.

Three more adult daughters and a young son, who willingly listen to me drone on and on about storylines and ideas while encouraging me to "keep going."

My amazing Beta Readers! Thanks to Barbara, Glen, Jim, Judy, Linda, Melonie, Tammy, and Tracy for your help in creating the final story. Your insights and abilities to see the things I miss are very much appreciated!

A special thank you to Kristy who gave me a peek inside the world of the Coast Guard and Forest Service. And also a special thank you to Tim, a specialist in all things that go boom, for always answering my questions and pointing out things I wouldn't even think about.

And to you, my readers, for spending your time on our new South Dakota adventure. If you have five minutes, you'd make this writer very happy if you could leave a review. I appreciate you!

About the Author

Millie Copper, writer of Cozy Apocalyptic Fiction and preparedness mentor, was born in Nebraska but never lived there. Her parents fully embraced wanderlust and moved regularly, giving her an advantage of being from nowhere and everywhere.

Millie Copper lives in the wilds of Wyoming with her husband and young son, tending chickens and attempting a food forest on their small homestead. After living off the grid for several years, they've recently gone back on the grid. Four adult daughters, three sons-in-law, and five grandchildren round out the family.

Since 2009, Millie has authored articles on traditional foods, alternative health, homesteading, and preparedness-many times all within the same piece. Millie has penned seven nonfiction, traditional food focused books, sharing how, with a little creativity, anyone can transition to a real foods diet without overwhelming their food budget.

The twelve-installment *Havoc in Wyoming* and six-installment *Montana Mayhem* Christian Post-Apocalyptic fiction series use her homesteading, off-the-grid, and preparedness lifestyle as a guide. The adventures continue with the *Dakota Destruction* series.

Find Millie at www.MillieCopper.com
Facebook: www.facebook.com/MillieCopperAuthor/
Amazon: www.amazon.com/author/milliecopper
BookBub: https://www.bookbub.com/authors/millie-copper